Sacred Lies,
Sober Truths

Sacred Lies,
Sober Truths

Kathryn Buckley Cowan

Sacred Lies, Sober Truths

Published by Wheatmark®
1760 East River Road, Suite 145
Tucson, Arizona 85718 USA
www.wheatmark.com

ISBN: 978-1-60494-896-7 (paperback)
ISBN: 978-1-62787-093-1 (ebook)
LCCN: 2013956071

My gratitude to
April Reed, Frank Babb, and Jane Johndrow,

And to the many friends who read my manuscript
and encouraged me to carry on

Part One

It took both of us to shove open the heavy wooden door. It was early Saturday morning, December 12, 1953. It was forty degrees in Wichita, and we were wearing our matching navy-blue wool coats. I had turned eleven that fall and my sister, Donna, would be nine in January. My sister was a blond pixie, exactly four inches shorter than me, with naturally curly hair, pale blue eyes, skinny arms, and what I called "toothpick legs." I was more substantial—not fat or even chubby—and Mom needed bobby pins or curlers to style my fine honey-colored locks. My eyes were bright blue, and I had rosy cheeks and a big flashy smile.

Donna and I had never set foot in an Episcopal church; Roman Catholics were forbidden to enter other places of worship. We knew we were breaking a rule, but Mom, sitting in the Chevrolet station wagon outside with our baby brother, said it was all right. She'd checked with our priest: "As long as they don't participate in the service," Father Fahey had warned her.

Mom always asked the priests for advice. She didn't ask our father, because he was a Protestant. He didn't go to church with us. He never talked about religion to us either. Early on Mom talked a lot about the church rules and sin. She showed us an Old Testament with colored engravings of ugly, misshapen figures leaping around in a flaming pit. Mom pointed her red-painted finger at the horrible creatures and said, "Here are the murderers being punished in Hell." She shuddered. "Murderers, evil men like the one who killed five college girls in Chicago."

The four of us—my Mom, father, sister, and I—had been sitting near the living room radio, waiting for our favorite mystery, "The Shadow," when we heard the brutal murders reported.

The words flew into our ears before Dad, who sat closest to the radio, could turn it off. Our parents frowned at each other, then at us, as if waiting for our reaction, wishing we hadn't heard the announcement. We didn't react. What could we say? Such a thing seemed remote, but that night I snuggled in close to Donna in the bed we shared. Restless, I'd think about devils and the flaming abyss until my stomach lurched and I'd clutch the little cross my grandma gave me and repeat rote prayers like the Our Father over and over until I fell asleep.

Now we peered into the dark, cavernous space. Dusty beams of light streamed through the stained-glass windows, giving the place an unearthly feel. It smelled like the oil Aunt Tilley used to polish her staircase. Donna grabbed my hand as we hurried up the aisle to the small open casket and stood on our toes. There lay Carol, our next door neighbor. She and her little brother Bobby had moved in two years before, and they became daily playmates, swinging and playing baseball in our yard. It was hard to see Carol so still. They had dressed her in a white lace-trimmed dress, her face was calm and innocent, her eyes were closed. Two days before, we'd read the obituary: *Girl, 8, Dies of Leukemia.*

The week before, we'd asked Carol's mother, Connie, how to find her daughter at St. Luke's Hospital, four blocks from our house. I wrote the room number in my special notebook, pretending not to notice her red-rimmed eyes. The next day after school, we set out.

We didn't tell anyone about our plan, except Connie. We entered a back door, checked right and left, and ran to room 113. Clasping hands, Donna and I tiptoed to the hospital bed where Carol lay propped on two pillows. Her face was ashen, as though they'd powdered it. Pink sores covered her puffed lips; they oozed like fever blisters. She wore a pale green gown patterned with little clowns. When she heard us, she opened her eyes and managed a smile.

"Carol, we want you to know we're praying for you to get well," I told her.

"Yes, get well, so we can play jacks again," Donna said.

"Be careful," Carol murmured. "If they catch you, they'll get mad. Bobby came in yesterday and they told him kids can't come in here." Bobby was only six, and I guessed that Connie had sneaked him in.

Carol tried to smile again, but appeared exhausted. She closed her eyes, and we crept carefully to the door, our hearts racing. We made sure the coast was clear, and we fled.

After Carol went to the hospital, Mom wrapped chicken casserole or beef stew in tin foil and took it to Connie and her husband John. One night Mom returned, head bowed, a wad of Kleenex covering her nose. We watched as she walked over to Dad. Her brown, wavy hair was pulled back over her ears, and she wore the dark green dress Dad favored because he said it showed off her slim figure. Though tears had smeared her makeup, she still looked beautiful, and on an ordinary day, Dad would have whistled. Dad was slight but taut with a warm Bogart smile, dark hair, and thick eyebrows. His hazel eyes, as always, looked kind. We were proud of our good-looking parents.

Now Dad stood up from his armchair and put his arms around Mom. She was sniffling, and we knew Carol was dying.

That night Donna and I picked at our stew and cornbread. We did the dishes in silence. Every day the following week I kept thinking about Carol. I'd look up at the big clock on the back wall of the classroom and wonder if she had died. After school I'd hang back. I wanted to walk home alone so I could let loose and cry. I didn't understand this dying stuff. I prayed. I knew God would take care of her.

Now we stared at her. She was dead. Neither of us had seen a dead person. "Look at her hair," Donna whispered. "It's done up fancy. She never wore it that way." Strawberry-blond curls framed Carol's face. Donna was right. Carol had favored braids or pigtails when we played in the backyard.

We used to pray for her because she didn't belong to our church. Standing there now, Donna said, "Look. She must be in heaven." She pointed at the gold medal around Carol's neck. It showed Mary, the mother of Jesus. "It's the same one Grandma wears."

"She must have converted," I said, and smiled. "She must be in heaven." I could hardly wait to tell Mom. Carol was safe.

I dreaded having my hair done up in Shirley Temple curls. It meant sleeping on bobby pins, but this was a special day. Wearing my hated white leather, high-topped shoes and my red strawberry dress, I was starting kindergarten at Our Lady of Sorrows School.

Mom pushed me into the huge room filled with rows of little tables and chairs, the ABCs displayed on an otherwise empty wall. I found myself staring at a pretty blue-eyed woman in a long black dress, her head covered by a black veil. Her shoes were just like my grandmother's, and I forgot to be embarrassed about my own. "Meredith, this is your teacher," Mom said. Sister Barbara smiled down at me.

"But where are your ears?" I blurted. The kids standing nearby giggled, then hushed to hear Sister's response.

The nun laughed and knelt, taking my right hand in hers. "Oh, I have ears. Here, feel them." I breathed in a starchy clean smell as I carefully laid my hand where she placed it on the side of her head. I felt the lump of an ear. As the nun stood, I decided—when I grew up, I'd be just like her. It was a childish, even silly idea, but it was one that would set the course of my life.

Only Catholics enter the kingdom of heaven. The day I heard this, straight from our pastor's lips, I raced out of our first-grade classroom and ran six blocks home. I was panting when I found Mom arranging fish sticks in the kitchen. Their unpleasant smell, like my cousin's aquarium, teased my nostrils. "Mom," I said, "Father Eck told us that only Catholics go to heaven. He said *only* Catholics." I tugged at her elbow until she looked at me. "What about Daddy?"

Mom wiped her hands on her apron.

"Meredith, your daddy is a very good man. Of course, he'll go to heaven."

"Mom, is something wrong with Daddy? Maybe you shouldn't have married him."

"Oh, no. The Church, well, they'd like everyone to marry a Catholic. When that doesn't happen, we can still get married, but it's called a 'mixed' marriage. We were married in the sacristy instead of the church."

I imagined my parents, all dressed up: Daddy in his best suit, Mom in hat and gloves, turned away by a scowling priest from the front doors of our church. "But why?" I persisted. Mom turned away. I'd spotted the glint of tears in her eyes.

"It's the way it is," she said.

"But . . .?" I started again.

Mom slid the pan into the oven. "Don't worry. Your daddy will go to heaven."

That wasn't the end of it. That night Mom followed my sister and me into our bedroom, and knelt beside us as we recited our prayers: "If I die before I wake, I pray the Lord my soul to take."

"Girls." She ran her hand over our shoulders. "Remember to ask God to bless everyone we love." The scent of her perfume touched the air.

"Bless Daddy, Mom, Grandma, and all our cousins," Donna piped up.

"And all the kids in first grade, especially Becky and Elizabeth," I added.

Mom bowed her head and covered her face with her hands. We could barely hear her whisper, "And please, God, convert Don to our one true faith."

Hearing Mom's prayer, I didn't believe for a minute that our dad was headed for hell, but I was determined to pray really hard just in case.

I was the only child of a mixed marriage that I knew of. I squirmed when the term came up in religion class; I thought it meant I was second-rate, maybe worse. So I never questioned the words we chanted three times each morning at Mass: "Lord, I am not worthy." I believed it.

Not long after my first confession I realized I was sinning all the time. I had hateful thoughts about June, the neighbor kid who pulled my sister's hair. I wanted to break her arms, or at least her fingers. And occasionally, when our teacher led the kids outside for recess, I'd sneak to the supply closet and grab a handful of lined writing paper, which I'd stuff in my lunchbox. Each time I stole that paper, I felt a thrill. I liked the feeling of breaking rules. We had so many rules, and sometimes I got tired of them. Still, racked with guilt, every morning before Mass I trotted into the confessional. "Father, my last confession was yesterday. I stole four sheets of paper."

After three weeks, our teacher, Sister Bonaventure, called me aside. She put her arm around me and leaned down. Her breath smelled sour. "Honey, you don't need to go to confession every day."

"But Sister, I . . ." My face flushed hot.

"Most people only go once a week."

I wanted to break away and hide. I stared at a piece of gum smashed on the floor.

"Maybe try not to go until next Saturday. Okay, Meredith?"

I nodded. Avoiding her eyes, I scurried off.

When the bell clanged one afternoon and the kids shoved their way out the doors, I headed for the library. It was a small room, bookshelves on every wall. In the biography section, I discovered a set of slim volumes—I counted thirty-six—with red, blue, and green covers. *Lives of the Saints,* "Andrew" to "Wenceslas." I pulled Bartholomew off the shelf, opened it, and cracked the spine. I inhaled what I would come to recognize as the smell of a brand new book, a subtle, linen-like fragrance.

I heard footsteps, and turned as Sister Geraldine, her gold-rimmed glasses falling down her nose, slipped into the room. "Good afternoon, Sister," I said.

"Well, here you are again, Meredith. How many books would you like today?" Her smile, with its one silver tooth, reminded me of the toothy grin of a jack-'o-lantern.

"How many may I have?"

"If you keep this between us, you may take six. I know you love reading."

Walking home, I decided to read one each night; I'd finish them in thirty-six days. In my bed at night I read gory descriptions of martyrs impaled on swords or having their eyes gouged out. I was fascinated. Three weeks later I closed the last one, eleven days before my deadline, and took up with Nancy Drew and the Hardy Boys. That summer the Bookmobile pulled up one street over, and I borrowed so many books I had to carry them home in a grocery bag. When the new public library branch opened only six blocks away, I discovered my new favorite writers: Louisa May Alcott and Charlotte Bronte. My passion for books fired up. I didn't know it, but it too would shape my life.

"Religious life is the highest way to serve God," a visiting Sister Bridget said. She told us she was a missionary, and she'd gone to Africa to convert pagans to the Roman Catholic Church. Her words ignited me. Next Sunday, as my family feasted on their Sunday fare of fried chicken, I announced my goal. I watched as half smiles played on my parents' lips, which told me they would be proud to have a daughter who wanted to serve God in the "highest way."

Weekday evenings, Dad rested before his night shift at Boeing Aircraft. Mom, with a cup of what looked like tea, settled into the floral armchair next to the big mahogany radio and listened to the news. On a February evening in 1952 she told us: "The king of England has died. They'll have a new queen soon, his daughter Elizabeth." We squeezed into the chair with Mom. Her breath smelled like the rum we'd been allowed to taste in Christmas eggnog. The bright red lipstick she'd applied after dinner accented the blue of her eyes. I snuggled closer, envisioning her as a movie star. Her tea always seemed to relax her, but she never offered us a taste. When she drank tea she even cracked jokes and laughed out loud at Donna's stories.

Come June, the three of us huddled next to the radio, listening to Elizabeth's coronation from Westminster Abbey. The music—organs and trumpets and violins—was the most beautiful I'd ever heard.

"Next week's *Life* will have a whole spread of pictures," Mom promised.

Donna and I waited on the front porch every morning. When the magazine finally arrived, we flopped on the living room floor and gazed at the cover: the queen in her beaded gown and bejeweled crown. We pored over each photo. I read the story aloud to Mom and Donna.

I finished, and Donna asked Mom, "Was your wedding like this?"

"Why, no, honey. It was wartime when your father and I married. And besides, a wedding like this is very expensive."

I turned away, remembering what Mom told me about having to marry in the sacristy, not in the church. Daddy was not a Catholic.

"Will I have a wedding like this?" Donna jumped up and leaned on the arm of Mom's chair.

"I'm sure you will, honey, if that's what you want." Mom stroked Donna's blonde curls.

Mom got up and went into the kitchen. I followed, and startled her when I came in. She was pulling out a bottle of rum from the top cupboard. I took the stairs to my room two at a time. I thought nothing of it.

In fourth grade, my teacher Sister Bertrand brought me a pamphlet showing young women in wedding dresses. "Nuns are brides of Christ," she said. "In a special ceremony we wear gowns, and then we receive our black habits. It's the first of July, and yes, you are welcome."

Later I begged Mom, "Please, please." When she smiled and said "I'll think about it," I knew her answer was yes.

On a hot muggy morning in July, Mother drove us across town to the imposing four-story Sacred Heart Convent. With Mom pushing us, we managed to squeeze into the crowded chapel as organ music thundered from the pipe organ. It felt like the whole building was moving.

I breathed in the intoxicating fragrance of roses that festooned the altar, and stared at the families around us: men in suits and ties, women in hats and Sunday dresses, teenagers in fancy clothes, and a handful of squirming young children. When the music's tempo picked up, fifteen women in long white gowns and veils began their entrance. I closed my eyes and saw my own family, bursting with pride, as I took part in this procession.

Donna and I inched forward as each nun-to-be was handed a pillow-sized bundle bound with blue ribbon. They left the chapel, and minutes later returned in full habits, identical to all the other nuns.

"Is it over?" Donna whispered.

"No—listen." I shushed her. The bishop's voice rumbled, giving each nun a new name, after a saint. Marilyn Bailey was to be Sister Mary Peter. That name put me off. It sounded so masculine, but I guessed she didn't have a choice.

When I heard Mom clearing her throat, we hurried outside. "Did you enjoy the ceremony?"

Donna grinned. I threw out my arms like I'd seen Doris Day on *The Ed Sullivan Show*. "Oh yes! But, Mom, wouldn't those veils be really hot in the summer?"

"Tie three scarves tightly on your head and see," Mom said, laughing.

"Oh, it would be stifling." Stifling was a new word for me, so I pronounced it slowly, waiting for Mom's face to register approval.

"Well, there's your answer." She smiled.

I resolved to get used to it.

At school, I was the only twelve-year-old with acne and buck teeth. I was almost used to the overbite which I'd lived with for years, but the acne had come on suddenly. "Puberty," our family doctor told Mom. "Tell her to avoid chocolate."

With a new outbreak of pustules erupting each morning, I felt hopeless. Before I slid under the covers every night I fell to my knees: Dear God, if you are omnipotent (om-ni-po-tent, I said it slowly to make sure he heard me), cure me. I pictured myself waking the next morning with a clear, smooth face, like the women in ads for Pond's face cream, but it didn't happen.

As for my protruding teeth, the orthodontist said braces would cost a thousand dollars. I knew my parents didn't have much money so I said, "It's okay, I'm only going to be a nun." Before I learned they were determined to fix my smile so I'd be "a pretty nun," I considered myself doomed to ugliness.

Wearing ugly silver braces that glinted in the sunlight, I felt so self-conscious that I tried to keep my lips closed, hard for a girl who loved to laugh. At night I'd lie in bed, ignoring the rubbery taste of the tiny elastic bands I wore to hasten the straightening process, and flick my tongue over the rough metal wires.

When the short, frail Father Patrick J. O'Malley showed up on April 1, we thought it was an April Fools' joke. Until then Sister Louise, our homeroom teacher, had taught us religion. A few weeks before, she'd gained our undying loyalty when she'd given a straight answer to Charlene's bold question: "Sister, what's wrong with being some-one's lover?" The room got still. We craned our necks to look over at Charlene, whose high-pitched voice made her sound like she was play-acting. I'd never heard of this term either, and I couldn't imagine how Charlene had come up with it.

Sister Louise, who had been sitting at her desk, stood, tossed her veil over her shoulder, and took hold of the podium. "Lovers are," she paused, fixing her large brown eyes directly on us, "people who have sexual inter-course outside of marriage." The air in the classroom electrified. Never had any of our celibate teachers used such explicit terms. She gave us a minute to digest her response before she added: "We can talk more about this when we study the sacrament of matrimony." We couldn't wait.

So we didn't understand why, instead of Sister Louise, old Father O'Malley showed up to teach us about marriage. What did he know that Sister Louise didn't? We'd seen him in the church when he tottered out to help distribute Communion, but this was our first up-close encoun-ter. His back was slightly curved, and he wore a box-shaped black hat with a tassel. A pair of rimless glasses perched on his Pinocchio nose, and his Irish brogue made him almost impossible to understand. This man intended to teach us about sexual intercourse?

"Young ladies, surely you've heard St. Paul's sacred words: 'Wives, be subject to your husbands.'" That's when he lost me.

No matter. I would never be a wife. I would never be subject to any man. I planned to give my life to God, as soon as I could.

When our neighbor Mrs. Murray asked me to babysit Saturday, I thought her timing was perfect. If the doddering priest denied us information on sex, I'd learn about it on my own. I knew the Murrays had shelves full of books, and their little girl went to bed promptly at 8:30 p.m. Surely they would have a book on sex.

At 8:30, after "Hansel and Gretel," and "Cinderella" twice, I tucked in the three-year-old and watched her eyes flutter and shut. I tiptoed out and softly closed the door.

From their bookshelves I grabbed a book entitled *A Catholic Marriage* by Reverend John O'Reilly, OSB. What would a celibate Benedictine know about sex? I scanned the table of contents, hit on a chapter called "Marital Relations," and found only a few illustrations of sexual organs. Finding nothing juicy to add to my limited knowledge about sex, I returned the book to its place and went to the kitchen for the piece of German chocolate cake Mrs. Murray had saved for me.

The summer before college, my cousin Georgiana gave me a stack of *Silver Screen* magazines. Georgiana was not only "well endowed" but she was also a cheerleader, which made her about the most exotic, attractive person I knew. I knew nothing about movie stars—the only movies we saw were old black and white films, shown on rickety projectors in the school auditorium. Still, the glittery world triggered new ideas for me. In my bed at night I'd pore over the pictures of beautiful people, some of them couples embracing, and ask myself: what if someday I met a man as good-looking as Clark Gable and he swept me into his arms as he did Vivien Leigh in *Gone with the Wind?*

What if I didn't become a nun?

This was the first whisper I'd heard from an inner voice suggesting I might not have a religious vocation. It horrified me.

Two weeks later, on August 28, our family made the three-hour trip to St. Catherine's College, and they escorted me to the end of the wide, polished dorm hallway. We crammed into 218, a small room with bunk beds, two desks with straight-backed chairs, and a pair of three-drawer dressers. We could barely move.

"Hey, Meredith, look—your roommate's already here." Donna pointed to the bottle of perfume and lipsticks on a dresser.

The card posted on the door read: Meredith Byrne. Eileen Donovan. "The letter from the dean of women said she's a sophomore," I said. "I hope she's not stuck-up, living with a freshman."

Dad and I lugged in my trunk—the same footlocker he had used in World War II with his name and serial number stenciled in white letters on the top: Donald Byrne, 48976, US Army Air Corps. Mom helped Donna wrestle my oversized suitcase to the other dresser.

Mom opened the closet to hang my clothes. "Your roommate has quite a wardrobe," she said.

I walked over next to Mom. Most of the closet space was already filled with Eileen Donovan's clothes: wool straight skirts with matching sweater sets, several blouses and more skirts, plus three winter coats. On the floor I counted five pairs of shoes and a pair of boots. Donna peered around my shoulder. "She must be rich!" I gritted my teeth and closed the closet door. Already I was feeling inferior.

"It's a little smaller than your room at home, honey." Dad was trying to make me feel good. "But my room at Oklahoma U in 1934 was just like this."

After lunch, I walked my folks downstairs to the Chevy station wagon and stood waving until they disappeared. I couldn't wait for them to leave. I ran up the back stairs to avoid bumping into anyone and into my room. I picked up Eileen's perfume: Je Reviens. French. As I caressed the narrow glass vial, images of Audrey Hepburn flashed into mind. Never in my life had I felt so out of place.

My whole first year at St. Catherine's, I felt intimidated by the crop of Easterners who'd chosen to study at our modest Kansas campus. My first roommate, with her classy clothes and pageboy hairstyle, was the quintessential sophisticate and compared to her, I felt the country hick. But in May Eileen returned to New York (to marry her boyfriend back home), and I slowly acclimated to college life.

Evenings I shelved books in the library with a guy from California, a place I only knew from the movies. When I'd first spotted him in calculus class, I'd admired his tanned skin and dark bushy eyebrows. He was the only Californian in our entire college. I wondered what he was thinking, enrolling in this nondescript place when he lived in the Golden State.

One evening I walked in to find him lost in a book covered in what looked like brown paper bag wrapping. It was bunchy at the corners and I guessed he might have wrapped it himself.

"What's your mystery book?" I said.

Glenn glanced up. "Promise not to tell," he whispered. "It's too racy for these nuns."

Now I was intrigued.

"It's called *Goodbye Columbus*, and you'll never see Sister Ludmilla cataloging it here." He laughed.

"Where did you get it?" I moved closer to him.

"Shhh." He put his finger to his lips and leaned into my ear. "The public library. Downtown."

After that Glenn became a kind of guru for me, mysterious and worldly, someone who knew about books like this.

He laughed quietly, thumping his fingers against the book. "Think you can handle it?"

Before I could say yes, Sister Ludmilla, her rosary clicking at her side, sauntered in. Unlike the other nuns, she cracked jokes and seldom frowned, even if we arrived late. Everyone liked her.

"Good evening, Sister," we said. Glenn tucked the book onto the shelf below him.

She chuckled, as though she guessed our secret and didn't even care. "What are you two up to?"

"It's quiet tonight," Glenn said. We grinned at each other as she disappeared into the stacks. "I'll give it to you Monday," he promised.

Goodbye, Columbus was not about Christopher. It told a racy story about the summer romance of a college couple ravenous for sex. I found it spellbinding. I had never read anything so explicit.

Later on, Glenn introduced me to books I'd never have found on my own: *Catcher in the Rye, The End of the Affair, A Clockwork Orange.* One by one these books and others claimed their place, each dressed in paper-bag brown, beneath my mattress. They showed me whole new worlds, far different from those of old classics we studied, such as *The Odyssey, Paradise Lost,* or *A Modest Proposal.*

In Modern Poetry I discovered poets like Sylvia Plath and Anne Sexton, whose fine-tuned verses I pored over trying to find a clue for their eventual suicides. Soon, reading threatened to take over my life, and I decided to major in literature.

Sophomore year a young man sat behind me in English Lit class. I didn't pay much attention to Mike until the monstrous Grendel attacked Beowulf. Then I heard a couple of low growls from Mike's direction and had to bite my lip to keep from giggling. Besides being funny, Mike was attractive. He was tall, with wavy brown hair and dark brown eyes. A small chip in one of his front teeth gave him an engaging smile. He favored long-sleeve plaid shirts like my dad wore, and, like me, he wore thick-lensed glasses with dark frames. A couple of weeks later when he asked me to the Homecoming Dance, I was ecstatic. Even though I was committed to becoming a nun, I desperately wanted to know what it was like to have a boyfriend.

By senior year I'd grown up enough to feel comfortable with my roommates, Barb, Julie, and Joann, even though they all hailed from New Jersey. One October night we lay in our beds, waiting for the nun to do lights-out check (10:30 p.m., no excuses) when Julie spoke up. "Hey, I've got an idea. Midterms are over Friday. Let's celebrate."

"Celebrate?" Barb asked.

"The Blue Lounge?" I ventured. The Blue Lounge, a ratty downtown bar, was popular for its cheap beer and free popcorn. Probably too pedestrian for the likes of Barb and Julie, but half the guys in our class called it their favorite hangout, and I'd even gone there a couple of times.

"No," Julie said. "I'm serious. Let's do something different—a picnic at a lake. We can drive to that place we visited last year."

"Oh yeah, Clark County Lake," Barb said.

Joann giggled. "Remember that line, 'a glass of wine, a loaf of bread and thou'?"

"Yeah, I'll get the wine," said Julie. She was twenty-two, old enough to buy liquor. I had a fleeting vision of her family clustered around the fireplace in a drawing room decorated in Louis XIV, each of them in fancy dress holding a snifter of brandy in one hand and a languid cigarette in the other.

My own experience with alcohol was an occasional mug of the

3.2-percent beer permitted eighteen-year-old Kansans. I hated the taste and barely sipped at a glass set before me, but I forced myself to drink it, just to fit in. As for wine, back when I was twelve helping the nuns in the sacristy, I waited until I was alone one day and opened the sacristy closet, unscrewed the lid on the heavy gallon jug, and took a big swallow. The sacramental wine smelled fruity, but tasted like vinegar. Unlike the altar boys, who regularly indulged, I never tried it again.

But that didn't mean I wasn't up for a real glass of wine with my friends.

Friday we climbed into Julie's '62 Chevrolet convertible and drove out to Clark County Lake. It was a perfect fall afternoon—cool crisp air, electric-blue skies dotted by an occasional cloud, and best of all, a deserted lakeside. Kansas had only nine or ten lakes, and Clark County would never make a list of "Best" places to visit.

It was the size of an indoor skating rink, surrounded by scraggly elms and swarms of flies and gnats.

On a little patch of green—more rocks than grass—we spread Joann's red plaid blanket and laid out our feast. Barb lit a cigarette. Jane pulled a corkscrew from her leather bag and opened the wine. "Help yourself," she said, pouring herself a half glass. She too lit a cigarette and took a sip of the deep red liquid. She closed her eyes when she tasted it, and her face seemed to relax. I wondered how I would feel.

Drinks in hand, we nibbled cheese and bread. The wine was tasty; nothing like the altar wine I'd swallowed years ago. It was almost like Kool-Aid, but not as sweet. Its aroma was nice, too, like the Welch's grape juice my grandma had served. I tried to imitate Julie and take only small sips. Soon I was gulping.

The lake appeared more tranquil by the minute, its plainness endowed with beauty I hadn't noticed at first. I gazed around, thinking of Wordsworth: "I wandered lonely as a cloud / That floats on high o'er vales and hills." There were no hills in Kansas, but the sky was puffed up with clouds like cotton candy. Soon I felt joy, bordering on ecstasy.

I poured another glass, this time a full tumbler. Why not? It was practically Kool-Aid, and so refreshing.

After an hour or so, we gathered our things and got back into the car. I was in the backseat when suddenly the world began to tumble and spin. I'd never been so dizzy. I started to say something but hated to embarrass myself. Then nausea hit me, hard. "Stop!" I cried. "I'm sick."

We lurched forward as Julie braked. I heard her high-pitched order: "Get her out of my car!" Someone pulled me out and I started retching, over and over again. Through squinted eyes I glimpsed traces of ruddy liquid mixed with the bread and cheese I'd eaten just minutes before. Then the world faded to black.

Two hours later, I awoke fully dressed in my lower bunk bed. I felt terribly weak, and my throat was scratchy and raw. I was alone. The clock on my desk read 7:10.

The door swung wide and a blond-headed fury stomped into the room. It was my sister Donna, now a freshman. Her blue eyes were wide with accusation and her face scrunched with frowns. She couldn't have looked more like our mother. "What's wrong with you?"

"I've got the flu," I said, hoping that she didn't know the truth.

"Well, Mike's waiting for you. What do you want me to tell him?"

Oh, no. I swallowed hard. My mouth was sour with the taste of vomit. "Could you tell him I have the flu?" I said.

"I'll tell him, but you know what, Meredith?" She moved in close and glared at me, her blue eyes bulging. "I don't believe for one minute that you have the flu."

She whipped away, slamming the door. I lay there, thinking what a liar I was. In a few minutes I fell asleep again. I didn't hear anyone come in that evening, not even the gravelly voiced nun doing bed check.

The next morning my tongue was cotton and my arms ached as though I'd been drawn on a medieval torture machine. When I saw my roommates after breakfast, they told me that after I'd stopped vomiting, Julie had driven us to the dorm's back door. Julie held the door and Joann and Barb lugged my dead weight up three flights of stairs, hoisting me by my armpits.

No surprise I was sore.

I never confessed to getting drunk. After all, I hadn't done it on purpose. I promised myself instead to stick to one beer, if and when I ever drank again.

The following weekend I ignored my distaste for beer and by the time I finished my twelve-ounce glass, I felt the tingling exhilaration I'd found at the lake. I felt prettier, funnier, smarter. I liked what drinking did for me.

For a couple of years at least, having one drink made me quite content.

I wanted to teach college English, so I needed a master's and a doctorate degree. In November of our senior year—1963, a week before JFK's assassination—I got serious about graduate school. Still a devout Catholic, I applied to Marquette, Fordham, and Carradine, all run by Jesuits. When a letter arrived from Carradine offering me a job as a teaching assistant to cover my tuition plus two hundred dollars a month, my decision was made.

A month before graduation, I grabbed Mike after his French class and led him into an empty classroom. "What's going on?" he asked.

"Ssshh," I whispered. "I have an idea." His eyes grew wide. He thought he knew me well by now, but I knew this would surprise him.

"We're never alone, and I have an idea, but it's risky. If we get caught, even our high GPAs won't prevent our getting kicked out."

"Well, what is it? I can't believe you—a rule-breaker?" He cracked his knuckles.

"Not never. Soon."

I whispered my plan. He would borrow his best friend's car for a Saturday night and we'd drive to Garden City, a tiny burg that Truman Capote's *In Cold Blood* put on the map. We'd get a motel, have dinner, and hold each other all night. I'd saved enough money cleaning tables in the cafeteria to pay for the daring excursion.

"Mike, I'm so sick of nuns sneaking up on us every time we hold hands. I want to be close to you. Close, only close." Months ago Mike had told me he didn't want me to experience sex. He'd implied it was so exciting that would cause me to change my mind about becoming a nun. But I wasn't a nun yet, and I yearned to bend the rules. Why shouldn't I know how it felt to hold a man—and be held?

Mike laughed. Then he guffawed. "I can't believe you, Meredith, you've got it all covered."

Thursday when I met Mike in the cafeteria, he was grinning. "Now I have an idea," he said. "We're staying in a motel, right?"

I nodded.

"Well, what if the motel clerk thinks we're not married?"

"I never thought of that."

He reached into his pants pocket and pulled out two fake wedding bands. "Look. I found these in the dime store."

I grabbed the smaller one and slipped it on my ring finger. A perfect fit.

"Meredith." Mike sounded serious now. "If I buy you something to wear that night, will you, uh, wear it for me?"

I giggled. Mike buying fake rings and sexy sleepwear? A new Mike was emerging to match the new me. With this getaway I'd break every rule in the dean of women's book, and I couldn't wait.

At noon, Mike parked the Chevy coupe in the back lot. I got in and we slowly drove away. Mike's hands on the steering wheel were trembling. "I got us a little something to celebrate," he said, pointing to a brown bag on the floor. A pint of Four Roses. "We can have this with 7 Up." Cocktails? I was excited.

Garden City was sixty miles west, more than an hour's drive. At Lights Out motel on Main Street Mike parked and shut off the ignition. We sat, staring at the purple blinking neon OPEN sign in the office. He lit his sixth cigarette.

"Are you sure you can do this?" I asked.

Five minutes later he emerged from the office, a key dangling in his hand.

"The guy didn't raise an eyebrow. He doesn't care who we are," he said, rattling the key in my face. "Let's go—room fourteen, down at the end."

Room fourteen was the shabbiest motel room I'd ever seen. It smelled like they'd doused it with a concoction of Pine-Sol and Clorox. A double bed with a blue chenille spread was pushed against the wall; a small table with a lamp sat beside it. The only other furnishings were a beat-up little desk with three drawers on one side and a straight chair, its seat covered in brown plastic. The bathroom had only a small tiled shower, a toilet, and sink. Everything reeked of cleanser. I stared into the cheap mirror to see a blurred version of my face. I looked expectant.

"Okay, so far, so good," Mike said. He was perched on the bed. "Come here," he invited, almost shyly. "Here it is." From a grocery bag he pulled out a white box tied with a large baby-blue bow. He watched closely as I undid the package. Wrapped in white tissue paper, I found a short, strapless gown, made of light blue chiffon with a white satin ribbon marking the cleavage.

"Oh, Mike, it's lovely." I felt genuinely pleased—but very nervous.

"Would you, uh, model it for me?"

As I turned to go change in the bathroom, I pictured myself as Doris Day in *Pillow Talk*. Shifting into the role, my nervousness disappeared. It was fun to feel sophisticated. A man. A motel room. "Make us a round of drinks, OK?" I said.

No one ever knew about our secret trip. No one would have believed that we'd done what we wanted to: we held each other all night long. But I had to admit, I'd felt ripples of a new kind of pleasure when we were making out, and was grateful Mike hadn't pushed me.

After graduation Mike was headed to Kansas State University, and I to Carradine. But not before he proposed one summer night, and I told him I still wanted to be a nun. He took my refusal with good humor, but I thought I saw a flash of disappointment in his eyes.

The week before I left for graduate school in St. Louis, I dressed in my new black knit suit and posed in front of the large mirror on my antique dresser. "Good morning, I'm Miss Byrne, your English teacher." I projected my voice as I'd learned to in speech class, and rehearsed several times. I decided my appearance was acceptable—I resembled some of my college instructors who weren't nuns—but I stepped in close and saw anxiety in my eyes. Oh God, I'll be teaching a bunch of eighteen-year-olds and I'm only four years older. And there was the fact of numbers: St. Cat's enrollment was eight hundred; Carradine's was twelve thousand. I was sick with worry.

I loved graduate school, especially Chaucer, Shakespeare, and the more contemporary Updike, Ellison and Baldwin. I loved sifting through ink-blurred newspaper accounts about the Mississippi River from Mark Twain's era preserved on microfiche in the library or having a beer and joking about nineteen-century bestsellers like *The Scarlet Letter* or *Moby Dick*. I didn't even mind trekking up and down three floors on the ancient, creaky stairs to the huge common room where we teaching fellows, as we were called, held office hours in this space which offered no privacy.

The next two years flew by. At the end of my first year my acne mysteriously disappeared and I bought contact lenses. I became a blonde with a stylish new haircut. I blossomed. For the first time in my life, I saw that I was pretty. So did several male colleagues.

Most nights I stayed up late reading student essays and writing papers on the blue portable typewriter my parents had given me. Weekends, my new admirers invited me to see films and drink beer in the handful of ancient, smoky bars near campus. Early mornings I raced across the street to the 6:30 Mass, where I always remembered to renew my promise. I enjoyed the male attention, but remained determined to be chaste and marry only Christ.

One afternoon after her last class, my colleague Gwen swept into our office. Of our group, only Gwen had a husband and a baby, and I caught a trace of the lavender scent she wore to hide the smell of drool. She threw a stack of books on her desk and turned to me. "You're almost finished here. Why don't you apply for a teaching position at Sumner?"

"But what about my exams and—my God!—my dissertation?"

"Do it in your spare time or during the summer."

I wheeled my chair to my desk and nodded. "I'll think about it."

Gwen picked up her books and started out the door. "Do it," she barked.

Sumner was a community college a few miles north of the university. I was intrigued, but I'd never set foot in an institution that wasn't Catholic. After long deliberation, I called for an application, having no idea how much my life was about to change.

For my first twenty-four years, I'd never wavered from my promise to become a nun. Certainly I'd flirted with carnal knowledge, but I knew next to nothing about sex.

Until one evening after I'd changed into my chaste button-up flannel nightgown, and my neighbor Judy knocked. I opened the door and she held out a book.

"I know it's dog-eared, but it's time you learned a few things. Read this book." I stared at the title: *Lady Chatterley's Lover.* I paused. I was dying to read it. Years before, I'd seen it on the Index, the list of books forbidden to Catholics.

D. H. Lawrence's steamy book left me conflicted: I started to savor the notion of sex. This strange new sensation was perturbing, especially since I'd long fancied myself celibate. But who was I kidding? Maybe I'd "preserved" my virginity all those years only because sex—and men—terrified me.

Connie Chatterley changed all that. Over and over, I studied the graphic account of Connie's liaison with her gardener Mellors. Lawrence's language and style seemed terribly old-fashioned, but the eroticism he described was irresistible. Mellors was "turgid," "quivering," and "inside her." Then "helpless orgasm" set her "rippling, rippling, rippling like a flapping overlapping of soft flames, soft as feathers, ... melting her all molten inside."

I felt as if a switch had been turned on in me. My face got hot and feverish. I began imagining myself having sex with every man I knew—even the Jesuit priests. Or at least the young ones. What would it be like? How would I get the nerve? I wanted what Connie Chatterley had—the ripples, the feathers, and most of all the flames.

The subject of S-E-X was forbidden to us youngsters. Good Catholics did not talk about it, we did not touch ourselves for pleasure (mortal sin!), and we certainly didn't touch anyone else. But now, a woman on fire, I began to examine and question my motives. I realized the promise I'd made at age five was more than uninformed, perhaps out of a romanticized idea about nuns, reinforced by the saints' biographies I'd read as a child. What little girl wouldn't be impressed by a nun who gave the pope orders (which he followed) and opened orphanages all over the world?

My curiosity got the best of me. I decided to see for myself what this sex thing was all about. But before I did, I went to see Father Theodore Westfall, the kindly Jesuit who'd taught me last year.

"I feel as if I'm letting God down," I told him. We sat in his second-floor office overlooking the quadrangle which nearly everybody on campus used as their meet-up place. It was winter and the huge elm was bare and stripped of its leaves.

"I wonder if any good person can let God down," he said in his strong, reassuring voice.

"But Father, how do I know for sure?" My tightly clasped hands began to sweat. I had to make peace with myself.

"My dear, over all these years, I've become convinced that God wants us to be happy and fulfilled."

"Then I'm no different than all these nuns who are leaving."

"No. And all of them—and you—are only following their hearts." He smiled, maybe wistfully.

I had to change my mindset. I was not disappointing God or anyone in breaking my promise to become a nun. But after more than twenty years, it wasn't easy. Every time I saw the nuns kneeling in the college church, a voice taunted me: "Well, you're too weak to give your life to God. You've failed."

That Catholic guilt haunted me for years.

In my third year of graduate school, I got involved with the handsome blonde Jack Elting. He had a fresh, jaunty look, as though he were out to conquer the world. And maybe he was. Jack had left the seminary after eight years. He took me out a few times, and we'd made it to heavy petting, but no further. After all, two months before he'd been a full-fledged celibate member of a religious community.

I played the chaste plain Jane until a colleague of mine jumped into the ring. Shelly appeared at a party one Sunday afternoon, twenty pounds slimmer than I'd ever seen her. She wore a colorful sundress with cleavage showing, fancy sandals, and a snappy new hairdo. In the two years I'd known her, I'd never seen her date or even get a letter from a hometown boyfriend. So when her perfectly made-up face broke out in a smile directed at Jack, I knew exactly what was up. It never occurred to me I needed to make drastic changes to my looks, and here came Anne Boleyn. I was devastated.

Then I met a man who would change my fantasies about sex. Though short and stocky, Nick had a sizzle I couldn't ignore. He and I went for pizza, and for a double feature at the drive-in. Our dates ended in heavy petting. One night, as we embraced, I touched his knee. He removed my hand and glared. "Do you know what you're doing to me?"

"What am I doing?"

"That's a turn-on. A huge turn-on. You can't do that to a man without repercussions."

"Oh, I'm sorry!" I was embarrassed at my naïveté.

"Never mind." He reached for me and we started kissing again. I made sure to keep my hand well away from his knee.

One winter afternoon we left the Pine Street Bar, climbed into the front seat of his Ford pickup, and began kissing passionately. I was tipsy, trying hard to ignore how eagerly my body was responding. Every kiss became more urgent until Nick was moaning softly. He put his hand through the opening in my blouse and began caressing my breast. I struggled against the stimulation, but didn't stop him. As we continued, the car windows steamed over.

I accidentally dropped my hand on Nick's thigh and he jolted, and pulled away. "That's enough. Let's go."

"Go?" I started buttoning my blouse.

"To my house. This is too much."

He turned the ignition key and pulled onto Lindell Boulevard. "Find something on the radio," he ordered. Trying to figure out whether he was angry or overcome with desire, I started thinking about Lady Chatterley's gardener-lover Mellors again. I found a radio station playing "The Beat Goes On." Neither of us said a word, but both of us knew. The beat was on.

Nick parked behind the ramshackle house he shared with two other men. He came around, opened my door, and pulled me by the arm through the front door and up the stairs. There was a strange odor in the hallway, but I didn't think it was the time to ask what they'd cooked the night before. Besides, I was beginning to get excited.

The late afternoon sunlight gave the empty apartment a shiny glow, like a stage lit with spotlights. Leaving his bedroom window shades open, Nick tore off his shirt, unbuckled his belt, kicked off his shoes, and shed his jeans. I watched, gaping.

"Well?" He sounded impatient. He plopped down on the bed.

I racked my brain, trying to remember the scene in the book. I had no idea what to do. I recalled Mellors had undressed Lady Chatterley, but here was Nick, stepping out of his underpants and making no move toward me. Not knowing what else to do, I removed my blouse and skirt, draped them over a chair, and stood awkwardly in my panties and camisole, a satin one my sister had given me for my birthday.

"Come here, come on," he said, holding his arms out to me. I lay down and he began kissing me so hard I could barely breathe. His whiskers scratched against my cheeks; his body was damp with sweat.

In a few moments it was over. What? So fast? Where was the pain of deflowering I'd read about?

Truth to tell, I felt almost nothing: no discomfort, only the sensation of something inside me and a heavy weight moving up and down. The bedsprings were squeaking. Before I could speculate further, Nick heaved a couple of huge sighs, shivered, and rolled off.

I closed my eyes, thinking perhaps he would hold me or kiss me again, but the next thing he did was get up. He padded away from me, down the hallway, and I heard running water and a toilet flushing.

Well, I asked myself, is that it?

Later, as I showered in my own bathroom, I asked myself if I needed to confess my sin. I thought the Church deemed sexual intercourse sinful because it was a pleasurable act before marriage. But I'd felt no pleasure. What was the point?

But when I went to confession, I told the priest, "I have sinned. I had sex with my boyfriend."

"Do you plan to repeat this action?" His voice sounded serious, even angry.

"Oh, no, Father. It happened because I had too much to drink."

"You'd best watch your drinking." He cleared his throat. "But the question is: do you plan to let this happen again?"

"No, Father."

So much for sex. A three-minute sweaty act and a penance of ten Our Fathers and ten Hail Marys. Nick's idea of lovemaking hardly resembled what I'd imagined after reading *Lady Chatterly*. It wasn't hard for me to promise I wouldn't do it again.

In May, 1968, two weeks after a grueling interview, I signed a contract as a full-time faculty member at Sumner College. I was told to report the last week of August for orientation.

When the time came, I had a dental emergency and arrived a day late. My first destination was the the dean's office where a dark-haired woman wearing Ben Franklin glasses welcomed me from a desk piled high with files and books.

"Hi, I'm Meredith Byrne. May I get my keys?" We shook hands and smiled.

"Hi, I'm Pearl. Good to see you." She scrabbled in her drawer. "Here's a key for your office and one for the mail room."

I barely had time to thank her when the dean's door flew open, and a big, burly, red-faced man emerged. "Ah, Miss Byrne, you're here. A day late?"

I blinked. "Oh, I called and left . . ." I fought back an angry reply.

"Well," he interrupted, "we'll have to deduct a day's pay from your salary. It's in the contract." He sounded harsh.

"Of course, I understand." I was determined not to be completely cowed. "And you are the dean?"

"Oh, yes. Sorry. Malcolm Bradway." He extended a beefy, moist hand.

"Pleasure," I forced a smile, pulling my purse strap onto my shoulder. "Well, excuse me." I ducked out the door. It's a good thing he wasn't on my hiring committee, I thought.

Pearl followed me. The dean's door slammed shut. "Don't mind him," she whispered. "He's not smooth, but he's OK." She pointed me south. "Your office is 32, on the right."

Halfway down the hall I ran into Greg Ellis, one of the professors on my hiring committee. He smiled broadly when he saw me. He was a couple of inches taller than me, with a wide face which dimpled when he smiled, soft gray eyes, and thick graying hair. Not handsome—but attractive, I mused, relieved to see a friendly face.

"Good morning, Meredith," he said. "Glad you made it."

With my new key I opened the door to a smallish room outfitted for two. The office smelled of floor wax and Windex. The windows on one wall stood floor to ceiling. Through the slat blinds I could see splinters of the blue August sky, bright green lawns, and farther out miniature cars dotting the parking lot.

"Your new digs," Greg said, easing into a swivel chair. He rolled closer to mine. "Meredith," he said "I was outside the office, and overheard Malcolm. I decided not to barge in, but do you mind telling me what happened?"

I told him.

"Hmmm," he said, taking a pack of cigarettes from his pocket. "Do you want one?"

"No thanks. Look, maybe I shouldn't have told you what Malcolm said."

He lit his Marlboro and shrugged. "Oh, don't worry." His boyish grin was reassuring.

Seconds later Gwendolyn Blake walked in. Her hair was a nimbus of red curls and she carried the same worn leather briefcase she'd used the past three years in grad school. It was Gwen who'd urged me to apply for this job, and we'd both been hired. Now we were assigned an office to share.

At 3:00, the three of us sauntered into a classroom for our first department meeting. As a new hire, I was keen to see the behind-the-scenes working of an English department. A minute later, a man in a rumpled shirt and green plaid Bermuda shorts ran in, panting hellos to his colleagues. Gwen whispered, "That's Andrew. I hear he's a Harvard man."

I rolled my eyes, but I was only going along with her. I had no idea what a Harvard man looked like. I barely knew what Harvard meant.

Near the end of the meeting Malcolm lumbered into the smoke-filled room. Everyone but Andrew, Gwen, and I was smoking nonstop. Malcolm fussed with his red scraggly beard as he droned on, enumerating our responsibilities. When he finished, he sighed and took a step toward the door. "Questions?"

Greg snuffed his cigarette and raised his hand. "I think the department needs to know how we've handled Meredith's absence," he said. Everyone turned to look at him. He stood and explained the issue, noting that my pay was being docked. He turned to face me. "Is that about right?"

My facing blazing, I managed to nod. Grumbling spread throughout the room.

"Come on, Malcolm," Andrew, the Harvard guy, said. "She didn't know the protocol."

"Yeah—give her a pass," said a bearded man.

Everyone continued growling at the dean, whose face had turned crimson. "All right, all right." Malcolm raised his hands in defeat. As he stepped out the door, applause erupted. "Way to go, Greg," called Laura, the professor who'd chaired my hiring committee.

Greg became my first friend at Sumner College and my new hero.

Our dean, believing that Gwen and I lacked experience, appointed Greg as our mentor. At first, we were indignant. Hadn't we already taught freshman English at the university for six semesters? To our surprise, Malcolm was right. Teaching at a white upper-middle-class Catholic university did not prepare us for the student population at Sumner, where 44 percent of our students were black, and more than 50 percent worked (sometimes full-time) and had their own families. In my own college years many of us worked, but only a few hours a week, and all of us lived on campus. At Sumner, a community college which required neither a hefty tuition nor a high GPA, my classes were full of people as new to the college experience as I was new to teaching them. I didn't know it then, but I was smack in the middle of one of the most significant shifts in American higher education. I had no idea too that teaching the "new" student population would be the most rewarding experience in my life.

Shortly after my class ended one night, Samantha Jones, a large-boned black woman toting her books in a worn black handbag, dragged herself into my office.

"Ms. Byrne," she said, "Ms. Byrne, I don't have my paper tonight. My little one, he's only four, got the croup on Saturday, and I couldn't get it done for his coughing and crying."

I looked into the eyes of a deeply pained, exhausted mother and nodded. "Do you work too, Samantha?" I asked.

"Yes'm, I clean in the Chase Park Plaza 'cause a year back my husband, he left. I'm on my own, but if I can make it through these classes I can be an assistant teacher." She sighed, shifting her purse to the other arm.

In those few minutes, Samantha taught me more than she would ever know.

Gwen and I began meeting with Greg the following week. Curious about him, we pummeled him with questions. We learned that he'd served a four-year stint in the Air Force, married a stunning brunette (he fished her picture from his wallet), fathered three girls (another picture), and studied at the University of Wisconsin with the Hemingway scholar W. C. Chase before moving with his family to Sumner.

Greg showed interest in us too. He called us his "bluestockings." When I said I'd considered becoming a nun, he bent over laughing.

The second week he invited me to lunch. He drove us to a little bistro with outdoor tables with yellow umbrellas where he ordered wine with our chicken salads. I soon realized that I'd never met an older man—particularly one so intelligent and articulate—who seemed intrigued with what I had to say. Sure, I'd had professors who knew literature and loved it as I did, but none had ever sat down with me to discuss Shakespeare, John Donne, or Faulkner. Some afternoons Greg and I went to the college library where he'd search for books he loved but that I was unfamiliar with, and bring them to me. I was fast falling in love with his mind—or so I thought.

That was September.

The first time my new supervisor asked me—only me, alone—out for an after-work drink, I hesitated. As colleagues, we had lunched a couple of times, but after-work cocktails?

Greg was an engaging man, but he was married. I found his eagerness for my company flattering, and I felt waves of desire when he was near me. I put him off a day or two, but he persisted. Finally, I gave in.

He drove us to the Fox and Hounds, a plush new lounge in midtown. Inside, the large dimly lit space was furnished in English drawing-room style, with soft leather sofas and chairs, coffee tables, and a fireplace at either end. Tapestries depicting medieval hunting scenes hung on the walls. I'd never seen such elegance.

"How's this?" He steered me to the most secluded corner. "I thought of you while I was teaching today," he began.

I groped around in my purse for my pack of Marlboros, feigning disinterest. With all the smoking around me at Sumner, I'd recently started.

"Roethke, you know his work?"

Shaking my head, I pulled out a cigarette, and Greg lit it. For an instant I could see his eyes. They were fixed on mine.

"I knew a woman/lovely in her bones," he quoted. "You know, maybe because the students are so young, they don't share my enthusiasm for Roethke's imagery. Listen to this: 'She stroked my chin/She taught me Turn, and Counter-turn, and Stand.'"

Embarrassed, I kept my eyes down, grateful that the soft lighting hid my blushing face. "Sounds like Donne's 'A Valediction: Forbidding

Mourning,'" I countered. "The twin compasses, bending with each other?"

At that moment the waiter arrived, and we ordered martinis. Wanting to steer Greg away from such sensual poetry, I asked him about the essay on Shakespearean villains he'd published.

As the alcohol loosened us, we began playing a literary game: one of us would recite famous lines from a play or novel, and the other had to identify the speaker. Greg kept choosing Shakespearean lovers. "I am dying, Egypt, dying," he called out, gesturing widely and laughing.

"That's too easy," I said.

"Listen to the passion in that short line!"

Of course I understood, but I was also aware I was walking a fine line. Passion was not an appropriate topic. By the time we'd left the Fox and Hounds, I'd steered the conversation to his daughters.

Still, I couldn't stop myself. A few weeks later I started studying in earnest for my doctoral exams, and Greg became my personal tutor, like a don at Oxford. I had a single-spaced twelve-page list of books I could be questioned on, and every afternoon, Greg would quiz me. More than once he told me I'd better work harder. And I did.

On another afternoon we rushed through a downpour and arrived at the Fox and Hounds sopping wet. I ducked into the ladies' room and stared at myself in the mirror: my hair looked scraggly and dark circles of running mascara haloed my eyes. I clipped my hair into a ponytail and refreshed my lipstick, yet still felt shabby. When I walked back to our corner table, there was Greg, martini in hand, smiling.

"I've never seen you so—" he paused, "bedraggled."

I groaned."No Isabel Archer today?" Isabel was the comely, spirited "lady" in the novel called *Portrait of a Lady*.

He covered my hand with his. It felt warm and dry. "No, my dear, more like Connie Chatterley. Remember, when she meets Mellors outside, under the trees?"

Listening to him, I was transported to another world—a world where I could talk about the books I loved with someone who cherished literature as I did. But deep down I knew the truth. We were talking sex.

Later in the week Gwen caught me alone in our office. "Mer, you're spending too much time with Greg. Do you know what you're doing?" Her face scrunched into a frown. I gave her what I hoped was a noncommittal look.

She was right, but I wasn't about to admit it.

One October afternoon, when all the trees were tinted in hues of red and yellow and orange, Greg and I walked across the street to Forest Park, a place I found especially enchanting because Tennessee Williams mentioned its famous Jewel Box, a mammoth greenhouse, in *The Glass Menagerie*. Fallen leaves swirled around our feet as we strolled under clear azure skies. The air smelled musty and smoky. As we walked, I asked about our colleague Martin and his wife, Tammie. I didn't know anyone like Martin. He was on his third or fourth marriage and had four children, none with his current wife. To me he was a wild, coarse man, bearded with black-rimmed glasses sliding down an oversized nose and loudmouthed at department meetings. Greg had known Martin for two years. I started analyzing him as if he were a fictional character.

"Do you think they really love each other?" I wondered aloud. "They seem so ill suited. I don't really know how to say it, but—"

Greg cut in: "You know, don't you, that we love each other?"

I flinched as though I'd been stung. What was I thinking? Worse, what was I doing? I was twenty-five years old, and considered myself a good Catholic. Now it appeared I was falling in love with a married man thirteen years older than I, who had three young daughters whom he adored. In my head I claimed innocent friendship. Didn't I recognize the feelings that surged when I was with him? Was I so damnably naïve?

Apparently. I had no words for my sin. I sat down on a stone bench a few feet away, and the world blurred through my tears. Greg did not follow me. When I finally straightened up and wiped my face, I walked over to where he stood and met his gaze.

"Now," he said, "all we need to do is stay out of each other's arms."

We walked in silence back to our offices. I felt relieved. We would avoid each other and be done with it.

Part Two

For weeks my university friends Pat and Moira Callahan kept after me to meet a friend of theirs. At first I put them off. "I've got one boyfriend already, and I don't need another." (Mike had joined the Navy, and though we kept in touch, we were growing apart). Moira spiced up her description: this Rob had spent five years in the seminary; he wrote poetry, loved books and music. "You two are perfect for each other," she promised.

The Callahans invited Rob and me for dinner in their apartment a few blocks from my place. I arrived first, sat on the edge of their overstuffed coach, and crossed my navy-blue stockinged legs. Moments later Rob appeared in the doorway. He was much taller than I expected—maybe a head taller than me, and slim, and he stood ramrod straight. He had a square face with a firm jaw. His high cheekbones and aquiline nose accented luminous light green eyes. His wavy blonde hair was neatly combed and a stray forelock played on his brow. But it was his eyes that captivated me, and his bright flashy smile. We locked eyes and he beamed at me. I hadn't expected him to be so handsome. I could hardly breathe.

At dinner he was bright, articulate, and funny. When he walked me home afterward, I had to look up to him, and guessed he must be over six feet tall. It seemed natural to invite him up to the flat I shared with my roommate, who hadn't yet returned from her weekend trip. Once inside he fell to his knees to examine my modest library, lined up against the wall on bookshelves I'd made from bricks and 1 x 10s. "Oh, Meredith," he laughed, and again I noticed his good looks, "we have the same books! I have these too." He was pointing to *The Blithedale Romance* and *Walden*. "And here's my favorite, *Leaves of Grass*." His green eyes danced.

A couple of weeks later Rob and I were holding hands in the Loft, a theatre that showed art films, watching Zefferelli's *Romeo and Juliet*. I wept when Romeo, preparing to take the poison, kisses Juliet's still-warm lips. Rob squeezed my hand. My tears continued unabated when Juliet plunged the dagger into her chest. As the last notes of "A Time for Us" faded away, Rob and I stepped into the cold night air, and I shivered. He put his scarf around my neck and led me away from the noisy patrons leaving the building. His breath felt warm as he whispered in my ear: "If anything ever happened to you, I'd do what Romeo did."

He may have been sure enough to make such a declaration, but I wasn't sure about him. We'd met only twenty days before.

That weekend we rambled through Tower Grove Park across from his apartment. It was November, the trees were mostly bare, and the air felt cold and brisk.

"I love this place," Rob said. "My dad brought me here when I was a kid. He's a bird-watcher, and he taught me to recognize different calls." He whistled.

"What is it? It sounds familiar."

"A warbler." He grinned and whistled again.

"Not bad," I said. "Your dad's a good teacher."

"You'll meet him soon, I hope," he said. He stopped and put his arm around me. "I want him—and all of my family—to meet you, Meredith. On Thanksgiving. I hope you'll come." He squeezed my shoulders, and I felt his excitement.

"I'd love to." My heart raced. Meet his family? Next week?

Later that evening we shared the poetry of e.e. cummings. Rob loved poetry as I did, and I loved hearing him read cummings's poems aloud. "Be of love a little more careful than of anything," and my favorite, "I'd rather learn from one bird how to sing than teach ten thousand stars to dance." When he drove me back to my apartment, he parked the car, drew me close, and kissed me. "Meredith, I have to be honest. I fell in love with you the instant I saw you." He nuzzled my neck. "There you were, sitting on the Callahans' sofa. I loved your smile. And you know what?"

I shook my head.

"You're just the kind of woman I need, Meredith. You're smart, you're Catholic, and you're beautiful."

I tried not to swoon. No one, not even Mike or Greg, had ever called me beautiful.

Thursday morning I woke with my stomach roiling. Putting on my robe, I padded across the hall and rang my neighbor's bell.

Judy, in jeans and blue turtleneck sweater, cracked the door. "Meredith—what's wrong? You look like you—"

I cut her off. I'm meeting Rob's family today and I don't know what to wear. Come, please; visit my closet. Do your good deed for today."

"Such urgency." Judy laughed and closed her door. She followed me into my bedroom.

"You don't want to wear a skin-tight sweater?" We started giggling, peering into my closet: two skirts, three blouses, one navy dress, a blue sweater, a pair of plaid wool slacks, a long winter coat, a light green wool suit, a black linen suit, and a dozen or so empty hangers.

"It's the navy blue again, I'm afraid. It's what I wore the night I met him," I said.

"I think you're right. Oh, well, let's at least dress it up. Where are your scarves?" I opened a drawer and Judy poked around, pulling out a red and white silk scarf. She tied it around my neck. "There! That will be perfect. Sort of—patriotic. Hey, what about this romance? Is it serious?"

I shrugged. "Maybe for him, but sometimes I feel like we're moving too quickly."

Two hours later I watched from my upstairs window as Rob parked his aging blue Falcon at the curb. At the last minute I decided to take a gift, a 45 RPM of "The Unicorn," one of my favorite songs by the Irish Rovers, to Rob's father, who had recently celebrated a birthday.

When I opened the door, Rob hugged and kissed me. He wore black dress slacks and a dark green sweater. I was glad I'd dressed up. "I remember that dress! It looks great with the scarf, Meredith."

I handed him the record. "Since your dad's birthday was last week and you said he enjoys corny, silly songs, I thought I'd bring him this one. You know it, don't you?"

"Oh," he said, laughing, "the one about the green alligators and long-necked geese? He'll love it!"

Rob's parents, Leonard and Evelyn Baird, owned a modest two-story in south St. Louis. As we pulled up in the driveway, my chest tightened. This is only a dinner, I told myself.

Rob took me first to his father, who beamed in the same way his son did. In gray slacks and a light blue sweater, Len was an older version of Rob. His hair was balding, but he had the same wide smile and light green eyes. His mother embraced me. I caught the scent of White Shoulders, the same perfume my aunt wore. "Welcome, Meredith, we're so glad to meet you." A thin, wiry woman, Eve stood nearly as tall as her husband; her auburn hair, in a French twist, was perfectly in place. She wore a brown wool belted sheath with a white collar covered by a soft yellow apron. Gran, Rob's silver-haired grandma, an apron covering her gray wool dress, sat in a chair by the window, smiling broadly as Rob introduced me to her and to his two little sisters, Jeanne and Fran. Sporting perky hairdos and short skirts that showed off slim shapely legs, the sisters rivaled their brother for beauty.

After dinner Rob's little sister Fran took my arm and led me into the spare bedroom, closing the door behind us. "Meredith, do you know?" Wide-eyed and conspiratorial, she bent over giggling. "Meredith, you're the first girl Rob has ever brought home." She leaned in to whisper in my ear: "I think my brother is serious!" She laughed again.

"I'm flattered," I said. I couldn't help but smile at her playfulness. Inside, I groaned. *I don't even know him yet.*

Still grinning, she added: "I thought you might like to know."

I wasn't sure I wanted to know, but I giggled with her as we went to join the family in the living room.

Friday night Rob brought his guitar to my apartment and we sang together. He knew all my favorites—"If I Had a Hammer," "Blowin' in the Wind," "Scarborough Fair." It was the first opportunity I'd had to sing harmony since grad school. I loved it.

Sometimes I had trouble believing this romance was for real. I felt as though I had landed in some fantasy world. At least twice weekly he mailed funny cards to my office. Soon he began sending me tender love-themed poems every day, written in large loopy script on fragile parchment. When we were together he often kissed and hugged me—a habit that endured even during some of the worst times that came later. We laughed a lot. I realized he shared my quirky sense of humor, but more than that, I really liked the person I became when I was with him. Best of all, every time I saw him, Rob's eyes sparkled and he held me close, whispering, "Do you know, Meredith, how much I love you?"

Monday after the holiday weekend Greg waited for me. When class let out, we joined the throng of students cramming the hallways. The rabble created such a din I had to lean close to hear him. "Lunch, later?" I nodded and returned to my classroom.

By the time we reached Ruggeri's, the Italian bistro Greg favored, the noonday crowd had disappeared and we had the place to ourselves. After we ordered, the waiter brought goblets of red wine.

"How was your holiday?" Greg said, raising his glass and sipping.

I had not told Greg much about Rob, only that we'd met and seen a couple of movies together. "I spent the day with Rob's family." I swallowed a big gulp of wine. It tasted robust and woodsy and felt warm in my chest.

Greg squirmed in his chair. "How did it go?"

"Great. He has a lovely family, Greg. His sisters—they're ravishing beauties. And funny. His parents and grandmother too—I think they liked me."

Greg nodded. "Of course they liked you, Meredith. Why wouldn't they?" He sat up straight, gesturing with his right hand. "Besides, he's perfect for you—you share the same Catholic upbringing, your schooling—and you're the same age." He shook his head, as if in bewilderment, but I got the point.

I reached out and touched his arm. "And your Thanksgiving?"

He raised his glass, took another sip of wine. "We went to my brother's. In Chicago."

"All the way to Chicago? Quite a drive."

"Yes, but all those hours I drove," he paused and sipped his wine, "your face was right in front of me. When we were there, I told my brother about you."

A ball of fear lodged in my throat. I took another drink of wine and wrung my hands. "Oh, Greg."

In the next moment the waiter arrived, carrying steaming bowls of pasta. I picked up my fork and began to eat. Silence filled the space between us.

On the way back to the college, we talked of the escalation of the Vietnam War. We shared no more of our personal lives.

Not that day.

"Mrs. Robinson?" I laughed, incredulous. "You had a Mrs. Robinson?" Rob and I were sitting on the floor in his apartment, paging through his high school yearbooks.

"She was a manager at the bank where I worked, the summer after I left the seminary," Rob said.

"Was she like Anne Bancroft? You know, slender, dark-eyed, and stunning?"

"Mmmm, she was. One day she walked by and brushed my shoulder. I remember being surprised because she'd seemed so aloof and sophisticated, but there she was, touching me. When she winked, I got it."

"Was she married?" I scooted myself to the wall so I could sit with my back straight.

"Divorced."

"Where did you go?"

"Her high-rise apartment downtown. But it didn't last long, Meredith. Hey, no more details; this is now and you're more beautiful than she ever was," he said, reaching over to touch my face.

I could easily imagine Rob in Dustin Hoffman's role. I pictured his Mrs. Robinson dressed in an elegant white silk suit, sipping martinis in her luxury apartment and offering Rob a smoke from her gold cigarette case. Abruptly I returned to reality and asked, "Were there a lot of others?"

"Oh, only about a hundred," he joked. "No, not really. Five—no, six. You?"

I counted on my fingers. "Three."

"Tell me about them. But only if you want to."

"My first time was with Nick. He was a social worker."

"Not the guy you said was your first true love, in college?"

"No, not him—that was Mike. But we were never lovers. Mike knew I wanted to be a nun, and he respected that."

"So . . . Nick?"

"We'd been dating and necking a lot for a couple of months, until one day he drove me to his apartment and said, 'Okay, enough of this.' It lasted all of five minutes. We broke up the next month."

"Good riddance?"

"Yep," I said, brushing a stray hair from my face.

"How about a drink?" Rob said. "Gin and 7 okay?"

"Sure."

As we sipped our drinks, Rob resumed. "Meredith, I—I've never had a serious relationship before. Those others, including the woman at the bank, they were about sex. I wanted to find out, to experiment. After all those years of celibacy,"

"I understand."

"There was one more, one that I've never talked about, not with anyone." He paused. "It happened one New Year's Eve in the seminary. Matt—my best friend at the time, and I, we'd been drinking gin and 7 Up for hours, and I remember feeling very lonely . . . Matt was there and, uh, we, well, it happened." He paused again. "We made love."

The words tumbled around in my brain. He'd said "made love," not "had sex." "But you were lonely," I said, as my fingers floated up to my throat, "and full of gin."

Rob nodded and lit a cigarette.

He made love, I thought. With a man. "I'm glad you told me, Rob."

"It's—it was—those circumstances. It wasn't as if we'd planned it."

"No, of course not." I flipped open one of his yearbooks. Longing to change the subject, I said, "This was your senior year?" I nodded in the direction of the book. "Let's find some more pictures of the young and handsome Rob."

He leafed through the pages until he found his senior photo.

"Look at that!" I poked him in the ribs, and we both laughed.

"Wait till we see *your* yearbooks," he teased.

Sitting on the floor with Rob, I remembered Mom, blushing with embarrassment, and her five-minute lecture on sex when I was twelve, but before that I'd heard only whispered rumors from my friends at Girl Scout camp. In high school my pals and I confirmed the rumors ("Mr. and Mrs. X must have done it twice. They have two kids.") From the nuns and the priests we heard all the rules that forbade kissing, touching, and even thinking about sex. Then I'd devoured Lawrence's racy book. But nobody had ever mentioned homosexuality. I vaguely recalled reading that my favorite playwright, Tennessee Williams, was gay. Now I had to consider: Was Rob gay? What did that mean for us?

Back in my apartment later that night I stretched out on my sofa. The streetlight flickered through the open blinds and shadows leapt like acrobats across the walls. I lit a cigarette and replayed the scene with Rob. "It was New Year's Eve," he'd said.

I asked myself: What did I know about sex? It was taboo for unmarried Catholics. But if Rob's homosexual encounter was about feeling lonely and getting drunk, I could certainly understand. Each one of my own brief sexual experiences had been alcohol-fueled. I smashed out the Marlboro and fell to my knees. God, let me forget what Rob told me. I am touched by his honesty, but that was the past and it has no bearing on our relationship. Holding that thought I fell into bed and pulled the covers over my head.

After that night I never allowed myself to think about Rob's confession. I never mentioned it to Margaret or Gwen, my two closest friends.

By refusing to speak of it, I believed I could make it disappear.

In early January while I was still on winter break, I came home from the library to a ringing phone. It was Rob inviting me to supper the following night.

When I knocked, the door flew open. Rob stood there, his face glowing. He wore a red-checkered apron over his light-blue shirt and jeans. "Welcome to Rob's Famous Midwestern Diner," he said. He threw his arms around me and kissed me.

"An apron—this is a first!" I laughed.

"Mom had an extra one. I hoped it might improve my culinary abilities." He helped me with my coat and laid it on a chair. Holding my hand, he ushered me into the tiny kitchen with its small wooden table, carefully laid: flowered tablecloth, two place settings, candles, and juice size glasses filled with burgundy.

"Oh, Rob, it smells so good." I inhaled audibly.

"Nana's stew recipe." He waved me to sit and took the lid off the cast iron pot on the stove. "Family secret, but I can tell you—there's a touch of horseradish in the gravy."

He'd also baked Pillsbury biscuits from one of those little cans you peel, rap on the counter, and six little rolls of dough fan out. As soon as he brought them to the table, we dug in, ravenous. "You get an A-plus on this dinner, Rob." I wiped my lips with my napkin. As we finished our wine, washed the dishes, and chatted, I realized I was beginning to feel at home with this man.

"This is my first cooking adventure," he said. "I wanted to do something special for you."

"I'm honored." I gave him a little curtsy.

"Now, let me escort you into my spacious parlor." He swept his arms in the air, gesturing like a salesman in a furniture showroom. In truth, his living room, like the rest of his apartment, was small, but his placement of sofa, reading chair, lamps, and wall hangings gave it an intimate, cozy feel, especially after he lit a red votive candle on the coffee table and turned off the overhead light. The smell of the burning wax reminded me of church. With Rob's body next to mine, I felt warm and safe.

He stroked my hand for a moment, kissed it, and laid it on his chest. "I carry your heart, I carry it within my heart," he whispered.

"That is the wonder/that keeps the stars apart," I said, finishing the lines. "Cummings—I love this poem."

We kissed, slowly, tenderly. The wine tasted sweet on his lips. I sighed, watching candlelight flicker on the wall. Outside cars swooshed along, and an isolated horn beeped. Inside we cuddled on Rob's secondhand green couch, letting quiet fall on us like a down-filled blanket.

When Rob spoke, I gave a little start. "Meredith, do me a favor, will you?"

Nodding, I turned to meet his eyes. Even in the darkened room they sparkled.

"Now close your eyes."

I wondered if this was some kind of game he'd invented, but I didn't want to be a spoilsport. I squeezed my eyes shut so tight I felt the skin on my face crinkle.

"Meredith, will you marry me?"

My eyes flew open. "Marry?" I blurted.

"Yes, my love, yes!" Rob laughed. "Of course, marry!"

"Don't you think it's—it's—a little premature? It's only three months since we met." I struggled to smile, or at least not to frown.

"But I know all I need to know. I've told you everything, Meredith. You know all my secrets."

I put my head on his shoulder. "I'm just surprised, but... Oh, of course it's a wonderful surprise—but I need... some time." I gently moved him aside so I could stand up, and reached for my Marlboros and lighter. "I need a little time. I'll go and have a cigarette. I—"

"Of course. Take whatever time you need." Standing beside me he laid his hand on my arm. "I'll be right here."

I walked into the study and stood at the window. Remnants of last week's snow were heaped in little hummocks around the yard. Across the street outlines of trees hung in the park, their leaves long gone. "Bare ruined choirs," I whispered, quoting Shakespeare's sonnet. Cars made squishing sounds as their tires rolled over the wet asphalt. Oh God, I ought to be dancing on air, but I'm frightened. After only ten weeks he's proposing.

Sure, I like him, I enjoy being with him, but there's so much I don't know. How can he be so sure he wants me forever? What about his homosexual experience? I can't allow myself to forget that. Still, as Greg said when I first told him about my budding relationship, Rob is perfect for me.

Suddenly, flashing on the image of Greg and me standing in Forest Park, I remembered the photos of his daughters on his desk. I knew what I had to do. I could not relinquish my Catholic principles by falling in love with a married man, destroying his marriage, harming his kids. I was so conflicted at this point I didn't even consider other options. I didn't consider sleeping on the issue, or taking a few days to think. I believed I had to give him an answer that very night. I took a deep breath. Rob's timely appearance—the week after Greg had broken his chaste silence—had to be an answer to a prayer. I believed God was taking care of me, giving me someone who loved me so much that I'd forget all about Greg.

I had no idea how naïve I was.

I walked back into the living room. Rob had scooted into a corner of the sofa, his eyes closed, his arms crossed over his chest. I nuzzled in close to him. I took his hand in mine and kissed his cheek. "Yes, Rob. My answer is yes."

His eyes flew open and he stood, pulled me close, and kissed me hard. "I love you, Meredith. I can't wait until you're my wife. Now let's go call our parents." That was fast, I thought. Why is he in such a hurry?

Later that night, I drove home. When I pulled the covers over me in my bed, my heart speeded up to double time, and I tossed and turned. Repeatedly I kept coming back to what I knew I didn't yet have with my future husband: the flicker of desire I felt whenever Greg came near. I hoped I was falling in love with Rob, but was it love? That passion I'd read about and dreamed about and felt so strongly with Greg—that spark with Rob couldn't come soon enough.

It seemed strange to ask God to give us lust, but that is exactly what I did.

We set an August wedding date. In June Rob had taken a position at Camp Williams, a camp for underprivileged children funded by Catholic Charities, where he'd been activities director the previous summer. I planned to spend my summer preparing for the first of three written exams for my PhD and teaching a night course to cover our wedding expenses. I didn't care how many months we waited to marry. Simply knowing we had a plan gave me the impetus to channel all my energies on my soon-to-be husband.

"I can't wait to introduce you to Ellen," Rob told me. "She's run this camp for the last fifteen years. I admire her more than anyone." I was eager to meet this larger than life woman, Rob's bona-fide hero.

The weekend after Rob's proposal, we visited my parents in Wichita. As we rang the bell, we heard footsteps as Mom and Dad hurried out to welcome us. Mom had done her hair in a soft wavy style that gave her a youthful look, and wore a navy blue A-line dress I'd never seen. Hugging her, I thought I smelled bourbon on her breath (now I knew the difference between rum, bourbon, and scotch), but I wasn't sure. My dad, who we always kidded for being a Humphrey Bogart lookalike, sported his favorite maroon corduroy shirt and a new pair of dark-rimmed glasses. When I hugged him, I smelled the pungent Old Spice he always wore.

We'd barely settled in with coffee and cookies when Mom began a litany of questions. "What degree are you working on? What does your father do? Does your mother work?" The moniker 'steamroller' didn't do her justice, and I blushed with embarrassment, relieved when my father spoke up. "Honey, he'll be here all weekend. You can ask more questions tomorrow."

I'd assumed that Rob's Jesuit training, which I'd mentioned to my folks on the phone, would be enough to quell any objections they might have, so her behavior annoyed me. But Rob handled her with gentle tact, and before we departed, my parents pulled me aside. "Mer, we think he'll make a good husband for you," Mom said. Dad winked in agreement.

A week or so later, Rob's parents invited us to dinner at their favorite German restaurant. We waited outside where the air was frigid, and we stared at our breath making puffy clouds in the night air. I pulled my coat tight around me, shivering as the Bairds' sleek Buick pulled up to the curb. Len and Eve got out. Eve threw her arms around me. "Oh, kids, we're so happy with your news," she said. Len smiled and kissed me, and shook his son's hand. Riding to the Gast Haus on Lindberg Avenue, I felt I'd found my new place in the world.

After we were seated Eve started up again. "Well, kids," she said, "we're ecstatic."

I stifled a nervous giggle and grabbed Rob's sweating palm under the table, recalling Juliet's whispering to Romeo that "palm to palm is holy palmers' kiss." Rob squeezed my hand and sighed.

"We can't think of anyone we'd love any more than Meredith." Eve was talking nonstop when Len started clearing his throat. Rob had warned me that his mother was inclined to prattle, but after my mom's barrage of questions, I certainly couldn't complain.

The waiter came with water and menus and lit the little candle. Its glow softened the edges of things.

"Will you have a honeymoon?" Rob's mother asked as we sipped our drinks. I saw Rob flinch.

"The Ozarks," Rob said. "We'll camp out so I can show—"

Eve cut in. "Oh, no, Rob, not for a honeymoon." She reached over and covered my hand with her larger one. I looked at the perfectly trimmed nails, polished in bright red. "Not for a bride. She needs, well," she paused, "facilities." She laughed nervously.

Len nodded. Rob seemed perplexed. "Okay, well, we can get a cabin, but I want us to have an outdoors experience, right, hon?" He met my eyes.

"Oh yes," I said. The Ozarks? It didn't occur to me to object—it was what Rob wanted. I flashed my most alluring smile. "Of course. I love the Ozarks too."

The waiter brought our plates and we feasted on rouladen and boiled potatoes slathered with butter, and chatted on. Eve described her first sighting of Len: "He had perfect teeth," she said. "That's what I told my mother."

After the waiter cleared our plates, Eve excused herself. When she returned she had freshened her lipstick and applied a flowery scent I didn't recognize.

"Before we go, kids," she started in. Rob and I exchanged a glance. "There's something we want you to consider. Why not schedule your wedding for early June? That way the two of you can spend the summer at Camp Williams."

The camp? For the summer? What about my plans to study? To teach? I peered at Rob in the shadowy light, trying to read his expression. He smiled and reached for my hand. "Would you want to come with me?"

My mouth felt dry. The words stuck in my throat. They were all staring at me. I smiled. "What a great idea." I kept smiling.

We drove back to my apartment. "I can't believe my Mom would come up with such a good idea," Rob said. "I didn't even consider that you might want to share the camp experience with me."

I hadn't considered it. I hadn't even seen the place yet. I remembered Girl Scout camp, sleeping on a hard, narrow cot, yes, but also tramping through the woods collecting leaves and flowers singing "I love to go a-wandering, along the mountain track." Crooning the chorus: "Valderi, valdera, a knapsack on my back," we'd get boisterous, marching like soldiers we'd seen in news clips. I remember savoring the clear coolness of dawn, breaking out in a chorus of chirping birdsong, free of the humidity that would stifle us by noon. And the evenings sitting cross-legged around the fire, devouring s'mores and licking warm chocolate from our fingers while we spun Poe-inspired ghost stories. Recalling these past Kodak moments, I figured Camp Williams couldn't be all that bad.

The following Sunday we drove east on Highway 64 out of St. Louis. The spring sky was blue and clear as we followed a winding road lined with elm trees to a cluster of wooden buildings that resembled old army barracks. We found Ellen's office in the largest one. When Rob knocked, Ellen Williams, the director, a petite woman with pixie-styled silver hair, opened the door. "Oh, I'm so glad to see you." She embraced Rob, kissing him on the cheek, and reached for my hand. "Rob's told me all about you, Meredith. Welcome!"

After she got us sodas, we sauntered outside for the campus tour. Besides the main building which housed the staff offices, the cafeteria, and a large auditorium, there were three dormitories for thirty campers each. On a green sloping hill to the north of the main building, four small log cabins were scattered several yards from one another. From a distance they looked cute and cozy, like the cabin my parents had rented on one of our Ozark vacations.

"Let's take a quick look at your cabin," said Ellen. "Guess you'll still be on your honeymoon when you arrive, won't you?" She chuckled.

We smiled shyly, and I was still feeling optimistic. Rob and I shared a fondness for Thoreau, who stayed a whole year in a Massachusetts cabin. Our shorter stay, I assured myself, would be a similar adventure.

As Ellen jerked open the door, a burst of musty air smacked us in the face. I sneezed, but forced a smile. Rob took my hand and pulled me inside. "Look, Meredith, our home away from home." There was an unmade double bed pushed against the wall, a wooden straight-backed chair, and a child's size dresser with a mirror over it. A stand-up lamp stood next to the bed. Rob flicked it on, and the cramped space took on a sickly yellow glow. The furniture crammed inside left scarcely an inch of wiggle room. The room was stifling. Home away from home? I struggled to keep my mouth shut against Rob's fatuous remark. In the next second, my optimism faded into despair.

"You won't need to bring linens and towels," Ellen said. "We'll provide them."

"Oh, it's fine," I said. "It'll be great fun." I smiled at Rob all the way back to St. Louis. Though it nagged at me, I was learning to be a good liar. When I asked myself why I had to lie, the answer was simple. I was afraid—afraid Rob would think less of me if I did not meet his standards, afraid to disappoint him, afraid that I would not be considered the good wife. But most of all, I was afraid that I would lose him, and I was willing to do anything to prevent that.

After I accepted Rob's proposal, I thought surely we'd make love. We spent a lot of time stroking and kissing, but he never pressed me to go further. One night during a particularly hot make-out session, I said, "Rob, don't you want to make love?"

"Of course! But I want to be unique. I think we ought to wait until we're married," he said.

"Isn't that sort of—old-fashioned?"

"Then let's be old-fashioned."

I considered it an odd response from a man, but again kept my mouth shut.

Unlike my high school friends, who'd pored over *Bride's Magazine* dreaming of their weddings, I had no ideas, no teenage fantasies. Only two years before, when I was twenty-four, I'd abandoned my childhood dream of being a bride of Christ. After Vatican II, when the pope challenged nuns and priests to become fully invested in social justice, thousands of them left their orders to work in the communities. One week on the Carradine campus nuns and priests rushed around dressed in long black robes, the next they appeared in clothes like everyone else's. Witnessing this exodus, I'd started seriously questioning my own vocation. With Father Westfall's help, I'd made my decision two years before.

When I'd fallen in love with Greg, I knew it was wrong. When Rob made his grand entrance and promptly began wooing me, I thought it nothing short of a miracle. He was sent to rescue me.

Rob and I planned a simple wedding, entailing costs we could take care of without our parents' help. For a wedding dress, I wrote Aunt Tilley to ask to borrow hers. Since I was a child I'd loved gazing at the wedding portrait of my aunt, resplendent in a satin gown, its long train spread out in front of her. Whenever I dusted in Mom and Dad's bedroom, I'd pick it up and stare at it, never considering that in the future I might wear that very same dress.

The day she received my letter, Tilley phoned me. "I've prayed for years that you'd change your mind about entering a convent, Mer. I'm thrilled you want to wear my dress!"

Rob secured the University Chapel where we attended Sunday Mass, and we invited five Jesuit friends to officiate. We wrote our own marriage vows, ironically omitting the part about the husband being the head of the wife. After all, we considered ourselves hip, part of a new generation that believed in equality.

Little did I know, we ought to have left it in.

"Now all we have to do is stay out of each other's arms." That's what Greg had told me seven months earlier. But I was unable to resist spending time with him, lunching with him in our Italian restaurant or sitting in his office talking about Hemingway and Fitzgerald as the sky darkened in late afternoons.

Somehow Greg and I managed to avoid physical contact. We knew we were playing with fire. As my wedding date approached, it was time for me to extricate myself from him for good.

On the first of April, right before noon, Greg knocked at my office door and poked his head inside.

"Come on in," I said.

"Lunch later?" he said. He was wearing a flowered shirt with full sleeves, and bell-bottomed beige slacks.

"New shirt?" I said. I stood but didn't walk over to him as I usually did.

"Jill bought it," he said. He was blushing.

"You're trendy."

For a long moment, neither of us spoke. I knew I had to hold my own.

"I have to stop seeing you," I burst out. "My wedding's only two months off."

He blinked a couple of times, opened the door, and exited into the hall packed with raucous students. I walked over to shut the door, barely able to keep myself from calling out to him. He's not yours to keep, I told myself, sitting in front of my typewriter. I needed to prepare an exam on *The Canterbury Tales* for the next day. Feeding the paper into the machine, I couldn't help thinking that perhaps I was playing the role of Allison, the young wife greedy for sex in "The Miller's Tale." I wasn't having sex with Greg, but not because I didn't want to.

After that I set a new routine. Arriving seconds before my class, I'd avoid my office, since his was next door, and go directly to my classroom. Right after my class ended at noon, I'd head down the stairs, my arms full of papers and books, and hurry to my car. Then I'd either drive to the university library or return home to pack. Since Rob had rented us a larger place, I was preparing to vacate my own apartment.

I was convinced that avoiding Greg would sever our connection, one that still sent a jolt of electricity throughout my body whenever I saw him.

During final exam week, only a couple of weeks before my wedding, Greg burst into my office without knocking. Two minutes before, Gwen had left and I was typing a letter of recommendation for a student.

"Meredith, we have to talk," he said. I spun around in my chair. He stared at me, wide-eyed. His normally soft and gentle voice sounded frantic. His arms were outstretched as though he was directing a symphony. Everything about him emanated urgency. As always, the current between us sizzled.

"Meredith, I can't let you do this."

I stood, speechless. My chair rolled back and crashed into the file cabinet. I almost laughed, but his face looked so serious.

"I had lunch with Andrew. He made me promise I'd talk to you," said Greg.

"Andrew?"

He nodded. "He begged me to stop you. He said, 'Greg, you can't let her do this. She's in love with you.'" Greg dropped his arms to his sides. His face fell.

I clenched my fists and took a step toward him. "But I must marry Rob. You know there's no other way." My thoughts rushed through all the reasons above the obvious one: to avoid ruining Greg's marriage. By now I knew Rob wasn't perfect, but I knew he was a good, kind man. I believed his love would carry us, with a little help from God on the way.

Greg closed his eyes and sighed deeply. "I promised him I'd tell you." His voice was a whisper. Our eyes met for a second. I turned away as my own eyes brimmed with tears. I barely heard the door close.

That was the last time I saw him until my wedding day.

The day before the wedding, my family arrived, and I settled them in at the Travel Lodge near the university. That night we hosted the rehearsal dinner at Rossino's, a landmark restaurant in the Italian neighborhood called "the Hill." Our happy crowd enjoyed steaming bowls of minestrone followed by heaping plates of pasta and loaves of fresh garlic bread, followed by homemade spumoni. And Chianti—I'd had to fight my urge to consume more than two small glasses.

I was soon rewarded for my efforts. After our guests piled into their cars, Rob swept me into his arms. "Tomorrow you'll be all mine," he said. As we kissed, I could feel a new tension between us. I was thrilled.

A few minutes later, driving myself to the home of my friends Nan and Ed in University City, I began to feel uneasy. Something was nagging at me. This wasn't the first time I'd felt as though I were in a play, but it was the first time I'd forgotten my lines.

Ed opened the door and Nan, holding a glass of beer in one hand, hugged me.

They were all smiles. "How're you doing? Would you like a drink?"

I nodded and settled into a wingback chair. I felt drained. Ed handed me a glass of white wine. I took a sip.

"How did things go?" Nan said.

"Fine, but—" I burst into tears. I put my head in my hands and sobbed.

"You're worn out," Ed said. "Why don't you go up and get a good night's sleep." He took my bag and started up the stairs. "Come on, you'll feel better after a good rest."

Drying my eyes, I trudged up the stairs and fell into bed. I tossed around, trying to find a comfortable position. Memories blurred my thinking: Greg's declaration in Forest Park, Rob's confession that he'd made love to a man. I was so conflicted. I wasn't sure that I truly loved him after all. I wondered if I'd pretended my way through our engagement. The idea terrified me. The tears returned, and I waited for sleep, praying for God's help.

I realized I had no idea what I was doing.

The next morning, I bolted up when Nan touched my shoulder. "Wake up, Meredith, here's some coffee. It's a beautiful day for a wedding." Sunlight streamed in through the short lace curtains. I could see a swath of green lawn and the tables and chairs below on the patio. I dressed quickly and grabbed my overnight bag. As I walked out on the porch, Ed snapped my picture.

I picked up Mom from the motel, and we got our hair specially done in a fancy salon in the Chase Park Plaza Hotel, then drove to the church to meet Aunt Tilley. Stepping into my aunt's dress, I remembered that earnest little girl who'd hoped one day to don first the white gown and later the black serge habit, giving her life to God.

Now everything was different. Without vows of poverty, chastity, or obedience, I was beginning a life I'd never even considered. All my high school friends who'd swooned over Pat Boone and Elvis Presley and papered their walls with posters of their favorite male stars were already married with one, two, or even three children.

I may not have planned for this way of life, but of one thing I was certain: I desperately needed to break free from Greg, and I believed Rob could help me.

I started back to reality, sensing my aunt's fingers on my back, fastening all thirty-two of the dress's tiny satin-covered buttons. "All right, you're buttoned up," Tilley said.

"Ready for the veil?" Mom said. "This is a long way from the convent, honey."

I nodded as she set the pearl tiara with its wispy white veil on my perfectly coifed blonde head. She got close enough for me to determine she had not been drinking. Her breath smelled of mint, or perhaps Listerine. "There." She and Tilley both sighed. "Now look, Meredith," they said. The three of us gazed into the full-length mirror, seeing a radiant bride with intensely blue eyes smiling to her mother and her favorite aunt. We made a comely threesome: Tilley dressed in a light-blue suit, Mom in a pale green silk dress, and I in creamy satin.

"Lovely, so lovely," Tilley said. "I'm so glad you decided not to be a nun. I've been so happy in our marriage, and I want you to know that happiness."

"I'm glad you found Rob, honey," Mom said, leaning against the wall, smiling.

Mom ducked into the hall and led Dad, wearing a deep frown, into the room. He hated being in the limelight. "Honey, you're beautiful. Now let's get this show on the road."

"You'll be off the stage in two minutes, Daddy." I hugged him to me, inhaling, as always, Old Spice.

Strains of "Sons of God, gather round the table of the Lord," an upbeat, catchy tune, were sung by the little choir of our friends, and I linked my arm through my dad's. At the rear of the church we paused. I locked eyes with my soon-to-be-husband, waiting for me at the altar. On the way up the aisle I spotted Greg, sitting at the end of a pew. He wore a brown suit and tie, his head tilted up to look right at me. His face was all creases and lines. He did not smile. Daddy and I moved on.

I made my vows, believing without a doubt that Rob and I would love each other forever. I had to believe it. I had to.

After the reception, Rob and I drove to the Holiday Inn on Highway 55, a few miles out of town. Tomorrow we'd begin our real honeymoon at Lake of the Ozarks, a six-hour drive, but we didn't want to travel far on our wedding night.

In room 132, around the corner from the swimming pool, we threw our bags on the floor. "Let's take a swim," Rob said.

Still too shy to do otherwise, I went into the bathroom to change. By the time I tugged on my suit and emerged, Rob was ready, holding towels for us.

"All set?" he said as we left the room. Hot humid air engulfed us as, still wobbly from the reception wine, we dove into the pool and splashed about. Since it was dinnertime, the pool was deserted except for an elderly bald man swimming laps. I began to swim laps in the next lane. "Oh, does this feel good!" I called to Rob, who waved at me from the diving board.

I heard the loud plop of my new husband's belly flop. After a few minutes, he swam underwater, grabbed me around the waist, and surfaced, laughing. "Hey, Mrs. Baird, how about a visit to my hotel room?"

"I thought you'd never ask." I giggled as we got out and wrapped ourselves in thick soft hotel towels. We hurried back to the room.

As he stuck the key in the door, Rob whispered, "Finally, finally, this day is here!" Once inside, he closed the curtains, took the towel from my shoulders, and began kissing me—lips, shoulders, neck—and moved me to the bed.

"Oh, I do love you," he said. He fumbled with my swimsuit, pushing it down to expose my breasts. "So lovely," he whispered.

I moaned softly, caressing his arms and shoulders. I wished I knew more about what to do, I realized, but Rob had more experience. I'd try to follow his lead.

"Wait, let me—" I pulled my suit off, and he his. We laughed at our childlike awkwardness and continued fondling and kissing. In the middle of a long ardent kiss, Rob stopped. "Oh, I almost forgot!" He sprung up and went to his suitcase, fumbled around and returned with an envelope addressed in his strong masculine script: "For my Meredith."

I took it and propped myself up on the pillows. Smiling, I opened the envelope and removed a page of heavy vellum. On it was a poem pledging his undying love.

That night I firmly believed him.

Embracing me again, he began stroking my breasts and kissing me passionately. The way we moved with each other was both tender and awkward, but at last I felt tiny flickers of the desire I'd been waiting for.

Much later, we shared a late dinner with a bottle of Dom Perignon Rob's dad had ordered for us. Tipsy from the champagne, we made our way back to our room. Rob lit a candle. As the light played against the walls and curtains, we fell into each other's arms.

The picture Ed took of me that morning shows a young woman dressed in Bermuda shorts and a white blouse, her hair disheveled. She's standing on the porch of a red brick house, clutching a makeup bag that in those days was called a train case. She's smiling at the camera. There is no sign that she's on her way to her wedding, or that the night before she cried herself to sleep.

Thirteen days after our wedding we loaded up our suitcases, books, and journals and headed for the camp. It was a Sunday morning, but we'd skipped Mass to make the staff orientation. On the way from the car to our cabin, I saw the first of two buses groaning up the narrow road. I watched as they stopped, the doors creaked open, and dozens of little kids stumbled down the steps to stand in the drive, their eyes wide at the first sight of their cabins in the woods.

At our first lunch, standing in front of Rob in the cafeteria line, I was full of ambivalence. This place was like nowhere I'd ever been. The room was a din, kids screaming, laughing, and shouting to one another, their bodies crowded around the picnic tables. A heavyset server, her stringy black hair stuck to her head and sweat pouring off her forehead, nodded at me. "Mac and cheese?" she said. "Okay," I said. She lumped the orangey stuff on my plate and threw a haystack of coleslaw beside it. "Thanks," I muttered as she plopped her last offering, a slab of cornbread, on my tray.

"My God." I started to say more, but stopped myself.

"What's wrong?" Rob's face scolded. "You haven't even tasted it yet." He'd felt my tension earlier in the day when we'd been given our chores. When I agreed to summer camp, I had no idea I'd be working there. I could only nod when upon arrival Ellen assigned me to pick up the kitchen crew at the bus stop five miles from the camp and drive them in to work at 6:00 a.m. each morning. I hated driving. I was insecure on the dirt back roads, and I would be carrying other people. Rob knew that. When the list was posted, he'd turned to me. "Oh, I'm sorry, honey." So much for marital equality. No one had even asked me.

But I was stuck. Tears had welled in my eyes and I'd turned away from him and returned to our cabin to unpack. At dinner he'd nuzzled up to me in the cafeteria line, gently teasing, "Hey, you can do this, you're okay, aren't you?"

I wasn't okay, but I wasn't about to tell him that. I'd wolfed down my food, said I wanted to take a walk, and left before dinner was over. I had to keep remembering that my job was to make my husband happy—no matter what.

That night after I picked up the keys to the van I hovered in back of the auditorium, watching as Rob strummed his guitar for the first round of campers, little tykes wearing tee shirts and shorts, their eyes round with joy. Their spindly bodies, caught up in the rhythms of the music, swayed slightly as though the irresistible force of music was making them into puppets, moving back and forth. "Michael row the boat ashore, Alleluia," they crooned along with Rob.

There he was, my husband of two weeks, alive, ecstatic. In his element, Rob's energy electrified these kids who'd probably never before seen a forest or a campfire. His whole body became incandescent as he sang, his eyes dancing with theirs. I had to smile over the rows of their little bodies, all the way to him on the stage. This will be an adventure for us, I resolved, and for me a huge challenge. I knew I had to be up for it.

Our private life inside that cabin was another story. In a few days' time we fell into a pattern governed by our responsibilities. Rob's day ran late, mine early. By 9 p.m. I found myself exhausted and longing to lie down, while Rob was just meeting with his staff of counselors to plan the following day.

Waiting in our honeymoon cabin for my groom, I'd get so sleepy that I'd drift off, and awaken to muffled sounds of Rob's creeping into the room and the slight creak of the bedsprings as he climbed in beside me. Despite a small electric fan buzzing on the chair, the room stayed hot and muggy. Too muggy to hug, too muggy for anything else. I kept myself very still, pretending to be fast asleep.

I grew to long for the two evenings each week I drove into the city to teach my class. I'd get into my Hudson, flip on the air conditioner, and wait for the air to cool my sweaty face.

Late one evening as I started down the dirt path to our room, I heard a rustling behind me. I turned and Rob folded me into his arms. "Surprise," he cried. "Finally we're both awake at the same time."

I pasted on my automatic smile. "Hi, honey." I told myself not to repeat what I'd heard on KWFR: that we were experiencing 100 percent humidity. As we walked, I tried to ignore the sweat beading on my forehead and the puddles forming under my arms.

Rob tugged the door open and turned on the lamp and the fan. The latter whirred to life but hardly cut the oppressive, stifling heat. I felt a small movement of warm air slide over my upper body as my husband began unbuttoning my blouse. "I was waiting for you." He was kissing me. "I thought you'd never come."

I tried to return his kisses. I didn't want to blight Rob's paradise. What the hell, I said to myself, and let myself go, ignoring the streams of perspiration making rivulets on our arms and legs, making us slither about. That night, he was an eager lover, and his excitement contagious. After a few minutes I no longer noticed the sweat or the heat and fell into the rhythms of the passion that quite surprised me that night.

If Camp Williams was a test of my flexibility, I did not pass. Five weeks in, I realized that except for a few dark encounters, I seldom saw Rob. As the activities director, he was occupied every minute: he had breakfast with his staff, visited each of the twelve groups in the morning, consulted with the director, and led singing around the campfire every evening. Plus, he had to be available anytime his counselors needed him. We could not have arranged a schedule more conducive to ignoring each other.

On the fourth of July, Len and Eve drove out for visitor's day. We waited for them in the cafeteria, the coolest place in the camp. All five standup fans were humming and a faint whiff of grease from the fried chicken we'd had for lunch floated in the muggy air. The Bairds wandered in, Eve waving her hand, trying to cool her face. Her gray hair was pulled back with a barrette, and she wore a sleeveless pink dress. Len's Bermuda shorts showed off sturdy white legs.

"Whew," Eve said. "I don't know how you kids stand it." She managed a half smile.

"Hi, darlin'." Len hugged me. He smelled like Dentyne.

Eve touched my arm and pecked my cheek, and reached over to hug her son. When her fingers first landed on his arm, now bronzed from frequent sunny hikes, Rob seemed to flinch, but only for a second. Then he recovered and kissed her on the cheek. Rob ran off to get us cold drinks, and we sat at one of the picnic tables. I watched as Eve's eyes roved over the tablecloth, fixated on a glob of what looked like gravy a few inches from her hand. "Golly," she said, "I never imagined this place would be so—" she paused, "primitive."

Time for me to smile again. Time for Rob to return, but no Rob yet. I sighed. "It's different, isn't it?"

"Well, this is a novel experience. What's the best part of it, Meredith?" Len asked me. In the face of Eve's demurring, he was trying for upbeat and positive.

"Ah, well." I paused. In my head I ticked off a list of negatives: the cabin, the food, our schedules, our growing separateness, what could I tell them?

"The campfires, the music. Rob loves to get them all singing. You should see him."

Rob walked up, hearing his name. "What do I do?" He laughed. Standing next to his father, I saw their strong resemblance. Vibrant, handsome men.

"You love setting this place ablaze with music," I said, reaching for the Pepsi he handed me. It felt cold against my hand, and before I opened it, I rubbed it on my cheek. I looked at Eve. She was rolling the can against her arm, on her neck, purring softly.

Rob toured us around the grounds. After we'd seen his office and the dormitories and strolled through a shady part of the woods, Eve stopped in her tracks. "Wait a minute, you're hiding something." She wore an impish grin. "You've got to show us your cabin. We can't go without seeing your love nest."

That morning I'd made up the bed, pulling the sheets tight and fluffing the pillows, making sure I replaced the wildflowers Rob had brought two days before. Now as we trekked down the path to our digs, the smallest glance passed between Rob and me. I was glad, so seldom did I feel connected to him in any way.

"Oh my!" Eve gasped as she peered into our little space. "No bathroom?" She looked up at her son.

He shook his head, avoiding her eyes. "I thought you knew that, Mom. It's right over there." He pointed at a wooden outhouse several yards away.

Eve shuddered, and gestured toward me. "How can this be for a bride? I'm so sorry I suggested you two share this experience." She looked bewildered.

I shrugged. "Oh, I'm back in my Girl Scout mode," I said. "You get used to it."

Rob blushed and steered his parents away from the door. "We're fine," he assured them. "You don't need to worry, Mom." I noticed Eve's eyes darting over to Len's before she looked at the ground and started walking back to their car.

After eight weeks, we celebrated the last night of camp. Flowers in her hair, Ellen showed up to lavish praise on Rob and handed out bottles of Budweiser. I was relieved it was almost over.

It was nearly midnight when I grabbed my flashlight, signaled to Rob that I was leaving, and set out for the cabin. I flopped on the bed, feeling a smug satisfaction. I'd done my best this summer, only once waking after 6 a.m. and making the kitchen crew late, and Ellen had quickly forgiven that. I'd managed to exit two nights a week for legitimate reasons. That time away had helped me get through the endless days when the temperatures soared into the nineties and kept me wet, sticky, and miserable. Weeks before, I'd decided to ignore our almost nonexistent sex life, chalking it up to the oppressive heat and humidity. Later, I thought, when we get home.

But sex was not the immediate problem.

The door opened and Rob came inside our cabin. In the yellow lamplight his face looked sallow. Maybe he's had one too many, I guessed. He stripped off his shirt and shorts and stood in his underwear, blocking the air from the fan. He was very quiet.

"Hey, that was a fun celebration, wasn't it?" I said. The air felt thick now, with the humidity and Rob's long silence.

"Yeah, yeah, I hated to see it end." He climbed in bed and arranged his pillow. He started to lie down, then sat up and looked over at me. I lay on my back, sticky in the diaphanous gown his sisters had given me, my arms and legs stretched out.

"Ellen asked me to come back." His voice was almost a whisper. "Next year."

My heart thudded. "Will you?"

He wiped a bead of sweat from his brow and shook his head. "No, no, of course not." He looked away, and started fooling with his pillow again. "You've ruined it for me. I know you hated it. I saw it in your eyes. Oh you tried, sometimes you tried. But I knew. It's over for me and Camp Williams. I should've known better." He slugged his pillow, moved away from me, and fell onto his side. My heart thudded. I was the one who should have known—what this meant to my husband. What was I thinking?

We lay there that night, tossing about, our bodies longing for the next slight breeze from the little fan. I realized that, in avoiding Rob so he wouldn't suspect my feelings, I had deeply alienated him. I reached out to touch his shoulder. He pulled away. "I'm sorry, Rob." The tears welled in my eyes.

Back in our apartment across from Tower Grove Park, with our books, our kitchen, our bathroom with tub and shower a few feet from our bedroom, neither of us spoke—ever again—of Camp Williams. I began a novena—a rosary every day for nine days—to guide my next steps. I refused to think about the camp. I didn't want to dwell on how I had failed Rob with my lack of enthusiasm. Maybe if I learned more about sex, I decided, he would forgive me. There had to be a good book somewhere. Now I just had to find it.

Most times when we made love, Rob's foreplay was a couple of long, sweet kisses. Neither of us knew a thing about foreplay. I barely had time to respond before he was on me, missionary style, until he finished. He'd always end by saying "I love you," but my sole pleasure lay in his desire for me, so more often than not I panted and feigned my own orgasm.

My imagination told me sex should be better than this. Every pop song spoke of it; I'd read dozens of books which led me to believe sex was fun, even ecstatic. The cover of every woman's magazine touted articles on how to arouse your husband to greater depths. But what about the wives? Something was wrong, and I didn't yet have the confidence to discuss it with Rob. Still, I was determined to ensure sexual pleasure for both of us.

I kept thinking of Connie Chatterley and her lover. Several times when Rob and I made love I'd felt glimmers of the ecstasy she enjoyed—and I believed he and I could find this ecstasy, if only we knew what we were doing.

What I didn't know was that most newlyweds, especially in the first months of marriage, made love two or three times a day, even when they were slathered in sweat and overcome by humidity.

In 1970 the Vietnam War invaded all our waking moments. Fearing that my eighteen-year-old brother would be drafted, my mother made constant novenas to St. Jude. A week before the lottery she wrote: "Pray that Denny draws a high number so he isn't called."

A few weeks before our wedding, Rob received his first draft notice. It had never occurred to me that he might be in line. He was older, in graduate school, and soon to be married. Driving home from the university one afternoon he brought it up.

"Meredith, you know I don't believe in war," he told me. I nodded. "If I get called, I'll file CO status."

"I heard that Jackie and Mark Reilly—my colleagues—are preparing to move to Canada. With a low number, it looks bad for him. But I'm sure you'll get the reclass." I wasn't sure, but I had to pretend.

Rob shrugged. "Our county has never issued a 1-0 conscientious objector status," he said. "But I'm sure to get it." He was trying hard to sound lighthearted. At first I couldn't respond. The thought of his going to a war we didn't believe in terrified me.

"Well," I said, smiling as confidently as I could, "you will be the first."

His second notice arrived the day after we returned from the Ozarks. He immediately filed his CO papers and received a date for his physical exam. When the date rolled around, I drove him downtown to the draft center at 7:30 a.m. All day long I tried not to think about what he might be going through, but fleeting visions of Rob being prodded and poked and made fun of for his opposition to the war ravaged my concentration.

At 5:00 Rob phoned. The exam was over. As I drove near the draft center on Main Street I peered through the car window. Several young men of various heights and colors were leaning against the building. It was dusk and I could hardly make out their faces. Suddenly a man waved and approached the car. Who was this? I barely recognized him. As he drew closer I realized it was Rob.

Pale, his face drawn and his eyes empty, he looked nothing like the man I'd dropped off eight hours earlier. I opened the passenger door and he got in. When I leaned over to kiss him, I felt his distance. "Was it bad?"

He nodded, avoiding my eyes. We said nothing for the five-mile drive home. When I put the car in park, he said, "I'll know in three weeks."

I tried to figure out why he was so upset. Maybe he'd seen some wounded soldiers, or had been shamed for filing CO status. Maybe they called him a coward.

He never spoke of that day again. I never asked.

Three weeks later to the day, I fished the envelope from the mailbox. I brought it inside, propping it against the picture of his mom and dad on his dresser. When he returned that evening, I stood when he opened the door. My eyes gave me away.

"Is it here?" he said.

"On your dresser."

He went into the bedroom and came back ripping open the envelope, scanning the letter. "I got it!" He read aloud: "You are hereby ordered to do substitute work at Our Lady of Mercy School for two years in lieu of service in the United States Armed Forces." He reached for me and we hugged very tight. "I did it, Meredith." As he went to phone his parents, I whispered a prayer of gratitude.

After our wedding I'd resolved once again to cut Greg out of my life. It worked the first summer, when we taught opposite schedules and seldom ran into each other. But as soon as the regular term began in September, I found myself unable to stay away from him. Fortunately he taught two evening courses. But that put us on campus together three days a week. I promised myself that I could see him only one afternoon a week, which didn't mean I couldn't go out for drinks with him in a group—with Martin and perhaps Andrew. Wise as I may have been in avoiding Greg alone, I would have been even wiser to avoid both the martinis and Greg.

One evening after I'd spent a couple of hours with Greg and two other colleagues at the Fox and Hounds, I told myself I'd only have one martini, but that didn't work. I had four. Very slowly I inched home to our apartment. Rob's car was parked out front. All the lights were on, and through a window I could see Rob moving around in the kitchen. I knew I was hammered and barely holding it together. I tried not to wobble as I made my way to the door and, my hand trembling, found the opening for the key. Knowing my breath reeked of gin, I gave Rob my cheek when he leaned over to kiss me. "You're home early," I said, throwing my books on the sofa and unbuttoning my coat.

"I couldn't wait till you got here! It's happened. So fast!"

My mind was so foggy, and for an instant in my blurry mind, I questioned: is he talking about Greg and me? Surely he couldn't know. "What? What's happened?" I said.

"Sit, please. Be right back." Rob hurried into the kitchen and returned carrying a bottle of champagne in one hand and two fluted glasses in the other. He was grinning as he set them down. "I wanted to celebrate this with you: *The American Scholar* accepted my article on William James."

I stood and threw my arms around him. "Congratulations!" I was genuinely pleased for him, and equally relieved that I wasn't in trouble.

"This is so exciting! My first major publication and I'm not even finished with my course work." Rob poured the champagne. "To us, and to more publications!" he said, handing me a glass and raising his own.

I took only a sip but my stomach lurched. As much as I wanted to toast my husband's success, I was afraid I was about to be sick and he'd start asking questions.

The phone rang and Rob went to answer it. "Oh, Mom, I was about to call you."

Trying not to teeter, I headed for the kitchen and quickly emptied my champagne down the drain, fighting the urge to vomit. I could hear Rob's voice, full of excitement and pride, as he told his mother the good news. Meanwhile, I was struggling to keep my eyes open. I was afraid that if I closed them, even for a second, my world would start spinning and I'd fall. I had no time to waste. Holding onto the walls, I tiptoed down the hall. Passing Rob, I kissed his cheek and pointed to the bedroom pantomiming exhaustion. He nodded, patting my arm. We can talk later, I thought, after he called his sisters. I will be okay as soon as I lie down.

"Oh, it won't be published for six months—they'll let me know the exact date," Rob was telling his dad.

I crept into the bedroom, dropped my clothes on the closet floor, pulled on my gown, and slid into bed. Before I could count to ten, the room started spinning and I blacked out.

I woke up the next morning, chastened by my bad behavior. Rob was buttoning his shirt. "Feeling better?" I nodded. "Oh, honey, I'm sorry. I wanted to celebrate but I was—"

Rob cut in. "So tired. Don't worry. I peeked in and you were sleeping so I called my sisters. I'm off early, to tell my advisor before class." He bent to kiss me. I gave him my cheek, thinking how foul my breath must be.

For a full ten minutes after he left I lay there. God, what is wrong with me? Why can't I stop after one or two drinks? I need more willpower. I know I'm disciplined. Where is my willpower?

I vowed to cut back.

The following Tuesday afternoon, I grabbed the newspaper from the porch and walked into our apartment. Rob wouldn't be home for another hour. I tossed my books on the sofa, kicked off my shoes, and picked up the front section. The headline read: "War Casualties." A sidebar listed 44,245 Americans, 400,000 South Vietnamese, and 90,000 Viet Cong and North Vietnamese, all dead. It was December 1970.

I laid the paper on the coffee table and put my hands over my eyes. Dear God, so many deaths in this sad, useless war. Please let it end. Thank you for keeping Rob here with me, and with the children at Our Lady of Mercy.

After praying, I picked up the telephone and dialed my friend from university days.

"Margaret, have you seen the latest stats? For every one of ours, they've lost countless more!" We groaned together.

"I heard that earlier today," said Margaret. "It's heartbreaking; I can hardly bear to think about it." She paused. "I hope you and Rob are coming tonight; it's supposed to be the biggest rally yet."

I pulled the phone cord to its full length and went to the sofa. "Yes, we are, and I think Rob may be one of the speakers. Yesterday Larry Fine, from his department, approached him, and you know Rob, he was thrilled."

"Do you want to come here and we'll walk over together?" she asked.

Three hours later we stood together in the packed auditorium, surrounded by hundreds of students and faculty. Many carried placards that read, "Vietnam: Unjust War"; "BRING OUR BOYS HOME NOW!"; "No More Body Bags"; and simply, "PEACE." The stuffy space smelled faintly of marijuana and sweat, and the din of voices made it impossible for us to talk.

We pushed through the wall of people to a front row marked "Reserved for Families," unbuttoned our coats, and sat. Carrying his guitar case, Rob came onstage with Father McDonough, the campus chaplain, and Rob's colleagues John and Larry. They sat on folding chairs to the left of the massive oak podium which stood in the middle of the stage.

Father McDonough stepped to the microphone and raised his arms until the crowd quieted; he read the invocation and introduced Rob as "one of our promising young professors." Rob moved quickly to the podium.

"Men and women of Carradine University," he shouted, "It's time for us to make our statement! As of today over forty-four thousand of our troops have lost their lives for this unjust war. And that's not all."

I readjusted my coat and sat up straight. Glancing at the people all around me, I saw that their eyes were fixed on Rob. I felt proud. This man was my husband.

When he finished, the roar of applause filled the room. Margaret leaned close to shout in my ear, "He's such a good speaker!"

At the end of the rally, Father McDonough announced the first Teach-In. It would take place the following Thursday, he told us, adding that we were following a precedent set by the University of Michigan. Thunderous applause erupted and everyone stood, waving signs and chanting, "We want out! We want out!"

At that point Rob carried his guitar to the podium. The crowd cheered as he began to sing "Where Have All the Flowers Gone?" As one, everyone joined in, "Long time passing..."

Afterward Margaret and I stood waiting until Rob left the stage. When finally he walked over to us, we both congratulated him: "Rob, you did that like a pro."

"They estimate eight hundred here tonight," said Rob, "so it looks like we're really reaching folks now." He shifted his guitar case from one arm to the other. "And more good news." His smile extended across his face. "We're going to start draft counseling soon. We need women counselors too. I'm hoping both of you will take the training."

We both nodded at him. "Where do we sign up?"

Rob laced his free arm through mine. "I'll pass on your names to Father McDonough."

We fell in with the scores of people shuffling to the exit. "I'm so glad there's a way to do something concrete," I squeezed his arm.

We walked our friend home and went to find our car, humming the songs we'd sung at the rally all the way home.

The next afternoon I dragged a heavy bag from the car up the steps to our apartment. Rob met me at the door, taking the bag and peering inside it. "Wow—these books weigh a ton."

Hanging up my plaid wool coat I said, "They're for my lectures next week. Look at them, All our favorite war protestors."

Rob knelt and set out each book on the floor. "Sure enough. Whitman, Thoreau, Emerson—these are great, honey."

I dropped to the floor beside him. "In our department meeting today Jerry—he's now the leader of the protest movement at Sumner—urged us to develop writing assignments using antiwar materials from great writers. He called on us to be 'Outspoken, with flair.'" I waved my arms in the air. "He ended his speech dramatically. 'Our students need our leadership,' he said, 'now more than ever. Remember, *educare*—from the Latin, to lead out.' You know Jerry, he loves to throw Latin around."

The following week, I walked into the classroom and wrote on the board: "War: Arguments FOR and AGAINST." I'd asked the students to bring in newspaper articles and editorials representing each position. Lucy Walton, a redhead with a strong Southern accent, raised her hand. "What's next? Does this mean we will have to write our own arguments?"

The other students stared at her, some with open hostility. The kids in the front row rolled their eyes. Lucy was notorious for her leading, and sometimes stupid, questions. "That's a possibility, Lucy. So listen carefully and take notes," I told all of them. I retrieved my grade book and pen and took a back-row seat.

In the next fifty minutes each student presented the main idea of the essay, first writing the author's name and title under FOR or AGAINST on the board. Their opinions were overwhelmingly anti-war. Then Phil Simmons, a tall, skinny basketball player, stood. "I have a pro-war polemic." Some of the kids hissed softly at his use of the word polemic but they waited respectfully for him to finish. At three minutes before the bell I returned to the front of the room.

"As Lucy guessed, your assignment is to construct your own formal argument, using both pros and cons you've heard today. I expect a four-page essay one week from today." The students moaned.

Lucy raised her hand again: "What if we write more than four pages?"

"Let's say no more than ten pages," I joked. "Seriously, keep it at four." The bell clanged and the students shoved books and binders together, picked up sweaters and coats, and headed for the door. As I was stacking my books, John Miller approached me. His brown hair was newly cut and a curl fell on his forehead, James Dean style.

"Could I talk with you?" he asked.

In my office he took the chair to the right of my desk. He waited until I sat to speak. "Dr. Baird, I—I'm being drafted in January." His voice was soft, almost a whisper.

"Oh, John, I'm sorry." I found myself clenching my fists.

"And the thing is, I don't know if I'm for or against war. My dad is so angry. He wants me to be rah-rah war, and when I come to class and hear these ideas, I get confused and honestly don't know what to do." He stared at the floor.

"Ah, John. That's a tough one. Would you like to talk to someone? Do you know you can get draft counseling here at the university?" I glanced up at the Sister Corita print I'd hung over my desk: a multicolored PEACE sign. "I can give you a number—"

He shook his head. "I don't know what to do. Dad gets so upset when he sees the protestors on the television, but I needed to tell—someone."

I stifled a sigh. "Your mother—can she help you?"

"My mom, she stopped arguing with him because, well, I guess it's not worth it. It really hurt her when I got a low number, and she—she—" he faltered. "She can't handle it. I mean my going."

We sat in silence. Footsteps thudded in the hallway outside, and John took a deep breath.

"I guess I'll be going now." He stood. I pushed my chair back. I wanted so much to hold him as a mother would.

"I wish I could say something to help you, John."

He looked at me, a wistful smile on his lips. "Thanks for listening." John walked out into the hall and I followed his footsteps down the stairs.

Sliding back into my chair, I lay my head on my desk, recalling Jarrell's poem: "From my mother's sleep I fell into the state . . . I woke to black flak and the nightmare fighters."

My students were about to become nightmare fighters, and there was nothing I could do.

As the war continued and protests increased across the country, an air of desperation pervaded my classrooms. One Monday afternoon Paul Donahue, a twenty-year-old sophomore in my composition class, came to my office. His face was sweaty, and he took a white handkerchief from his pressed gray slacks to wipe it. His head bowed, he sat.

"Paul, how can I help you?" I could feel his insecurity. After a moment he met my eyes.

"Dr. Baird, I can't get below a C in this class or I'll be drafted." His words tumbled out and his dark eyes welled.

"Let's look at your grades." I reached for my grade book, running a finger under the row of Paul's stats. "Pretty good, Paul. All Cs and, oh, a couple of Ds here."

He pressed his hands together. "I know—one was from that week, um, when I got my notice."

My heart raced. "Paul," I said, reaching out to tap his arm for emphasis. "Paul, you can do this. Why don't you revise the argument essay? Find some material in the library to support your main points. Bring it in Friday, and I'll go over it with you."

He nodded, mumbling "Thank you," and headed out the door.

I hoped he would stay on track, but, even if he couldn't, I knew I could never send anyone to this war.

In the spring Rob accepted a full-time position at the University of Missouri campus not far from our apartment. There he made friends with Gene Lawson, a new economics professor, and his wife, Ginger, a willowy brunette with huge brown eyes, a curvaceous body, and a heavy South Carolina twang. After the four of us met for dinner to celebrate our anniversary, Rob couldn't say enough about her. "Wow, that Ginger is really something, isn't she?"

I had to agree. While she was Ava Gardner gorgeous, she seemed genuine, not the least bit conceited or pretentious, and I'd enjoyed meeting her. "Yes, Ginger is really lovely," I agreed.

Rob responded, "Oh, more than lovely—she's perfect. She's built like a ton of bricks. How did Gene get so lucky?" I felt a twinge of anger, but I let it go.

On another evening, driving home after a second dinner with Ginger and Gene, we stopped for a red light at Grand and Lindell. Rob turned to me and said, "Why can't you have breasts like Ginger's?"

"Luck of the draw," I said. I struggled to stay calm. This was a side of Rob I'd never seen. Of course I felt jealous, but it wasn't Ginger's fault that my husband might fancy her figure. My breath caught as I stifled a sigh. The light turned green. We drove on.

Sitting in the bleachers at a Cardinals game a few Sundays later, Rob openly stared at each large-bosomed woman who passed by. So blatant was his ogling, he plainly wanted me to notice. When the game ended he puffed out his lips like a pouting child. This time I couldn't hide my reaction. "What's the matter?" I said. But when he ignored me, I purposely ignored him back. He sulked all the way home.

Back in our flat, Rob went to work at his desk, leaning over his papers and writing furiously. I escaped into a book of John Updike's short stories. Maybe the fictional couple, the Maples, still newlyweds, could teach me something of marriage. Later on, when I told Rob "Good night," he did not respond. I was so worn out from the day, I went straight to bed and quickly fell asleep.

The next morning I woke to find Rob gazing at me like a little boy pleading for cookies. Slivers of sunlight streamed through the venetian blinds and I could hear the traffic rushing by on Magnolia. Rob reached out and put his arms around me, pulling me close. "You know what I wish?"

Still groggy, I shook my head.

"I wish you had big breasts," he said, pushing me gently back to my pillow and staring into my eyes. He smiled, his green eyes eager as if I might instantly sprout mammoth enlargements and make his wish come true. I tasted bile in my mouth and I wanted to shove him away or even slap him in the face.

Instead, I said in the gentlest voice I could manage: "So...you no longer think I'm beautiful?"

Turning away, he got out of bed and stomped into the kitchen.

While I was showering, he stuck his head in the door. "See you later; I'm going to the library." Before I could respond, I heard the front door slam.

Exiting the shower, I felt my blood run cold. Something was happening, and it was out of my control.

We saw the Lawsons frequently that fall and winter at department socials and dinners in each other's homes. In June the four of us flew to Mexico for a week. By day we toured Teotihuacán, the cathedral of La Virgen de Guadalupe, and the parks and *mercados*, and by night we drank margaritas and ate *mole y pollo* in lively restaurants with mariachis.

It was no vacation for me. The day we arrived Rob began dogging me. "What about exercises?" he pleaded. "Can't you do something?" He began finding fault with me in other areas, too. "Meredith, you're not walking fast enough, can't you pick it up?"

The first time it happened I ignored it. But when Rob started up again in Puerto Vallarta, my heart fell. "Meredith," he said, "why don't you practice walking in a sexier way? You know, the way Ginger walks. Kind of slinky? You walk like a tomboy." He said this after dinner, when we were in our hotel room.

Longing to change the subject, I spotted a gecko scampering along the walls and said, "Oh my gosh, there's a lizard. In our hotel room."

"We're in the tropics, what do you expect?" He sounded exasperated. I couldn't tell if it was with me or the gecko.

Rob's directives had begun a few months after our wedding, but after we flew home from Mexico his criticism became chronic. I took every suggestion seriously. My husband was physically fit and Hollywood handsome, and because I was so proud to have him on my arm, I was willing to do anything to keep him.

One afternoon Rob breezed through the door, his arms full of department store bags. "Meredith," he said, beaming, "Look! These are the kind of things you should wear." I examined all the clothing he'd bought. There was a clingy yellow blouse with a scoop neck, tight stretchy tee shirts, a brown suede miniskirt and a snug brown sweater, hot pants, five pairs of pink bikini underwear, and three pushup Maidenform bras in size 32D. Nothing I would ever have chosen for myself.

He pulled the scoop-necked blouse from the stack and handed it to me. "Model this, honey, and don't forget the new bra."

I threw off what I was wearing, and started with the bra. He watched as I hooked it. I studied the effect of an almost hollow shell encasing my small breasts. "Rob, this looks strange, my breasts are hiding in this D cup."

He grabbed a bunch of Kleenex, stuffing each side with a handful of tissue. I thought the cups looked unevenly filled. "Are you sure this looks okay?" I asked.

He threw the blouse over my head, adjusted it so that my cleavage, such as it was, showed, and stood back. "Now there's a sexy wife," he said.

I wore all the clothes and took pains to stuff the bras. Since Rob continually admonished me never to leave home without doing my eyes, I painted myself with eyeliner, mascara, and bright blue eye shadow. I also tried to walk quickly and swing my hips as seductively as Ginger did. Then I dyed my hair platinum blonde. From that time on, at parties, when the rum warmed Rob to me, he'd encircle my waist and whisper, "You are the most beautiful woman in the room, and you're mine."

One evening, on our way home from a party, I lost it. Rob had started singing Ginger's praises again. "Now there's a woman," he began. "You need to be more like her—she's so calm and relaxed."

I bit my tongue while we were in the car, counting to a hundred as Aunt Tilley had taught me. Once inside our apartment, though, I exploded. "Damn it," I threw my purse in the chair and ripped off my jacket. "If you hate me, then say it. I can't stand this constant picking. I'm not enough this, I'm too much that, wear this, wear that, say this, don't say that. I hate living like this."

Rob gawked at me and shouted, "What have I married?"

What have I married? I countered in my mind.

I sobbed myself to sleep that night and woke the next morning with a heavy heart. Our marriage was in bad trouble. We needed help.

I'd been trying so hard to do everything my husband wished. In his recent complaints he'd referred to me not as who but what, as though I were a thing—an object of derision. His words had cut me.

We'd been married a few months shy of two years when I begged him to do marriage counseling. For the first time I started to ponder the possibility that Rob might leave me. Before, the idea of divorce had never entered my mind. We were Catholics and Catholics didn't get divorced. I was terrified of divorce—the shame, the loss of respectability. But Rob's recent behavior had alarmed me. I was relieved when he seemed amenable to getting help.

"Maybe we can see Bill O'Dowd. You know him, don't you?" The priest had taught him in high school and was known for his role as advisor to the Sodality, a national group of high school students devoted to Mary, the Mother of Jesus. Years before I'd heard him speak at a convention in Detroit, and I still remembered his charisma as he spoke from the podium to an audience of a thousand.

As cradle Catholics, it never occurred to us to seek counseling outside the Catholic Church. The Church was in our bones. We believed that the Church, through the counsel of a good priest, was the only the place to seek advice.

Rob made an appointment for the first Saturday in February. Three days before, the city was blanketed in a heavy snowstorm, and the TV news warned of black ice. So he drove slowly, the ice crunching beneath our tires, down Grand Avenue.

Gazing out the window, I was daydreaming: what if the black ice spun us out of control and we didn't have to do this? "Do you think we should have made some notes?" I said.

"Notes?" he chuckled. "Like a list, for a class assignment?" He laughed again.

I didn't see the humor. "I have no idea how to do this."

"Remember, Bill's been a counselor for ages. He was at Jesuit High for at least ten years before I knew him. You don't need to worry."

But I was worried. My husband had said a terrible thing to me, and here I was, about to bare my soul to a priest I scarcely knew. And what were we doing, sharing our relationship issues—including the fact that I, at least, thought we had problems with sex—to a celibate who had never been married? But I kept my own counsel, taking a moment to pray to a God I was finding more and more elusive: what were we doing here?

Rob parked the car and we hurried into the four-story brick building at the corner of Pine and Grand. Years earlier, the building had been quite the stylish place, a grand hotel with a spacious lobby and lovely rooms appointed with antique furniture. Now it housed fifty or so priests associated with the university.

As we entered the vestibule, I noted how purposefully my husband strode. He walks like a man who knows exactly where he's going, I thought, hurrying to keep up. The lobby, with its Persian carpets and heavy maroon drapes, was dark, and the odor of stale cigarette smoke hung in the air.

Threading our way through the silent hallways, we located room 160 and knocked. A priest wearing a long black cassock opened the door. He was a stocky man with a wide, ruddy face. His rimless glasses had slipped halfway down his broad nose.

"Come in, folks. Rob, and you must be Meredith?"

Rob reached out and shook the priest's hand. "Yes, this is my wife, Meredith."

I nodded. For a second we stood awkwardly.

"Well, sit, sit," invited Father, gesturing at a worn flowered couch as he slumped into a leather Barcalounger across from us. An enormous oak desk and two straight chairs sat on the other side of the room. I was glad we'd been invited to take more comfortable seats. I felt weak and vulnerable. The couch felt soft, cushiony, and supportive.

A fish-shaped ashtray was on the coffee table in front of us. Father Bill took a cigarette from a soft pack of Lucky Strikes and lit it. "Feel free to smoke, kids. Now what's this about you two having problems?"

Rob leaned forward. "We're having trouble fitting together."

The priest raised his eyebrows. I noticed a spot of dried food on his sleeve and wondered if he would get the sexual innuendo.

"We got back from Mexico a few days ago. It should have been fun, but in Mexico she constantly complained about the heat, the lizards in our room..." He sighed audibly. "We don't seem to be getting along anymore."

Now it was my turn. Defending myself was not my strong suit. "During the last two years I've tried to do everything as Rob wished. I do feel sad sometimes, but I try not to show it."

The priest coughed. "What do you mean 'sad'?"

I was afraid now that I was disappointing Rob. "Down in the dumps, Father."

He puffed on his Lucky Strike. "Well, you know what you have to do, don't you?"

I did not know.

"You need to learn to sidestep your feelings."

"What do you mean?"

"Well," said our counselor, "sometimes you have to simply do the right thing and wait for your feelings to catch up."

"I think . . . I mean, I guess I understand, but Father, what's the right thing?"

The priest straightened his glasses. "You'll figure it out. Don't forget, Rob can help you."

What was he talking about? I felt over my head and I began to weep, very softly. Rob made no move to comfort me.

The rest of that first session dissolved into blur of tears and cigarette smoke. Soon Rob was ushering me out the door, guiding me as if I were disabled. "See you in two weeks, Bill," he said.

When we got home we made drinks and acted as if nothing was wrong.

One rainy Saturday evening Rob suggested we see *Women in Love*, at the Highland Art Film Theatre. We both admired Glenda Jackson's work in *Marat/Sade* and were eager to see her in a new role. But we hadn't bargained for what we got: a film so full of sexual tension that it was palpable throughout the audience. Afterwards, strolling out of the building, Rob did not take my hand as he normally did. "Did you like it?" I asked.

He turned away. "I don't want to talk about it."

In the car driving home Rob stayed quiet. I started picking on a ragged fingernail and tried to figure out what had affected him so deeply—the graphic sex between Oliver Reed and Glenda Jackson or the intense wrestling match of the two men in front of the roaring fire.

In our apartment, as if I were not there, he hurried into the bedroom and got into bed. He made no overtures to make love—as he often did after sensual movies—and by this time I was blaming myself. Was his silence the result of something I'd done—or not done—sexually? As I struggled to sleep, my mind raced. I knew our sex life didn't come close to that of movie characters. I couldn't remember a single time, even on our honeymoon, when either one of us was ravenous to make love.

Maybe it was my naïveté. I was a novice and I did not know how to please my husband. I'd been so overwhelmed with grading papers, I'd put off the research I'd wanted to do. Tossing about, I threw the bedspread off and peered at the clock: 1:15 a.m. I'd been wrestling with the issue for nearly two hours. When Rob's breathing became shallow and I knew he was sleeping, I relaxed, letting go and allowing myself to sleep.

A few days later I was rolling my cart past the A&P magazine display when a *Cosmopolitan* headline caught my eye: "Sensuous Woman Tells All: Revolutionary Sex."

I grabbed the magazine and sat on my heels, leafing through until I found the article touting the book by "J" as the first "how to" book for "the female who yearns to be all woman."

That was enough for me. I raced through the store for eggs, cheese, butter, ground beef, and milk. It was 4:13. If I hurried I had almost enough time to get to a bookstore and buy my own copy of *The Sensuous Woman*.

By 5:05 I was driving home, the book stuffed in the bottom of my purse to read later, in my office or the library. I sure didn't want Rob to see it. I feared too that Gwen might see it and suspect (rightly so) that the sex I was having with my husband a couple of times a week was less than fulfilling.

I couldn't discuss it with anyone. Not with our marriage counselor who was a celibate priest, not with a man whose desire I sensed every time I passed him at the college, not even with my women friends to whom I simply could not admit this sort of failure. And certainly not with my husband.

The next day after classes, I told Greg I had errands and was leaving early. He and I had started chatting again, after our classes, and I found it comforting to spend time with a man who never criticized me. Once again, I rationalized our growing closeness as a shared love of literature. I knew it was dangerous, and that perhaps it was the danger that kept us going.

But I had to put all my energies into saving my marriage.

In the library I studied the book described on its flyleaf as a "detailed instruction manual of sexuality for women." "J" declared it was time for the "good" girls to find out what they were missing. She claimed that all women had sufficient erotic resources to set off fireworks in the bedroom. In a lengthy chapter with graphic drawings, she extolled the joys of self-arousal "even before he comes to the bedroom."

I kept reading. I didn't know if I could implement any of these suggestions, but I was willing to try. Finally I circled the one on page 45.

I scheduled it for the following Wednesday afternoon when I'd get home first and have plenty of time. That morning during my classes I tried not to think about what I was about to do. I flew out the door the minute my last class ended and drove to the A&P to make a single purchase, one I hoped would change our lives.

At home I drew a bath, sprinkling rose-scented oil in the water. Afterward I smoothed Ponds cream all over my body. I prayed: God, help me to make my body desirable to Rob. I brushed my hair long and straight, as he preferred it, and carefully applied aqua blue eye shadow and heavy dark mascara. I looked in the mirror. My eyes were luminous. Then I ripped open my package.

Wrapping myself in long sheets of Saran Wrap, I envisioned Rob's dark eyes shining with lustful delight when I answered the door. I got tingly feelings as I rehearsed the scene. I kept thinking about "J's" promise: her guarantee that this raunchy little technique would spice up the dullest sex life. When I pulled the last piece of Saran Wrap tight against my neck, I posed in front of the full-length mirror on the back of the bedroom door. What I saw horrified me so much that I scrunched my eyes closed. Who was this woman? Exposing myself this way felt so uncomfortable. But I couldn't allow my feelings to dissuade me. Nor could I let Rob sense my discomfort. This, according to "J," was what it took to be a "real" woman.

A second glance so filled me with revulsion that I wanted to peel the wrap off, stuff it into the trash, and be done with "J." What did she know about my marriage anyway? Instead I breathed slowly, ten or twelve times, in and out, and remembered the Stanislavski method. Become your character.

The problem was I didn't know what character I wanted to become. This Saran-wrapped version certainly wasn't me.

Finally an image of Ann-Margret, the bosomy actress who'd dazzled my husband in *Carnal Knowledge*, popped into my mind. I peered into the mirror and tried to smile seductively, as she did in the bedroom scenes with Jack Nicholson.

I checked the time. Ten minutes. I primed myself: think Anne-Margret.

I heard the key rattle in the front door lock and went into the living room. He was early, but I was ready. My heart raced as I took stage center for his entrance.

And there he was. First reaction: eyes narrowed, disapproving. A blank face, followed by a scowl. Finally, he spoke his lines, sounding harsh and disgusted: "What are you doing?" he growled, sweeping past me and disappearing into the study. I heard the thud of his books as he threw them on the desk.

I began to see where Betty Friedan was right: our patriarchy relegated women into roles that stifled us. We were never told we could perform many of the same jobs as men.

For her landmark study, *The Feminine Mystique*, Friedan had interviewed a large group of married women and discovered that most of them found their lives deeply unsatisfying. This was a first. No one had ever questioned the role of women so boldly.

I was excited about her insights, remembering back when I'd questioned my Mom about why fathers got praised for being the workers while the mothers, who worked so hard too, were largely ignored.

Although I was no housewife and I considered my husband liberated—he encouraged me to finish my doctoral studies and continue to teach and was always willing to help with household chores—I had to admit I often felt "less than" in his company. When we visited the Dodge dealership to look at cars, Rob took me along. But it was Rob who took the test drive. He never bothered to ask me if I wanted to try out the car and I'd been too cowed to ask. It was as though I didn't exist. On other occasions, after political discussions with friends, he'd take me to task for my silence. The truth was that I lacked the confidence to argue politics, but that didn't stop him from expecting me to join in. For Rob it was one more area in which I was lacking.

As I sat on the sofa reading Friedan's book, I felt conflicted. Here I am, I thought, an educated woman who speaks articulately in my classes and with my colleagues, but with my husband and his friends, I can barely open my mouth. What is wrong with me? Why didn't I ask: "What's wrong with him?" Why couldn't I?

I was glad Rob had not yet come home, so I could have a drink—well before happy hour. I loved how the alcohol blurred reality for me, and, almost instantaneously, my world brightened.

One morning I again woke to find Rob staring at me. As I stretched my arms and smiled at him, Rob said, "Why can't you have breasts like Ginger's?"

My answer came out in a rush: "Whatareyoutalkingabout? Where's this coming from?"

"Can't you do some exercises and maybe they'll—"

I turned away from him and stood, covering my chest with my arms. "I don't know what you've read or what ads you've seen, but there is no way that I know of to change my bust size." I stomped into the bathroom, slamming the door.

That weekend everything spun out of control. Friday night, I couldn't stop vomiting. One, two, three times I stumbled to the toilet and gagged. I'd had only two gin and tonics that evening, hoping to avoid a hangover.

When I returned to bed for the third time Rob reached over, and when he touched my hand, he bolted up. "Mer, you're blazing hot." He laid his hand on my arm. "I'm getting aspirin."

He returned and helped me raise my head to drink. Afterward I lay on my damp pillow and slept most of Saturday.

Sunday morning I still felt awful. Rob brought tea but I barely sipped it. "I feel so weak," I whispered.

"I don't know what you've got, honey; maybe I should stay home today."

"Oh, no, please. Go on and keep your racquetball date. It's really okay." I tried to smile.

"Well, I'm going to call Mom and see what she thinks."

A couple of hours later Eve showed up with chicken soup, Alka Seltzer, and 7 Up. "Try sticking to liquids, honey."

On Monday I phoned the college. "I have the flu, but I hope to be back Wednesday." Later that morning Rob drove me to Dr. Redmond's office. As soon as he heard my symptoms, the doctor asked, "Have you been out of the country recently?"

"We were in Mexico two weeks ago. Do you think—?"

"I can't make a diagnosis until after we've tested your blood. I'll call you with the results."

Dr. Redmond phoned that afternoon and asked us to return to his office. "I'll give you details when you get here," he said.

My diagnosis: infectious hepatitis. Probable cause: raw fish in Puerto Vallarta.

Treatment for me: complete bed rest and quarantine. For Rob: a hefty shot of gamma globulin.

I'd been out for three weeks when Greg showed up at the apartment bearing a gift wrapped in shiny bright green paper. "They took up a collection, Meredith, and gave me the money. They told me to buy you a book." I ripped the paper off. Joyce Carol Oates's latest novel: *Wonderland.*

"*Wonderland.*" I looked at him. "Is the title meant to be ironic?" In my current sickly state, any notion of paradise seemed absurd.

"Maybe." He smiled. "I haven't read it yet." He put his arm around my shoulders and gave me the gentlest squeeze. "I'm glad to see you."

I felt only the slightest flicker of desire, so small I almost didn't notice it.

My recuperation was so slow that Dr. Redmond finally prescribed steroids. "I must warn you, common side effects are weight gain and moon face." When I winced, he added, "Meredith, you need this medication." The drugs reacted like amphetamines in me. I couldn't eat, I couldn't sleep, and I couldn't read. My hands shook. Nothing but Marlboros and hot tea sustained me. By the fifth week I'd shed twelve pounds. My days were full of television. My nights were full of Valium and Seconal.

One morning Rob's mom brought me some of her books. None of them were the type Rob and I read, but I felt grateful. I'd confided in Eve my frustration at being caged in our four-room apartment. When Rob came home from the university that afternoon he saw the books on my bedside table. He picked up one by Barbara Cartland and scowled. "You can't be reading this stuff? Where did it come from?"

"Your mom."

"What is she thinking? This is housewife escape fiction. Look at all the books lying around here you've never had time to read." He pointed to a stack in the corner. On top were *Silent Spring* and *The Rise and Fall of the Third Reich*. "Why don't you read them?"

I was afraid to tell my husband I was too sick to read.

One afternoon while I was still home recuperating, the doorbell rang. I opened the door to find a package. I couldn't tell where it was from but I took it inside and tore it open. Under the plain brown wrapper the words YOUR NEW MARK EDEN REVOLUTIONARY BREAST DEVELOPER flew out at me. Inside the box was a plastic contraption hinged with heavy wires. It was Pepto Bismol pink and resembled an oversized clamshell. The accompanying directions promised: "Now you, too, can have breasts like the movie stars! Simply grip and press 30 times in the morning and again at night. Soon you will be amazed!"

I stared at the words, recalling Rob when he first broached the subject of my breasts: "Can't you do something?" I reexamined the directions and read again, "Thirty times in the mourning." I thought it said "mourning"! Stuffing the apparatus back into the box, I shoved it in my bottom dresser drawer underneath my sweaters and flicked on the television.

When Rob returned, I told him I'd received his gift.

"Where is it?" he said. He sounded elated.

"In my drawer. I hid it. I can't believe you believe that stupid ad! Rob, I weigh ninety-five pounds; it's not likely my breasts will suddenly expand. Look at Twiggy; she's bone thin and flat-chested!"

"Meredith, I honestly believed it was a good idea. Maybe you'll feel better about it later on," he said. I felt the tears start and quickly wiped them away. I didn't want him to see me cry.

The next night Rob walked in the bedroom as I was undressing. "Meredith, you look like a boy. How much weight have you lost?"

Since I'd told him only yesterday, I realized he had not listened to me, but I chose to ignore that. "Fifteen pounds, maybe more." I stood and stared at myself in the mirror on our bedroom door. What I saw was a hollow-eyed stick woman from a third-world country like one pictured in *National Geographic*.

An hour later Rob made love to me. It felt different than before. More tender, more erotic. I was confused. Maybe he was trying to make up for his thoughtless "gift." Maybe he understood I couldn't help what my body's become. At the time, it never even occurred to me that he might prefer my body with its new boyish look.

After eight weeks I was still quarantined, and our tiny apartment felt like a prison cell. Steroid injections were steadily bolstering my blood count, but their side effects continued to make me agitated, anorexic, and insomniac. Every morning I telephoned Greg a few minutes before 9:00, when I knew he'd be in his office, and begged him to visit me.

He visited only reluctantly, and not every day. Those afternoons when I knew he was coming, I'd set out a bottle of gin and mix him a drink, trying to recapture the afternoons we'd spent at the Fox and Hounds during the first year I'd known him. But now I was a nervous wreck. The drugs had stripped me of any passion, and Greg became only a kind gentleman caller who sat on a straight-backed chair while I lay propped on pillows in the bed I shared with my husband. I was no longer the ingenue delighting in sharing literary insights with a scholar, now merely an emaciated, sickly colleague.

One afternoon, Greg dropped by early. "I've done my homework," he said. "I brought you something."

I poured his drink, and we settled on the sofa. The smell of the gin disgusted me, but I wanted to be a proper hostess. "What did you bring me?"

"A list, from the newspaper. The fall TV shows."

"Television?"

"You told me it's been hard for you to read lately, Meredith."

I tried to hide my disappointment. Since I'd been able to plow through *Wonderland,* I'd been hoping for another good book. I smiled anyway. "OK, let's hear them."

I didn't mention that Rob disapproved of my watching so much television, or that he'd walked in and frowned at me one day when I was watching a soap opera.

In the evenings I always told Rob if Greg had visited. If he minded, he never showed it.

"You're getting better, Meredith," Dr. Redmond said, reading the numbers on my lab report. He took off his glasses, set them on the counter, and met my eyes. "How much weight have you lost?" he asked.

"Twenty-one pounds."

"Let's check your heart," he said. The stethoscope felt like a piece of ice on my chest. I shivered. I'd removed my blouse and was staring at my body in the mirror; the bones in my back seemed to be protruding in unnatural ways. "I'd like to stop this weight loss, but we'll gradually get you off these steroids. You're not exhibiting any of the typical side effects—weight gain and moon face. It's puzzling, though I'm glad to say you are better." He moved away to write notes on my chart.

"Am I still confined to quarters?" I said, trying to sound light-hearted.

Dr. Redmond ignored the question and looked at me sternly. "Okay, Meredith, you've had to take prednisone simply to get your blood count to begin coming down. By no means is it where we want it to be. So, no, you're not ready to go out. You're still quarantined, but you can do some small things like cooking a meal or straightening the house."

"Ah, I'd been hoping I could get back to housekeeping," I joked, forcing a laugh. My doctor did not smile.

That night I put on a pair of slacks and a sweater and waited for Rob on the living room sofa instead of in our bed. In my hand I held the grocery list I'd prepared as soon as I got home from Doctor R's office. The door rattled when Rob pushed it open shortly before 6:00. He smiled when he saw me.

"Mer, you're out of bed?"

"I'm better." I walked over to kiss him. His cheek felt cool and smelled like Lifebuoy. "Look!" I said, "I've made a grocery list."

The simple act of setting the table made me feel better. At least it was something more constructive than lying around waiting for the hours to pass. I did not want Rob to consider me—the skinny asexual rag doll I'd seen at Dr. R's office—a burden. Besides, I had an idea.

After dinner that night we sat together in the living room, the first time in nearly two months. "It must be hard for you," I said, "sitting here with me night after night. Why don't you go out and have yourself—what do they call it? A boys'night out?"

At first he balked, but two weeks later he brought it up himself. "Remember what you mentioned, about my getting out on my own? I think I'd like that," he said. "I hear there's a new lounge where they play folk music after 8:00."

The following evening I sat watching as he changed into a blue button-down shirt and the soft gray sweater I'd bought him for Christmas. He looked in the mirror, combed his hair, glanced again in the mirror, peering in close to straighten his collar, and turned around. "Are you sure you don't mind?"

"No, I only want you to have some fun, Rob." As he swooped down to kiss me, I questioned my trust. He's so handsome, what am I doing? I thought. But then I reconsidered. He keeps telling me how much he loves me. I have to believe him.

After my blood tests at the end of November, Dr. Richmond's nurse phoned. "You're good to go, Meredith," she said. "Congratulations. Doctor says you can return to work next week, but be sure to take it easy." I yelped with joy and phoned the college.

That next week as I prepared my lesson plans, I raised all the window shades in the study and sat at our desk. Swaths of sun fell around me, and I hummed along with Carly Simon's rendition of "Anticipation." It didn't take long for me to sink into my work, and two hours passed. When Rob came in, he walked over to me, grinning. Seeing me at the desk he said, "Are you cleared to teach again?"

"Yes, my blood count's normal. I go back next week." He leaned down to kiss my cheek.

"After four months, I'm so glad. I know it's been hell," he said.

Hell was an understatement. But it was nearly over, and I longed to get back to my students and my life as a teacher. I didn't know yet how I'd feel about being near Greg again, but what was uppermost in my mind was a return to normalcy.

When I entered my classroom the following Monday, the students stood, clapping and cheering. On the board someone had written in huge bold letters: "Welcome back, Dr. Baird." On my office desk lay a small bouquet of pink carnations wrapped in green tissue, and a card signed by all the students in my class.

I was back.

On mornings after Rob's nights out, he always told me about meeting some nice guys and listening to good music. Since the bar was near the university I assumed that he met other academics there. But I never asked pressed him for particulars, and thanks to the Seconal and Valium I swallowed every night, I was always sleeping when he returned.

A few weeks into this new routine, Rob mentioned that he'd made a new friend. "You'll like Rick," he said. "We really had a great time last night, and I told him all about you."

The following week he said, "I really want Rick to meet you, Meredith."

When he told me Rick would be coming by Saturday afternoon, I shrugged. "I'll be happy to meet him, but, since I've been freed from captivity, Margaret said she'd come by and we'll go to the library. But that won't be until about two."

At 1:00 on the dot Rob leapt up to open the door for Rick. For some reason I assumed Rick would be beautiful like Rob, but he was only an average-looking man in his early twenties, wearing brown slacks and a beige sweater that seemed to dwarf him. He had curly brown hair and I didn't even notice the color of his eyes. Rob introduced me with a flourish: "This," he said, grabbing my arm, "is Meredith, my wife."

Rick took my hand and pumped it. His smile was warm but his palm felt sweaty. "I've heard so much about you, and you're as lovely as Rob said." His grin showed off his crooked teeth.

After the hellos and have-a-seat-please, I went to make tea. From the kitchen I heard the two men talking as Rob showed Rick around our apartment. From the window of our study Rob pointed out the advantage we had, living right across the street from Tower Grove Park. "I'd heard about this park since I was a kid," Rob said. "My dad always stops here on his way to work. He loves to talk to the birds—and he swears that they talk back!" They laughed. I could hear the joy in my husband's voice. I was glad he'd invited his new friend to our home.

I served tea in blue mugs that were wedding gifts, and we sat and chatted. Rick's family had moved to St. Louis three years before and they lived far north, so he was unacquainted with midtown where we lived. Rick worked for an insurance adjuster.

In a boisterous voice Rob regaled him with stories about our meeting, our wedding, and honeymoon. After about an hour, I excused myself and went outside to wait for Margaret.

As we drove down Grand Avenue I told her about Rick. "He's a new friend of Rob's."

"Someone from the U?" Margaret asked.

"No, I think he met him in that new music lounge on Clark Street. He seemed nice, and Rob was really glad to see him. Rob's been telling me for a couple of weeks that he wanted us to meet."

Margaret parked and we got out of her car. As she was locking the car, I remembered something else: "It was interesting, too, because Rick, well, he came off as—kind of effeminate."

"Really?" Margaret and I began strolling up Pine Boulevard. Both of us fell silent, and I thought no more of my remark.

Monday morning as he left for school, Rob complained of a sore throat. When I finished classes I came home to find him in bed huddled beneath the covers, burning with fever. Aspirin, tea, and even my loving attentions failed to revive him for the next three days. On Tuesday he asked for the phone. "I have to call Rick. I can't go out tonight." Although I had completely recovered, Rob still went out solo on Tuesdays. I brought the phone to him and went into the kitchen.

Later that night Rick called to check on Rob. The next afternoon Rick phoned again, and again the day after. "He's a very thoughtful guy," I said to Rob. None of Rob's other friends called so often.

After that Rob talked of Rick less, and I never asked about him. It was more than a year before I thought of Rick again.

I suppose it was inevitable. When I was sprung from my sick room, we resumed our visits to Father O'Dowd's drab, smoke-filled office.

As soon as we sat, Rob started. "We're still having trouble, Bill. But I think we've gotten through a rough spot with Meredith's being so sick."

We never addressed our problems on our own. We reserved them for this tired inner sanctum, and I never knew what to expect from Rob—or myself. Now I wondered what he meant: got through a rough spot but still having trouble. Trouble? So far, trouble always seemed rooted in my behavior. I squirmed in my chair.

Each of our sessions followed a pattern. Rob stated his concerns. Father Bill asked me about mine. I gritted my teeth and reminded them that I was trying. When Rob complained of my moods, Bill admonished me, "Sidestep your feelings." He'd shake his finger at me: "That's what you must learn to do." This went on for two months. The end of most sessions left me dissolved in tears. How would I ever please my husband?

Strangely, I began to feel closer to Rob. I believed the counseling was helping. At least I had a chance to hear what was on my husband's mind and try to alter my behavior.

We changed our morning appointments to afternoons. That way it was easier to go home and have a couple of drinks, and there were fewer hours to get through before we went to bed. Always, the next day, we'd soldier on as though the session had never taken place.

A few nights later when he reached for me, I pulled away and went to my dresser. In the top drawer, tucked underneath my bras and panties, lay the little white plastic container holding my diaphragm. Rob had barely touched me in days, and I could sense his urgency. I thought perhaps he was feeling better about us. I was excited. I returned to our bed and to Rob's welcoming arms. After we made love, we slept in our usual spoon fashion. It felt good to me. Promising.

Weeks later I woke early and watched Rob sleeping. Lying faceup beside me in the warm glow of morning light, he was the picture of contentment. I slipped from bed and tiptoed into the kitchen to make coffee. Opening a can of Folgers, I inhaled the tantalizing aroma. The next instant, I doubled over. I dashed to the bathroom and vomited. I tried to be very quiet, but our bed was only a few feet from the bathroom and soon Rob tapped on the door. His hair was tousled and he'd put on an undershirt. "Honey—you okay?" He watched as I stood over the sink, dabbing at the sleeve of my chenille robe. "Oh, I'm fine, it's probably something I ate," I said. "I'll be out in a minute."

I dressed and poked my head into the kitchen. Rob was eating a bowl of Cheerios. "I made toast for you," he said, pointing to the plate. "Did you eat something strange yesterday?"

I shook my head. "I don't think so."

"I hope you're not catching the flu," Rob said." He tipped the bowl to get the last spoonful of milk.

"No, no. Besides, I don't have a fever." I broke off a corner of toast, put it in my mouth, and touched his arm. "Got to run, class at nine."

At Sumner College I ran up the stairs and hurried into the office. Gwen was already reading at her desk. She glanced up and smiled. "Hi."

I tossed my purse on the desk. I picked up my folder of essays and tapped her on the shoulder. "Gwen, do you have a second?"

She put her book down as I described the nausea. "Gwen, you've been pregnant. Could it be?"

She smiled. "Hey, it could, but do you have any other symptoms? Missed period? Breast tenderness?"

"Nope." I shook my head.

"Probably not. Maybe it was food poisoning. You want some Tums?"

"Bought some on the way here, but thanks." The bell rang. Gwen grabbed her bag, and we headed for our classrooms.

The following day I woke up without a trace of nausea, but when I rolled over to stand up, my forearm grazed my breast. I winced.

From my office I phoned Dr. Redmond.

The next afternoon waiting in the doctor's office, I stared at a picture of snow-capped mountains. I thought they resembled little white breasts swelling to the sky. Doctor Redmond ordered a pregnancy test and patted me on the back. "Seems like your marriage is going more than well," he said. "I'll call you later with the results."

How could this have happened? Did my diaphragm have a hole in it? Had I not applied enough jelly?

I couldn't ignore the clear signals my body was sending: my breasts were swollen and tender and I was voracious. At lunchtime I could easily devour two whole sandwiches when normally I'd eat only a half. And I was tired, so tired that I'd doze off before 9:00. I told Rob nothing about any of this, including my doctor's appointment.

The next day when the phone rang, Rob was already home reading in his armchair, the lamplight chasing shadows from his face as evening closed in. I grabbed the ringing phone and stepped into our bedroom. "Hello? Okay . . . Oh." My voice was fading away from me. "Okay, I will. Thanks for the call."

I stood in the doorway until Rob glanced up from his book. "That was Dr. Redmond," I said. "Rob, I'm pregnant."

My husband's eyes widened. "What?" He reached for his cigarettes. A moment slipped past as he lit one, inhaled, and met my eyes. "Oh, well, you'll have to do something about that."

A tinny acidic taste filled my mouth. "What do you mean?"

"Do what Jeanne did. It's not a big deal."

"I thought, before, you said—" I'd felt as if he'd slugged me.

"Did you honestly think a baby would solve our problems?" Rob paused and sat up very straight. "Besides, I don't want your children."

Feeling a knot of ice form in my chest, I swallowed hard and retreated into the bedroom, shutting the door behind me. I lay on our bed sobbing. God, how did this happen? What have I done? I believed being married meant eventually we might have children. I never dreamed Rob would respond this way. When she was only eighteen, Rob's sister Jeanne had gotten pregnant. Rob's parents had acted swiftly, terminating both the boyfriend and the pregnancy. I didn't know all the details of Jeanne's story, but I knew I was not Jeanne. I cannot do it, I thought. Abortion is against everything we've been taught. Struggling to get hold of myself, I forced my husband's ugly words out of my mind, determined to talk him out of this insanity. Then I cried my eyes out again.

After a few minutes I dragged myself out of bed, staring in the mirror at my mascara-streaked face and red eyes. I was numb, but I carefully dried my face, applied a light coat of powder, relined my eyes, brushed my hair, and returned to the living room. When I sat on the sofa I saw that Rob's lips were slightly pursed and his eyes were fixed on the window. This was the look he wore when he was upset. "Rob, please," I said. "I've been thinking. We need to talk to Father Bill. He's been advising us for months, and I need to hear what he has to say."

He nodded. "Okay, Meredith, we can see him, but don't take it for granted that I'll change my mind."

"No, no, of course not. Will you call him or shall I?"

"I'll call while you're in class."

I felt relieved. Surely the priest would talk some sense into him. How could my Rob, who was raised Catholic and spent four years in a seminary, even consider abortion? I couldn't even entertain the possibility.

When we first stepped inside Father Bill O'Dowd's office at Carradine University, the musty windowless room had reminded me of the setting for *No Exit*, the bleak Sartre play I'd recently studied. Now, after months of sessions here, the impression intensified.

After three years of marriage, Rob and I had reached an impasse. I begged to see the priest who'd advised us for months only because I believed he would change Rob's mind.

I sat on the couch in front of the large oak desk. Rob listened from a brown faded armchair, staring straight ahead, avoiding my eyes. In the dim lamplight, his face appeared flat and gray. Behind the desk the priest looked massive, his face a map of creases. Under his black cassock and cardigan, his broad shoulders loomed. I glanced at the crucifix on the wall. Next to it was an image of Jesus looking me in the eye, his index finger on his exposed heart. On a calendar below it I read May 1972. My eyes traveled to the priest's desk, cluttered with stacks of papers and the fish-shaped ashtray half full of cigarette butts.

Father Bill spoke so softly I leaned in to hear him. "How far along are you?"

"Almost four weeks," I said, trying hard to read my husband's expression. "Rob thinks, Father, that I should—"

The priest turned to me. "How do you feel about your marriage, Meredith?"

"Before last Thursday, Father, I believed we were better. I've tried to improve; we've talked about what I need to—" My eyes brimmed.

"And we were better before you decided—" Rob stammered and gripped the arms of his chair.

"I didn't decide anything. I don't know what happened."

"Rob," said Father Bill, "let's talk marriage first. Let's see how that goes."

I blotted my eyes with a Kleenex. "I thought we'd mended some fences. I saw positive signs. We felt—I'm searching for the right word here—close again. Rob wrote me a romantic poem a couple of weeks ago, and last week when I wore the dress he gave me, he said I looked beautiful." My face burned, and I couldn't look at either of them.

"I feel—" Rob cut in again. The priest raised his hand.

"Rob, give Meredith a chance."

For a moment no one spoke. The only sound was the priest puffing on his cigarette.

I felt stronger but my voice came out as a whisper: "I am trying. We've been working with you. The signs seemed positive."

Rob turned to face me for the first time. "How could you, Meredith?"

"I told you, I didn't do anything, Rob."

"I don't believe you. I've been trying, too, to make our marriage work, and I did want to stay married." He paused and sighed. "Now, I don't know."

I could not believe what I was hearing. "You mean it's either or?"

Rob averted his eyes again. He took a hard pack of Marlboros from his pocket and started fidgeting with it. Wanting to hide, I shut my eyes and saw black spots. Some invisible weight pressed on my chest and suddenly I knew I was close to fainting.

Father Bill shifted and his chair groaned. "Is it time for you two to have a child?" I opened my eyes to see the two men staring at me.

"Are you suggesting that I have an abortion, Father?" The room swirled around me. I had been experiencing nausea, and now the acrid smell of the ashtray made my stomach lurch. Breathing deeply, I tried to hold myself together.

Father Bill sighed, toying with a pen. "Well, I may have something that will help you."

Rob leaned forward. I held my breath.

"Frankly, I don't think it's a good time for you kids to have a child."

A half smile played on Rob's lips. I knew what the two of them were thinking. My hand moved to my throat as the priest stared at his desk calendar.

He cleared his throat and looked up, first at Rob, then at me. "Do you want to save your marriage?"

We nodded, like children in catechism class. "Yes, Father."

"All right, what are you willing to do?"

I felt anger surfacing again. No one was asking me if I wanted a child. It was two against one and I was losing. I could not believe that my husband was willing to sacrifice his religious principles to get his way—and that Father Bill O'Dowd, a Jesuit priest, was taking his side.

Father Bill swiveled his chair to face the bookshelves and pulled down a thick tome. "I assume you're familiar with Augustine." As he began leafing through the pages, he made a slight humming noise. Dust motes flew around him in the lamplight. "Here." He pointed to a passage. "This is significant for our purposes. Listen to this." He glanced over his glasses to make sure he had our full attention. "Kids, this is from *The Confessions of St. Augustine*. 'The law does not provide that the action [abortion] pertains to homicide, for there cannot yet be said to be a live soul in a body that lacks sensation. Ensoulment occurs at forty days for males, ninety for females.' This passage," the priest coughed and raised his voice, "clearly illustrates Augustine's doubt that the soul enters the body at conception." He let the book thud onto his desk. "I think we can safely say that if Augustine, Father of the Church, believed a four-week fetus lacked a soul, so can we."

"Here." He pushed the open book toward me and I balanced it in my arms. Staring at the pages, my eyes watered and the print blurred. The book smelled old. "Take the book with you," the priest said.

I was speechless, but at the same time, slightly hopeful. Saint Augustine doubted that the soul entered the fetus at conception. No soul. No human being. What was stopping me from having an abortion? Maybe it was the only way to save our marriage. But I wasn't ready to give in that quickly.

I stood and faced the two men. "When did Augustine write that book, maybe five hundred years ago? You two forget that I've studied theology too. I'm not sure I can accept his theory, even if he is called a Father of the Church."

The priest's voice became very gentle. "Take some time and consider this, Meredith."

"Consider this? If I do what you want, I don't have much time."

"Yes, that way, we have time so that later—" Rob said. He looked relieved.

"Later what, Rob?" I fought back my sarcasm. "After you said you didn't want my children, are you now promising me children? If I do what you want?"

Not bothering to check Rob's reaction, I pulled my purse over my shoulder with one arm and clutched the book in the other. I was about to turn when I noticed Rob and the priest nod and catch each other's eyes. Rob shrugged, and Father O'Dowd pushed his chair back and stood.

"Wait, Meredith—one more thing."

I snapped, "Yes, Father?" I felt uncomfortable deferring to him, addressing him as Father, yet years of model Catholic behavior forced it out.

"Remember, feel free to come by after, and...um...confess, to me." He waved his arm in the air like a magician performing a disappearing act.

My mind tumbled, trying to find the logic in his offer. Confess what? If I was to accept Augustine's theory, why did I need to confess?

I spun around again, and soon I was outside on the sidewalk. Rob ran to catch up with me. He tried to put his arm around me but

I walked faster. "Come on, Meredith, take it easy," he begged. He unlocked the doors and we got into our Plymouth. When he turned the key in the ignition, the radio was playing "Moon River," a song we'd sung together many times. I reached over and flicked it off. We rode home in silence. Rob lit a cigarette and blew the smoke out his open window. I held the book close to my chest. As we pulled to the curb, I jumped out and hurried around to the driver's side.

Rob got out and met me halfway. "What are you doing?" He sounded angry.

"I'm going out." I slid into the driver's seat, set the book on the floor, and used my own key in the ignition. In the rearview mirror I watched my husband, his hands on his hips, receding into the background, getting smaller and smaller until he became a dot and finally disappeared. I wished he would disappear, at least until I could get clear on what I ought to do.

I drove onto highway 255 South. I felt sick inside, recalling the priest's offering me confession, treating me like a child, promising that an act of contrition would make everything better. At Turner's Grove, I exited and followed a tree-lined road down a narrow lane and pulled into the parking lot a few yards from a sign that read Carmelite Convent. Slowly I climbed the stone steps of the imposing three-story brick building, and rang the bell.

The chimes reverberated. I stared at my reflection in the glass: a slight girl/woman with long blonde hair, the A-line red dress scarcely covering my knees. It was the dress Rob bought me for my last birthday. I couldn't see my eyes, but I knew I had applied the mascara and eyeliner Rob had chosen for me.

The massive door creaked open. "Hello, how can I help you?" An overly tall, bone-thin nun dressed in the long brown Carmelite habit and open-toed sandals smiled at me, revealing stubby yellow teeth. Her gray eyes were soft. If she knew my secret, I thought, she'd never let me in.

"I'd like to pray in the chapel, please, Sister."

The nun opened the door wide. "Of course, come in. I'll take you there." I stepped into a large foyer where a statue of Saint Teresa of Avila stood on a table. The nuns in school had taught me about Teresa's courage in standing up for what she believed was right. When she thought nuns were too lax in observing their vows of poverty and chastity, she took action. She confronted her superiors in her conviction that reform was necessary. Now, some five hundred years later, here I was in one of her convents, facing a crisis of my own.

I followed the woman down the wide, highly polished hallway. The only sound was the clicking of her rosary beads as she glided ahead of me.

She stopped at swinging doors. "Here you are," she whispered, "stay as long as you wish."

I tiptoed into the spacious chapel, empty except for an elderly nun sitting in the back row, bent so far over her prayer book, I wondered if she was sleeping. The scent of candle wax and incense wafted down from the main altar where a tiny votive burnt in front of the gold tabernacle. I slipped into the first pew and covered my face with my hands.

I felt close to gagging, as I had on my one and only roller coaster ride, when I'd climbed into the car directly behind our teacher, Sister Angela, believing she would keep me safe. Terrified, I felt my throat close as we inched to the top and plummeted down, once, twice, three times. When we rolled to a stop, I staggered from the car and stared at my hands. They were red from clutching the safety rod and they reeked of its metallic odor. I raced to the bathroom and vomited the Cheerios I'd eaten for breakfast.

Now I felt like I was on a roller coaster again, my thoughts pulling me to the top of the curve in one second, in the next, crashing me back to earth. I was sad, angry (what's happened to my husband?), bewildered (how can I abort our child?), and devastated (where is the God message I needed from the priest?). I didn't even consider talking to another priest. The secret weighed too heavily. I felt as though I was blind, feeling my way down a long, dark hallway. One that never ended. My heart thudded.

Was I that second grader so determined to understand Church teachings that she started asking questions every day. Nobody else did, and my questions were not well received. One morning Sister Mary Mark was smack in the middle of repeating for the third time that, to get to Heaven, we had to be baptized in the Holy Roman Catholic Church. She was using her most serious voice, the one we knew meant "shut up and listen." But I couldn't stand it and waved my hand. "Sister," I blurted: "Sister, what about babies born dead?"

When I said "dead," the room got still and I suspected I had crossed a line. But I had to know. I'd heard Mom tell Aunt Tilley about a woman who'd had a "still birth," which she explained to me later.

For a minute Sister Mary Mark kept staring at me, her eyes blurry through the thick lenses of her glasses. I should've known better, but I kept on: "Sister, those babies have no way of getting baptized, so if they aren't allowed in heaven, it really isn't fair."

Nobody made a sound. Sister pulled from her sleeve a big white handkerchief like the one my daddy used. When she blew her nose, it made a small honk and the kids in back of the room snickered. After she put her handkerchief away, Sister frowned. "Next week we'll learn about limbo. Limbo is where those babies go. Now let's get on with this lesson," she said, turning her back on me.

I looked around and the old nun had left the chapel. My watch read 4:33, but I was not ready to go home, back to our apartment and

Rob. I walked to the side altar and knelt before a statue of the Blessed Mother, her cloak and eyes cobalt blue, her narrow face placid. The marble floor cooled my knees. I fought back the urge to scream. Mary, give me a sign. Dead babies? Limbo? Our teacher never did explain limbo. Am I about to kill a baby? Is that why the priest brought up confession? What about Augustine? I began to cry, and there was no stopping until I ran out of tears.

When I left the deserted chapel, I felt light-headed. No one was around, so I pulled the front door shut until I heard the lock click in place. I stood on the porch and gazed out on a darkening sky, asking the question that would haunt me the rest of my days: what happened to the little girl who wanted to give her life to God?

Father Bill had taken Rob's side, urging me to ponder St. Augustine, and my hopes had disappeared. When I'd first told him I was pregnant, his face had turned stony. Now, only a few days later, he came through the door, his excitement palpable. His expression reminded me of an earlier time, when that giddiness was about us alone. "I've got the name of a doctor who'll facilitate this. You'll have to see him to get the process started," he said. He tossed his jacket on the chair. "You can't have it here legally, but you can in New York." Rob was talking fast now, almost breathlessly. "So after he sees you, his office will make all the arrangements with a clinic near the airport. You fly up there in the morning, have the procedure, and fly back the same day." He laid a note with the phone number on the table in front of me. I nodded and picked it up. He came and sat beside me, taking my hand in his. "Listen Mer, I know this is hard. But I'll go with you. I'll take care of you."

I shook my head. "I don't need you for this. I'll do it on my own." I glanced over at the crucifix on the wall next to the door. God help me, he's got it all planned out. And he wants to take care of me? But I wanted to stay married to him, and I knew I had to do it.

He walked away and hung his coat in the closet. "Oh, I wish it were over," he said. "I know that afterward, we'll be all different, all better." He smiled and strolled into the kitchen.

It, I mused. He's reducing our child to a two-letter pronoun. Our baby's gender is now neuter.

The following Friday Rob drove me to the doctor who confirmed my pregnancy, the office nurse gave us the paperwork required by the Evans Company (a discreet name for a group that handled abortions), and she booked my flight to New York City for the following Wednesday. On Sunday I woke to find Rob watching me. The beginnings of a thunderstorm were rumbling, and as soon as he saw I was awake, he stood and threw open the shutters. "I brought you some orange juice," he said. He sat on the edge of the bed.

I propped myself up and took a sip. "Thanks."

"How do you feel?"

I couldn't meet his eyes. "Like I'm living a bad dream. How else could I feel?"

"Hey, it's only two more days, Meredith."

I took the orange juice, sniffed it, and set it back down. "I know," I said, throwing the sheet back. "I hope you remember our talk last night," I said. I put on my bathrobe. No one, I'd begged him, no one must ever know. I'd put my finger to his lips and he'd nodded his promise.

"Do you want to visit Bill after? I mean, right away?"

"I don't know," I whispered. But if it's not a sin, why? I was so sick with rage I felt like throwing the glass of juice at him. I was relieved when he left the room. I didn't want him to know that nothing was right with me. The question teased me now: How well does he know me?

I showered and put on a navy blue skirt and a white cotton blouse that strained against its buttons. I walked into the kitchen where Rob was buttering toast.

"Want some?" he asked. He gawked at me. "Wow, honey—look what's happened to you! I'm sorry they hurt so much." His face was luminous. At last I was the buxom blonde he'd longed for.

"I can barely fit into my bra," I said. "But while I'm still this way, you'll probably want to take a picture, something to remember. It's ironic, because this is what you wanted, isn't it?"

And that's exactly what he did. Rob posed me in the courtyard outside our apartment. The photograph he took shows me standing in a tight-fitting jersey top, a very short miniskirt, and brown heels, my blonde hair cascading over my shoulders, a halo around a smiling face that masked anger and betrayal. I'd dressed carefully because I knew this photo would be special for him. Rob would want to remember me like this: a big-breasted blonde with spindly legs. Afterward, whenever I studied the picture on his bedside table, I thought I appeared oddly misshapen. With such swollen breasts and skinny limbs, I looked exactly like a Barbie doll.

Twice during the drive to the airport Rob reached over to squeeze my arm, but neither of us spoke; it was as though we'd made a pact not to talk. The car radio was playing the Beatles, "Eleanor Rigby" and "Lucy in the Sky with Diamonds." The songs brought back all the evenings Rob had played his guitar and we'd sung them in harmony. Naively I believed with all my heart I could bring all that back.

At the American Airlines entrance I grabbed my purse and a copy of Sylvia Plath's *The Bell Jar* and hurried from the car, avoiding Rob's reach. "Tonight at 9:30, okay?" he said.

Nodding my goodbye, I turned and headed into the building. After checking in, I went to Gate 12 like an ordinary passenger taking a one-day shopping trip to New York. There a gray-haired man in a dark suit stood holding a placard: Evans Group. Five women hovered nearby. I nodded to the man and studied the women. Why, they're only girls, I thought, wide-eyed, tight-lipped teenagers clutching purses and rolled-up magazines, each one of them much younger than my twenty-eight years. None of us said a word. I glanced at my watch. Ten minutes to boarding.

Another young woman walked up. Her hair cut in a pixie, she wore a bright yellow miniskirt and tight black leather jacket. Her patent leather shoes looked new, but her purse was worn, even ragged. I watched as she approached the man with the sign, and not at all shyly introduced herself. "I'm Roberta Weiner."

The Evans man nodded, put the placard in his briefcase, and took out a notebook. Clearing his throat, he gestured for us to move closer. "Looks like we're all here, and we'll be ready to board." He read only our first names: Lee, Anne, Jean, Patricia, Lorna, Roberta, Meredith.

I requested an aisle seat at the rear of the plane near the bathroom in case I got sick. But when the stewardess announced lunch service, I waved her over. "Could I possibly have two meals?" I whispered. "I'm starving." I felt terribly embarrassed, but I was so ravenous I didn't care. When she brought a second lunch tray I looked up to thank her. She knows. I bet she knows, I thought.

Deplaning at JFK, our group merged with the crowds. The scene reminded me of "A Thousand Clowns," with its depiction of the teeming sidewalks of New York. I'd never seen so many people, and I was terrified, as if I were about to be trampled to death. Motioning for us to follow, the Evans man led us outside to a white van. We climbed into the backseats, and our escort announced that we would arrive at the clinic in forty-five minutes.

Roberta and I were sitting next to each other. "Ever done this before?" she asked. I shook my head and swallowed hard. The city's smoggy air was stirring my nausea.

"I have," said the girl behind us, and we turned to face her. She had mousy brown hair and wore a leather minidress. "I first got pregnant two years ago, when I was sixteen," she said, "still in high school. My parents were furious."

"Well, what was it like?" said Roberta.

The girl giggled. "Oh, it's okay. Doesn't take long."

When the others began chatting, Roberta told me about her own pregnancy. She'd met an older man in the law firm where she worked. "He—he made a lot of promises," she said, laughing self-consciously. "Yeah, that's why I'm here now. You're married?" she said, pointing to my wedding ring.

I twisted it from my finger and held it so I could read the inscription aloud: "Come Share My Life."

"Sounds good to me. So why are you here?" Roberta asked, tugging down her skirt.

Loading my voice with sarcasm, I said, "This isn't a good time." It was a good enough answer. I couldn't tell her anything close to what Rob's first response had been or I'd burst into tears.

"Oh, one of those. I am sick of men who think they can control everything." Her words came tumbling out: "Especially ones like my guy, who fed me all those lies, and I was stupid enough to believe them and he's not even married, so what's his excuse? 'Oh, I do love you,' he told me." Suddenly she flushed bright red and her eyes brimmed. "I'm so damn mad...at myself." Her tears fell and she covered her face.

When Roberta spoke again she sounded hoarse. "In the end, this is all due to my own stupidity." I knew what she meant. I reached for her hand and held it tightly. The other voices in the van had quieted and the only sound was the swooshing of hundreds of cars and trucks passing us on the freeway.

We parked in front of a two-story brick building and filed into a stark white waiting room full of chairs with green padded seats and backs. They were lined up classroom style. I counted thirty-two of them. Business must be good.

On the corner tables I noticed the only magazines were beat-up issues of *Life* and *Time*. Crazy, I told myself, we're using time to... I concentrated to find a gentle verb for what we were doing. To surrender life.

I picked up *The Bell Jar*, but when I reached the part where Sylvia first attempts suicide, I had to close the book. I wondered why I'd chosen such a depressing book. Leafing through one of the magazines, I tried to distract myself with pictures of Pat Nixon on her world travels. Seated beside me was the girl who'd told us it was her second time. Whispering in my ear, she said, "You seem... really okay with this?"

"I hope so," I said tentatively. "You?"

In response she burst into tears. I moved to put my arms around her. After a minute she looked up at me, her face blotchy and mascara-streaked. "Oh dear," I said. "What's your name?"

"Patty," she said, sniffling. She blew her nose, but the tears kept coming. I held on.

"It's that—well, Keith doesn't even know I'm—" She buried her face in her hands and folded over.

"Oh, Patty."

A tall blonde in a peach-colored suit opened a door. "Patricia?" she called. As Patty started out, I raised my hand in a gesture of what I hoped was solidarity, and watched as the door closed behind the two women.

I gave up on the magazine and sat contemplating our ride from the airport. From the girls' chatting I had guessed right. None of them was over twenty. They had lots of time for more babies. Suddenly I felt exhausted and closed my eyes. My head drooped to my chest and I fell into a light sleep. I was little again, and Mom was doing my hair up in pin curls. I was bracing myself for the pain I always felt when she pulled the comb through my tangled locks. A door slammed, startling me out of my reverie. In the next moment the fear resurfaced, turning my stomach upside down.

Soon I was the only one left. I reached into my purse, fumbling around for my rosary. Our Father, Who art in heaven, forgive me . . . I could barely grasp that I was thousands of miles from my childhood innocence, about to do the unthinkable. Forgive me. I clutched the silver crucifix so tightly it cut into my hand.

The door opened and a young nurse in a stiff white uniform called my name. She led me into an office where a sweet-faced woman introduced herself as a social worker: "I'm Ms. Stanton, Meredith." (Why hadn't she called me Ms. Baird?) She motioned for me to sit. "I need to know, Meredith, if you understand what you're about to do."

"Of course! I've come all this way..." I clenched my jaw. Why didn't they get on with it?

"Meredith, I'm concerned about possible psychological effects." She tried to stifle a sigh. "I see you're married?" She tapped her pen on the forms I'd filled out.

I met her gaze. "Yes, but my husband knows, if that's a concern."

"But the decision is ultimately yours." She clasped her hands as if she were praying. "And you realize that you may experience aftereffects?"

I nodded.

"We want to be sure you're convinced this decision is right for you, for your life."

"Yes, yes." I was getting impatient.

"All right. Follow me." Ms. Stanton led me to a dressing room, where I had another moment to ponder what I was about to do. I recalled the mantra I'd invented the week before: St. Augustine doubted, St. Augustine doubted?

"Remove your clothes and put on this gown," said the social worker. "The nurse will come for you."

I started unbuttoning my blouse—stopping at the third button. Grabbing my purse I flew from the dressing room, through the waiting room, out the front door, and onto the sidewalk inches from the street.

As the cars and trucks flew by, hot humid air enveloped me. What am I doing? How did I get here? A semi roared past, blaring its horn. I jumped at the wailing sounds. So much noise made me yearn for the silence I had found in the cloister. Only last week.

Now I stood on the sidewalk feeling sick and disoriented as pedestrians streamed past. The sun was blazing so brightly, I had to shield my eyes. I was breathing raggedly. A bus drove by, its fumes coating my face, and I had to swallow hard. What am I doing? Maybe I'll walk right into the street. It wouldn't take long; I'd be hit instantly. In one second this would be out of my hands—over. I closed my eyes and saw the faces of Rob and the priest scowling at me. Horns bleated and brakes squealed. I felt a tap on my arm and turned to see the nurse.

"Meredith," she said, "you don't have to go through with this." She took my arm.

Feeling a near tsunami of nausea, I covered my mouth with one hand and stared at my feet, overcome with embarrassment. "I'm sorry, I'm so sorry."

Back in the dressing room, "I was wrong to run out," I told the social worker, "and I apologize. Please, let's get this over with." I felt blank, numb. Smudging my tears, I changed into a pale green gown and paper slippers.

The nurse led me into an operating room and stood beside me as I lay down on the table, helping me get my bare feet into cold stirrups. As the Valium raced through my veins, my mind started up again, spinning circles around the teachings of the Church. Oh God, do not forsake me now, I prayed, trying to breathe slowly, willing my mind to go vacant.

A white-haired man wearing a surgical gown came into the room and, leaning over me, took hold of my right hand. "Hello, Meredith, I'm Doctor Graham. I want to explain how this procedure works." He seemed calm and gentle. Pointing at a small machine on the table next to him, he continued, "This machine sounds like a vacuum sweeper. You may experience some cramping, but the Valium will calm you. It will be over in a few minutes." He let go of my hand and patted my arm. "Do you have any questions?"

I shook my head. He walked to the end of the table. "Now take a deep breath."

I awoke in a spotless white room. I lay on a white bed with white sheets and blankets. The nurse held my hand and told me to try to rest but the tears kept coming. I was sure that God had deserted me because I had done an awful thing. I had let them kill my child.

On the way to the airport I wore my sunglasses, hoping nobody would notice what a disaster I'd made of my face. And of my life.

When I boarded the plane I searched the faces of the stewardesses. Did they suspect anything? A group of young women traveling in tandem, on a one-day trip to and from New York. Surely, they knew.

I settled into my seat and the cramping started. The huge Kotex felt bulky and awkward. I started worrying that I might be bleeding through it. After the pilot announced we could move safely around the cabin, I skittered to the bathroom. I was okay. No need to worry. The worst was over, I told myself. But was it?

I stared into the night, preparing myself to see Rob, trying to gather my wits to appear cool and confident. I had done this terrible thing to please him. Now I wished I never had to see him again.

When I stepped from the plane I saw Rob waiting at the gate. I steeled myself, remembering what my college drama coach had taught us: step into your role and act as if. I knew I had to ignore the echo of his cruel words about not wanting my children or I'd never be able to touch him again. I had to forget, too, how I'd let the priest control me, blindly accepting his simplistic rationalization so that I could stay married to someone I hardly knew. Someone perhaps I'd never known, maybe didn't like, or didn't like anymore.

Back in our apartment Rob made Manhattans to toast our new life. And so I raised my glass to his. Liquor was our communion that night. I caught sight of myself in the light reflected off a picture frame. Who is this woman? I wondered. Who would guess she's relinquished a principled life for love of this man?

Rob held out the pack of Marlboros. "Want one?"

I shook my head. "No thanks." I stared at the amber liquid in my glass as I struggled with my thoughts. Stop, I told myself. Stay here. From now on, I will play the role my husband directed so that I can continue to share the stage with him. I'd made my decision, and I had to live with it.

Rob sat with me on the sofa and lit a cigarette. "Tell me everything," he said. I shook my head. I would never tell him.

The bourbon stung my tongue and throat. About two seconds after my first sip, I drank again, this time a big gulp. I wanted to feel the liquor's calming heat. Rob's question still hung in the air between us. Finally I turned to face him. "I can't talk about it."

"Oh." He frowned.

He crushed his cigarette in the ashtray and I tried to read his expression. I hoped my silence wasn't annoying him, but I did not dare divulge how I really felt—awash in despair and loss. I thought of how we looked now, the two of us sitting cozily together, like sweethearts sharing drinks after work. As if that were the whole picture, I imagined Rob asking: "Well, darling, how was your day?"

I almost laughed aloud at this image because it was so forced. Cozy implied comfortable, and I felt no comfort in being here with this man. My day had been horrible. I didn't even know how I could keep up my pretext—that everything was all right between us, that somehow we were pushing a button on our marriage that said "RESTART."

Rob stood. "How about another drink?"

"No, thanks. I think I'll sit here and relax for a while."

"Do you want me to sit with you?" He was trying hard.

"No, please, you go on to bed. I'll be in soon."

Rob moved in close and kissed my cheek, gathered our glasses, and took them into the kitchen. I heard water running, then his footsteps as he went into the bedroom. He left the door open.

I stretched out the length of the sofa and yawned. My watch said ten minutes to eleven. Lying there warmed by the bourbon, I remembered the main character in Joan Didion's *Play It as It Lays*. Hers was the first description of abortion I'd ever seen, and I'd read it wide-eyed with curiosity. At the time, the notion that one day I would be in that woman's shoes had never entered my mind.

I tried to remember the character's name. When it would not come, I tiptoed to the bookshelf and located my worn paperback. I stopped and listened for Rob's breathing, heavy and relaxed, telling me he was sleeping as deeply as he always did.

I walked softly to the kitchen, opened the cupboard and pulled out the bottle of Maker's Mark Rob had just put away. I took my glass from the dish rack and in the dim light from the hallway, half filled it with the magic elixir.

Holding the drink near my heart, I crept back into the living room. I took a swig of bourbon and shivered. With the drink to calm me, I knew I'd be certain to sleep. With another gulp I started leafing through the book to find that woman's name, though I knew it might as well have been Meredith.

The next thing I knew I was standing over Rob's sleeping body, armed with a carving knife we'd received as a wedding gift, slashing him, over and over. His blood was spurting everywhere and when a glob hit me in the eye, I woke, horrified. I ran into the bathroom, switched on the light, and checked my face. The nightmare was the first of many in the following weeks. Each time I'd bolt awake, stretch out my hands, expecting to see them bloodied. Then I'd peer into the dark and listen to Rob's peaceful breathing.

By night my mind spun visions of violence, but by day I worked hard to restore our life. I resumed going to Mass during the week and made visits to the Carmelite chapel. I knew I was returning to a kind of childhood faith, begging God to help me mend the mess of our marriage, but I needed a miracle.

At work and at home I always made sure I dressed carefully in the clothes Rob had bought for me and did my hair and makeup exactly the way he liked it. I also started reading up on current events like Nixon's possible run against McGovern so I could better contribute to conversations.

Very slowly, I thought, our relationship began to heal. I never stopped to question whether both of us were playacting. Once in a while we watched a movie together and our eyes would meet, and again I'd feel connected to the man I thought I'd fallen in love with three years earlier.

The night I'd returned from New York, Rob and I had begun a new ritual—evening cocktails at home. Usually we'd each have a Manhattan or two. I was still so troubled by what I had done, I needed those drinks. I didn't know how Rob felt about our new habit, but I was quite content to have his company and an excuse for a couple of strong drinks at the end of the day. He hadn't touched me in weeks. My nightmares may have revealed my dark side, but I desperately wanted a sign that Rob still loved me. I wanted him to make love to me. I kept hoping.

A month after the surreal journey, our friends Lou Ann and Randy invited us for a Friday evening of Scrabble. While I was changing into Rob's favorite sweater (a tight one) and a leather miniskirt, I reminded myself to limit my drinking. I swore I would definitely stop at three. And I did.

For about fifteen minutes. Savoring the last sip of my third Manhattan, my resolve disappeared.

By the time we put our coats on and got into the car, I realized both Rob and I were drunk. "You okay?" I asked him.

His eyes stayed glued to the road. "I'm feeling pretty good," he said. He squeezed my hand, turned up the radio, and sang along with Simon and Garfunkel: "Like a bridge over troubled water . . ." Lulled by the pleasant music, I dozed off.

At our apartment building, Rob had to rouse me from a deep sleep. "We're here, Mer. Wake up; I'm coming around for you."

As he opened my door I moaned. "I'm so tired." I tottered up the sidewalk, leaning against my husband. I was still clutching his arm when he shut the front door and clicked the deadbolt into place.

"Let's get this off," Rob said, helping me out of my coat. He threw it on the sofa and took me in his arms. "My beautiful wife," he whispered, cupping my breast. His breath was heavy with whiskey and tobacco, but his touch felt electric. I fought to remain awake and alert. Maybe this was the miracle I'd been praying for.

Clinging to each other, we stumbled into the bedroom and fell in a heap onto the bed, giggling. Rob managed to pull off my sweater and unhook my bra while I fumbled with his belt buckle. Naked at last, we clung to each other. Rob was breathing hard, his hands tracing my back and hips. Suddenly he shoved me away. "My God, Meredith—we almost forgot—"

I leapt up and we finished his sentence together: "—the diaphragm!"

First I held the appliance to the hall light to make sure I couldn't see any holes. As quickly as I could—I didn't want him to lose interest—I carefully applied the spermicide and inserted the diaphragm. I took my time but soon I returned to Rob's embrace, feeling exuberant. My husband was back, and he wanted me.

From the time I'd met Greg, I'd walked a tightrope with my relationship to him. But when Rob began nagging at me, and especially after my traumatic visit to New York, I knocked on Greg's door. I rationalized spending time with him, telling myself I had to feel comfortable with someone, and we always had our poems and books to share. But I never told him about the nightmares—slashing my husband to bits—and refrained from discussing our sexual dysfunction, my desperate need for alcohol, or our marriage counseling sessions. I also didn't reveal my gravest concern: whether Rob and I could ever love each other again. I knew that sharing any of those revelations with Greg would smash everything I'd worked for into little pieces.

Close as I allowed myself to be with Greg, divorce was anathema, and I was determined to make my marriage work.

I hadn't been alone with Greg in almost a month, and then he invited me for a drink after a department meeting. When weeks before I'd broken my resolve and told him about the abortion, he had frowned.

"You can't do that, Meredith. That's against everything you believe in."

"But it may be the only way to save my marriage," I said.

A month had passed and I accepted his offer. Shortly before 4:00, we arrived at the Fox and Hounds and ordered Welsh rarebit with our martinis. I wolfed down the cheddar and bread, hoping a full stomach would save me from getting thoroughly drunk. When the meal was finished—and after several rounds of martinis—I checked the time. "Oh, God, Greg, look at the time—it's almost six!" Realizing we'd sat there for more than two hours, I bolted out of my chair, took one step, and stumbled, catching myself on a nearby couch. Greg got up to help me regain my feet. "Hey, I'm not sure you should drive," he said. He had his arm around me, propping me up as if I were a paper doll.

I tried to pull away. "I have to get home. Rob will be there by now."

"Look at you, Meredith," he said, pulling me close. His gray eyes were full of concern. "Look me in the eye and tell me you feel competent to drive."

I closed my eyes, feeling a wave of dizziness. I shook my head. "You're right. I'm not doing so well." I flopped back into my chair. "I've got to call Rob."

"Maybe you ought to stall a few minutes and—"

"No." I peered again at my watch. "I must call. Now." I stood and hoisted my purse over my shoulder. Greg followed me as I wove my way through the bar, stopping a couple of times to steady myself.

When we reached the lobby, I turned to him. "Now you go away, I can't do this with you hovering around." I pushed him away and watched as he disappeared into the men's room.

Standing in the phone booth, I rooted in my purse for change. When I came up with only a nickel and three pennies, I staggered to the hotel desk to speak to a clerk wearing a dark jacket with a name badge I couldn't read. Philip something.

"May I help you, ma'am?"

"Change," I said, waving around a ten-dollar bill. "I need to make a call and I don't have any change." By now I was so panicked about getting home late, I was almost shouting.

Another man appeared. "Anything wrong here, Phil?"

The clerk was fumbling in the cash drawer but not fast enough for me. I squinted at the other man. "I need change. Right now. I have to call my husband."

They glanced at one another as Phil handed me a bunch of dollar bills and some dimes and nickels. I stumbled back to the phone booth. As I inserted the coins, I heard the men talking.

"Can you believe her? She's so drunk she's falling down. Says she's got to call her husband."

"Well, do whatever you need to," said the other man. He sounded gruff. "Call a cab if you have to, but get that drunk woman out of here."

I wondered whom they were talking about—what drunk woman? I didn't see her out there, I realized, listening to the ringing of the phone and picturing Rob rushing to answer.

He didn't answer. I was reprieved.

Despite Greg's protestations, I tottered out to the parking lot. I turned once and saw him, framed in the light from the entrance, watching.

When I reached the car, I barely found the lock in the rain. From the glove compartment I took three sticks of peppermint gum and stuffed them in my mouth. Even with the wipers going full on, the world of lights and moving vehicles blurred before me like a surrealistic painting. The radio was playing "I Want to Hold Your Hand," but I turned it off and began chewing in earnest. The minty flavor filled my mouth and, with both hands, I clutched the steering wheel.

I parked in front of our apartment and took several deep breaths. When I stepped from the car, rain slapped at my cheeks and legs. I raised my face to the sky, allowing the downpour to soak my hair and rinse away my makeup. By now I surely resembled a pitiful waif; at least I hoped my husband might view me that way.

The second I turned my key, Rob flung open the door. "What happened to you?"

Soaked to the skin, puddles were forming where I stood in the tiled entryway.

"Come," said Rob, drawing me inside and helping me shrug off my sopping coat.

"I thought I could beat the rain!"

"You're drenched! Better get out of those clothes, right now. I don't want you to catch cold."

"Okay, yes," I said, hurrying to the bedroom to strip.

Rob called from the living room, "Who all went drinking with you tonight?"

Inwardly I groaned. "Marty and Greg and James," I told him. Liar, liar, pants on fire, scolded my conscience.

"I'm going to heat some soup, but first—do you want a drink?"

I looked in the mirror and saw stringy hair, mascara streaks on my cheeks, an ashen, distorted face. "Oh, no, thanks," I said. "But the soup sounds really good." Another lie.

After knotting my hair into a bun, I struggled into my jeans and my warmest sweater. In the kitchen, I sat ramrod straight as Rob ladled Campbell's soup into my bowl: chicken and noodles floating in fatty yellow broth. Eating was the last thing on my mind, but I needed to show a modicum of normalcy.

The first spoonful tasted salty and warm, much better than it looked. I smiled at Rob as he watched me eat. "This really hits the spot." It was true. The soup was delicious, and my secret was safe.

I never said a word to Rob about the afternoons I spent drinking with Greg. The last thing I wanted to do was dampen my husband's fervor, and anyway, I kept telling myself I was doing nothing wrong. After all, Greg and I weren't lovers. At times, I squirmed. What would Rob say about these long talks? Who was I kidding? I was in the wrong and I knew it. But I also chose to ignore the fact.

In spring that year our colleague Laura was named president of a national association of English professors. When she told us in a faculty meeting, we all clapped and cheered. Our own Laura was making a showing on the national scene.

At the next meeting, our department chair announced that because Laura's presidency was a stellar accomplishment for the whole college, the president had allocated travel funds for the entire department. A conference? In Cincinnati?

When I heard that, I sat up and gave the idea serious consideration. "The conference is the last weekend in March, and we can carpool to Cincinnati," said our chair, "since all of us will go."

After the meeting Gwen and I returned to our shared office. "What do you think? Do you want to go?" she said.

"I've never been to a conference. I'd like to. You?"

"I can't leave Davey yet," she said, speaking of her toddler. "He's too young, and Ed would kill me."

"He'd have to take care of everything, I guess."

She yawned. "Oh, well, the price of motherhood. You can tell me all about it. I'm off now, see you tomorrow." She closed the door behind her.

Less than a minute passed before Greg knocked, as if he'd been waiting for Gwen's exit.

"What about this trip?" I said. "You going?"

He looked determined as he took Gwen's chair. "You bet. This is the first time we've been given more than a pittance for travel, and besides, I really want to support Laura."

"I'd like to go, too," I said. "It would be my first convention."

For a moment neither of us said anything. The air thickened with tension.

Greg said, "Andy is going to drive, and maybe Martin. Who would you like to ride with?"

"I don't know." I was thinking: None of them, Greg. You know. I want to ride with you. But I knew that idea was farfetched.

He put out his cigarette. "Let's get more information."

On Friday Greg caught me on my way to class, walking near the wall, as I always did.

"Hey, little nun," he called out. He'd never forgotten that long ago I'd promised to be a nun. I smiled, and we fell into step together.

"Wait a minute," he said, taking hold of my arm. We stood facing each other in the crowded hallway.

"What is it?"

He squeezed my arm. "I've decided to drive to Cincinnati."

"In your car? With room for only one passenger?" A year earlier, Greg had bought his dream-mobile, a sleek bronze Datsun 280Z.

"Yep," he said, speaking close to my ear. "I'm driving. With you. I don't care what anyone says."

"Even Jill?"

"I don't care what anyone says," he repeated. "See you after class," he said, heading down the hall toward his office.

That night at dinner, I told Rob. "The college has funds so all of our department can attend the conference. Can you believe it? We can all go, to support Laura."

"Oh good, honey, it ought to be fun. I'm glad you're going."

I waited until one night after we'd made love to tell him I was riding with Greg. He didn't even blink.

On a rainy Wednesday at the end of March, Rob drove me out to Webster Groves, the suburb where Greg and Jill lived with their three daughters. The girls were in school. Jill was folding laundry in the kitchen when we entered the vestibule. The aroma of coffee hung in the air.

Greg and Rob walked out to load Greg's car while Jill and I chatted.

"I guess this is a real big honor for Laura," Jill said. "Greg told me he felt, out of loyalty, he had to go."

I nodded. "She said it would mean a lot to her if we were all there," I told her. "So we're giving her full-on support. Only Gwen's staying home, to be with her son."

We heard the front door slam as Greg and Rob came in. "Ready?" asked Greg, nodding in my direction.

"Okay." I took Rob's hand and walked him out the door, so Greg and Jill could say goodbye.

Outside Rob and I put our arms around each other and kissed, warmly, sweetly. "I'll miss you," he whispered, opening the passenger door of Greg's car. "See you on Sunday."

I climbed in. My driver and his wife came out and Greg slid into his seat. Jill stood beside Rob on the sidewalk. No brows were creased. No one seemed worried. All of us waved at each other until we were out of view.

When we moved onto the freeway, I glanced over at Greg, his eyes fixed on the road. "Greg, I have to tell you something," I said, as gravely as I could. "I don't want anything between us to change on this trip."

He reached over and stroked my hand for a couple of seconds. "Oh, my dear little nun," he said. "I know."

At the Cincinnati Hilton we each had a reservation, but when the clerk asked for my name, Greg spoke up. "Let's cancel your room. We're going to be together all the time anyway."

I blushed. He'd said this right in front of the clerk. "No, I want to keep my room," I said. The clerk, whose hair, a mass of gray permed curls, reminded me of Medusa. She was tapping her pen on the desk. I felt rushed with my decision but I had to act fast; I realized I was about to repeat my pattern and let a man decide for me. "I'll sign for my room, please." I nodded at the clerk.

I took the key she handed me and looked at Greg. He was lighting a cigarette, and I picked up my suitcase and he followed me to the elevator. Both rooms were on the fourteenth floor, five doors apart.

I stopped when he did at room 1412, a dark, musty room with a double bed near a window overlooking the exterior of a red brick building. A worn brown armchair and a brass lamp sat in the corner. The space was so cramped, he had to maneuver around me to set his suitcase on the bed.

Peering out the smudged window, I said, "I see you got a room with a view," and laughed nervously. It was the darkest, shabbiest hotel room I'd ever seen.

"I need to change," Greg said. He opened his suitcase and pulled out brown slacks. I started skimming the program. "But we'd better hurry if we want to hear Laura."

Greg stood looking over my shoulder. "Auditorium A," I said, handing him the program.

"Give me a minute to change," he said, opening his bathroom door.

"I'm going to my room," I said. "Come and get me."

My room was worse than Greg's. Its walls were papered in oversized navy blue and bright pink flowers, the bedspread a washed-out blue. It reeked of cigarette smoke. In the black and white tiled bathroom I pulled out my brush, ran it through my hair, and stared at the blonde in the mirror. Her hair wispy with static, she looked disheveled, but beautiful in a careless sort of way. A dark blue silk blouse accented the blue of her eyes. Her eyes? Quickly I turned away, before she could remind me: You are married. He is married. What on earth are you doing? Well, I promised myself, I'd definitely return to my own room.

As I stepped away from the mirror, Greg knocked. He'd changed into slacks and a beige sweater. He'd slicked his hair back and his face looked freshly washed, as if he were ready for a job interview. At once the room disappeared and I saw only him. With me. Alone. As I threw my bag over my shoulder, I had only one thing in mind: getting out of there. The air pulsed with possibilities.

"All set?" I asked. "The Grand Ballroom on the Mezzanine."

We were late. We scooted into seats at the rear of the auditorium just in time to hear Laura's opening address. After we joined in the thunderous applause, we waited near the exit doors for Andy and Martin, who'd driven over together the night before. "Laura's invited us to her suite for drinks," Andy told us. "Room 1502, and wait'll you see it—talk about swanky."

He hadn't exaggerated. Comfortable dark leather sofas and chairs were arranged in conversation groups. Also adorning the room were a marble-topped coffee and end tables with dimly lit lamps, beige carpets, heavy velvet drapes, four pink-tiled bathrooms with enormous showers and tubs, and two master bedrooms, each containing two double beds, mahogany chairs, dressers, and televisions. I counted five huge bouquets of scarlet red roses on the polished tables. A bar was set up at one end of the living room with two young men outfitted in black slacks and white shirts ready to serve. We were first in line.

"Two dry martinis," I heard Greg say. "Olives are fine."

For the first minutes, only our colleagues showed up. When Laura, dressed in gray slacks and a red plaid blazer, entered the room, we stood and clapped. Martin, Andy, and Greg whistled. She came over and put her arm around Greg. "I'm so glad both of you could make it. Hello, Meredith." She pecked my cheek and moved on, the acrid odor of cigarette smoke in her wake. Then the room began to fill so that soon we could hardly hear each other.

Greg got up to fetch more drinks and peer from the tall windows that overlooked the city sparkling beneath us. All around me people clustered in little groups smoking, drinking, and laughing. The scene was so picture-perfect, it looked like a movie set.

Standing in front of an enormous gilt-framed mirror, I took out my Maybelline lipstick and began applying it. Greg came up behind me, holding the drinks, and the two of us gazed at our reflections. For a moment, neither of us spoke. Greg said, "I never could understand how women do that. How strange to be painting your lips." He continued to stare.

I stared back, not moving. I was still sober enough to recognize the intimacy in his gaze, and it frightened me.

Martin waved us into one of the bedrooms. Carol, our latest hire, was sitting on a bed, her long legs crossed in front of her. A full bottle of Chivas Regal sat on the bedside table beside an ice bucket. "See what we found?" Marty said. "Want some?"

Greg laughed and shook his head. "Ordinarily I'd go for it, but I'm into gin tonight. I don't want to get blitzed." What was he talking about? We were already guzzling gin—was he implying that gin wouldn't make us blitzed?

We chatted with our colleagues as the room filled. I talked with a book agent I knew, and Greg with colleagues from his previous work. Carol came over and bummed a cigarette. I waved at another colleague and Carol got lost in the crowd. A few minutes more passed and Greg nudged me. "We need to get something to eat. Let's go."

"Shouldn't we include Martin or Carol?" I asked.

He shook his head and steered me outside the suite. As we left the hotel, the lobby clock read 7:23. "The concierge told me there's a little French café in the next block," Greg said.

The cold air smacked us in the face. I let Greg take my arm as we sauntered along. Snowflakes landed, melted, disappeared on the sleeves of my navy blue coat. I saw Greg's face luminous in the flurry. Once more I reminded myself: I don't want anything to happen.

We'd done well staying out of each other's arms—for nearly three years. Day after day, we'd confined ourselves to only abstractions, sharing literary loves and lines, barely touching. To exonerate myself I'd become an expert in denying my feelings. I was married, and I was not in love with this man.

At the restaurant we ate sole meuniére with new potatoes and salad, and were back outside in less than an hour. Ten more minutes and we were taking the elevator to our floor. "Come in my room," Greg said. "For one drink. I promise."

"You promise? Greg, remember what I told you in the car." But I'd already had enough gin to feel relaxed. I believed I was in control. I followed him into his room where we doffed our coats and Greg picked up the phone.

"Room service? We need a fifth of Tanqueray and a bucket of ice to room 1412 please."

A fifth. I worried.

When the bottle arrived I did not protest. We drank. He talked and talked. His stories of circling the world in the Air Force kept me spellbound. He spiced them with details of some sexual conquests he'd made along the way. No more poetry. This was sex tonight. Only sex. He took on a James Bond aura as we sat smoking his cigarettes, then mine. We drank some more. I talked and talked. I found it so easy to talk to him, about almost everything, but never the jeopardy of my marriage. Or of his.

He was sitting in the overstuffed armchair. I was on the floor, leaning against the bed, a besotted Desdemona to his Othello. The only light in the room came from the lamp in the corner. The blackout curtains were pulled tight. Any notion about placing myself in the path of sin flew in and right back out of my already gin-fogged brain. "I think I need to find my room," I said.

All at once he knelt beside me, cradling my face in his hands. "Oh,

God, I want you," he said. He was kissing me, and the all too familiar bolt of desire hit me. We stood, our kisses burning with urgency.

"Oh Greg." I pushed him away. "We can't do—"

He moved me to the bed. I wanted to pull the bedspread down, but that idea disappeared as he began to unbutton my blouse. He touched my breast and I moaned with pleasure. "You are so lovely," he whispered, kissing my neck. We tugged at each other's clothes until we lay naked. So this is passion, I thought. Then there was only Greg and a body I'd only dreamed of possessing, filling my moment. Completely.

The next morning I opened one eye, tasting cotton in my mouth. The room was dark. Turning, I saw that I was alone in the bed. Our clothes lay all over the floor. I threw on enough clothes to look decent and staggered down the hall to my own room. I locked the door and stepped into the bathroom. In the mirror I looked the same, but I knew I was different.

However I tried chastising myself, it didn't work. The irony was that I remembered almost nothing about our making love. Only the foreplay. The rest had blacked out.

I wrapped a towel around myself and stepped back into the bedroom. Greg knocked and called to me. I opened the door, and he walked in carrying two cups.

"Coffee?" He set my cup on the dresser. He did not look at me. "See you downstairs," he said, closing the door behind me. The next night we did not repeat our performance. The electricity was still there, but it was clear to me that Greg was remorseful. Together we attended several sessions, but we did our serious drinking with our colleagues in the bar. That evening we retired to our own rooms, and there was no calling room service. Both of us were drunk enough to pass out.

The next day we were riding along in Greg's Datsun, about an hour from home. We were both silent. I was mentally rehashing the minutiae of our encounter to make sure we didn't slip up. Rob and Jill could never know. I rehearsed what I'd say to Rob, who was probably already on the highway, driving out to meet us. I replayed every detail of the morning after, over and over. I knew I had missed something, but what was it?

"Why are we so quiet?" Greg said.

"Well, I'm thinking. I don't want us to make any mistakes." My tongue was still thick from all the cigarettes and gin. "Oh, God," I whispered.

"What is it?" Greg's brow furrowed.

"When I went to my room the morning after—our—uh, I didn't bother with underwear. I don't remember seeing my black panties. Could they possibly be in your suitcase?" I said.

"That," he said, "is worth checking out. We'll stop soon."

A mile after we reached the city limits, he pulled over and we both jumped out. Greg opened his suitcase, revealing a mishmash of disorder. I watched as he pulled out every item: underwear, handkerchiefs, socks, rumpled shirts, slacks, toothpaste, toothbrush, convention papers, and half a pack of Marlboros. He kept pushing things aside. When he found two packets of matches from the French restaurant, he handed them to me. "Throw these in that trash can," he said.

We found no panties, nothing of mine.

By the time we reached his house it was dark. We entered to find Rob and Jill sitting on the sofa. We all smiled and kissed and hugged and I tugged on Rob's sleeve. "I'm beat, Rob. Let's go home." Soon we were out the door, in our own car, driving along the freeway.

I told Rob about Laura and the parties, and the workshops on teaching composition and ebonics, the controversy around black speech patterns, and that, even though it was spring, it had snowed our first night there.

He asked me no questions. I told him no lies.

Back in our apartment, he brought my suitcase into the study. Kissing him again, I said, "I think I'll take a shower and go to bed."

"Oh, sure," he said, "I know you must be tired."

I went into the bathroom and closed the door. In the shower I mused about Rob and me. We'd reached a sort of truce, determined to make a life together. We had sex, not a lot, but frequently enough to convince me we were on solid ground again. Blaming my lapse in judgment with Greg on too much alcohol, I realized—though I abhorred the thought—I was drinking a lot these days. Where was my self-control? After I had one drink, the compulsion took over and I never considered stopping after two or three anymore. Perhaps I needed to cut down, but certainly not today.

Tucked into my bathrobe, I rubbed the steam from the mirror and stared at my reflection, recalling Anna Karenina, the adulteress Tolstoy created. That thought horrified me and I walked away from the mirror and began thinking about the various colleges where Rob and I had submitted teaching applications. Since we both had our doctorates, it was time to move on. Together. We had to get out of St. Louis. In the hazy smudged mirror I met my eyes, assuring myself: tomorrow is another day.

When the letter offering us jobs in Louisville arrived, Rob and I hugged and laughed. The next day I took it with me to the college, laying it on Greg's desk before he came in. At the end of my second class, I found him standing outside waiting for me, holding the letter in his hand. His face looked ashen. I said, "Well, now you know."

"Congratulations. You're being promoted to department chairman."

I nodded. "And Rob's chair of philosophy." When I met Greg's eyes, I saw his hurt.

"Let's get out of here," he said. He hurried us down the stairs and out to the parking lot. Dozens of students and faculty were spilling from the building, rushing past us.

I grabbed his arm. "Greg, I thought—"

"Wait till we get in the car," he said, unlocking the door. He cracked the window, lit a Marlboro, and extended the pack to me. I waved it away. "Oh God, Meredith," Greg said, putting his hand over mine. "I always knew you'd go, but somehow I didn't think it would be so soon. I should have prepared myself; I knew you had positive interviews. Anyone would be a fool not to hire you—and Rob, for that matter."

"You can't think it's easy for me," I said, tears welling.

Greg pulled on his cigarette. "But you're the one leaving. You'll have a new life and I'll be stuck here in the old life, without you."

"There's no other way," I said. "You know that."

His Adam's apple moved as he swallowed. He snuffed out his cigarette and drew me close. His breath reeked of nicotine and smoke.

"Greg, we're out here in the middle of the parking lot where anyone can see us."

"Let them," said Greg, burying his face in my neck. Then he sat up. "Let's get Andy's keys. At least in his apartment we can be alone."

I started to cry. "I can't, Greg, I can't."

Moving day was five days away. I knew all too well I needed to leave as soon as possible.

The day we left St. Louis, Greg came over to help Rob load the trailer we'd hitched to the back of our Plymouth. Piled in the living room were our bed, dresser, a desk, four captain's chairs, the kitchen table, and sixteen boxes of books. We'd donated the rest of our furniture to Rob's sister, who'd recently moved into her own apartment. The walls were bare and our voices echoed through empty rooms.

We were cleaning the kitchen floor when Greg called, "Hi, guys," and walked through the front door. "How does it feel to be embarking on a new adventure?"

"Great!" Rob said. He shook Greg's hand. "Thanks for coming."

I finished scrubbing the scuffed linoleum and said, "Yes, thanks for helping today." I was taking no more risks. I avoided Greg's eyes as I closed and bolted the back door.

They began by loading our bed and the dresser. Next Greg carried out a chair and Rob followed him with another. I took boxes packed with sheets and towels, and a few lightweight cartons of books. They're moving as if they'd worked together all their lives, I thought, watching the men hoist the last of our chairs.

I hurried down the stairs and got into Greg's car. He would drive me to rejoin Rob at my in-laws'. Neither of us spoke. I was so filled with anxiety, my chest hurt. We rode along Grand Avenue, past the Severeno's restaurant where Rob and I had staged our wedding reception three years before, past the university and into South St. Louis. A block short of our destination, Greg pulled over to the curb and parked.

"I can't believe this is happening," I said, bursting into tears. I was a tangle of emotions. I couldn't tell him that I felt relieved—that I wanted to extricate myself from the web of duplicity we'd woven, and anticipated the opportunity to make a life away from him. He had become my addiction, and unless I left, I could never fully belong to Rob. At the same time I hated leaving.

Greg held my hand, stroking it. "I can't tell you it'll be all right."

I continued sobbing.

"Come on, Mer, I've got to get you over there."

"Will you write me?" I asked, wiping my face.

"Of course. You know that." Removing his hand, he restarted the engine, leaned close, and embraced me, kissing me hard. "My little nun," he whispered, still holding me tight, "I've got to remember, you're not mine."

He pulled into the street and two minutes later we were standing in front of the Bairds' bungalow, Rob shaking hands with Greg, Greg turning to hug me chastely, and me fighting back more tears.

I did not watch Greg drive away. Instead I ran into the house, threw cold water on my face, and hugged Rob's parents. Eve and Len hugged me, and she handed me a bag of cookies.

"Now, you kids be careful." Rob's parents embraced him. "Call us when you get to Louisville." Rob turned on the ignition and the radio. "Bye, bye, Miss American pie," sang Don McLean. "Drove my Chevy to the levee but the levee was dry . . ." He headed our Plymouth south on I-55, leaving the city where he'd lived his whole life. I was still on the stage with him, saying my lines.

I sobbed for the first thirty miles as we raced our way toward our new life.

Not once did Rob ask why I was crying.

Arriving in Louisville that afternoon we drove to the apartment we'd rented, a spacious three bedroom in a complex near our college. With the help of our new landlord, we hauled in the few things we'd brought from St. Louis. We dropped our goods in the empty rooms that smelled of a recent paint job and headed over to the college.

Our dean, John Nichols, a short, stocky balding man, met us as we entered the foyer. "Hey, welcome folks." He smiled. "Hope you're getting settled in." We chatted as he led us through a long narrow building renovated to accommodate classrooms and offices. "As you can smell," John said, laughing, "the painters have been here and today the telephone systems were installed." He escorted us to our offices and gave us our keys.

The next day we loaded our car with books and stacked them on our office shelves. Then the endless faculty meetings began, tempered only by happy hours with our new colleagues. Even though we'd made a few friends, Rob told me one night as we cuddled under the blue chenille bedspread we'd bought before our wedding, "This move is so easy. You're right here beside me." Hearing those words I couldn't have been happier.

This brand new college flooded with students opening day, and our intensive work began. For the next sixteen weeks we became whirling dervishes, our lives consumed by classes, grading, and meetings. We didn't even have a chance to visit Eve and Len in St. Louis for Len's birthday.

In our new home we celebrated our first Christmas on our own, without family. The last year had been challenging, to say the least. Six months ago I'd renewed my commitment to our marriage by agreeing to everything Rob wanted, including the abortion. Later, when we got these jobs, we'd agreed it was the perfect opportunity to start over. I'd heard only once in three months from Greg since we moved, and to my surprise I scarcely missed him.

The day after Christmas I pulled to the curb near the American Airlines entrance, and Rob got out of the car, bending in to kiss me. He was headed to San Francisco for the national conference of the American Philosophical Association.

Mist shrouded the gray sky. It was only ten in the morning, and I had the whole day ahead of me. In fact, four whole days. I rolled down the window and savored the brisk air, considering possibilities. Since it was semester break I had no teaching responsibilities. I'd drop into Macy's and look over the after Xmas sales. I didn't need any clothes since I was still wearing the wardrobe Rob had chosen for me a couple of years before, but perhaps I might find some bargain gifts for next year. After that I'd buy myself a rare treat from Wylie's Bakery, a loaf of the raisin walnut bread that I loved. At home later, I'd have dinner and curl up with Larry McMurtry's latest book, *Moving On*. From the first scene I connected to the main character, Patsy, who was struggling with both her marriage and graduate school. It wasn't long before I lost myself in the book.

That was day one.

By the second day I'd flown halfway through the eight hundred-page novel, so when I first opened my eyes, I sat up and began reading. I loved indulging myself this way, submerging myself in another world. It was nearly 11:00 when I got up, made myself a pot of tea, and brought it into the living room. When the phone rang I was startled. My colleague Jennifer was inviting me to a small celebration to welcome the new college librarian. Jennifer's call broke my impulse to read all day. Instead I threw on a pair of jeans and a sweater and drove to the grocery store. I bought bread and Swiss cheese for the party, and onions, garlic, zucchini, tomatoes, and pasta to make Aunt Tilley's recipe for Italian country soup.

Drinking a few too many B&Bs at the party left me headachy the next morning, but I couldn't wait to sink back into McMurtry. After a couple of hours, I nudged myself out of bed, threw on my jeans and sweater, and went to type letters to my family, describing our Christmas and the dinner that Rob and I had cooked together. We'd been proud of our cuisine: a chicken roasted with rosemary, au gratin potatoes, green beans cooked with bacon (my Mom's recipe), and an apple pie. The crust had been our greatest challenge and we'd even called Rob's grandmother to make sure we had it right. I knew my family would be pleased to know that I might be evolving into a chef, of sorts.

The letters sealed and stamped, I clipped them on the mailbox. I wanted to change the bed. Since we'd moved, we'd enjoyed a new closeness, and I was anticipating enjoying my husband the following night, between fresh sheets.

While the laundry was washing, I cleaned the whole apartment. I prepared the vegetables for the soup and put them in a Dutch oven to simmer. Having played the good wife, I could return to my book without guilt. I changed into my well-worn chenille robe, poured two or so inches of Jim Beam over ice, and walked into our study, observing its comforts. A rocking chair with its red embroidered pillow, a gift from Rob's parents, stood in the twilight shadows. The huge oak desk from Rob's teaching days at Lady of Mercy faced the double windows. The plaid love seat we'd purchased as newlyweds sat against the opposite wall, a brass reading lamp beside it. I loved sitting there evenings while Rob played his guitar in the living room.

The top of my husband's desk was bare except for his journal, a large black notebook with corners worn soft from years of use. I reached to turn on the desk lamp. Our marriage is going so well, I thought. We haven't needed Father Bill for months, and we've got new jobs and a brand-new place to live.

It felt good to be far away from Greg Ellis and the apartment that housed memories of my pregnancy. I felt hopeful, even peaceful. Rob and I had spent our first five months exploring Louisville like two little kids, riding our bikes all over town on weekends. Some afternoons after work we joined friends for drinks or attended faculty events. My nightmares had all but disappeared, and we were making love again and—at least on my part—I was feeling, maybe for the first time, a real sense of intimacy with Rob.

Never before had I considered reading Rob's journal. Standing in the lamplight, I flipped it open and leafed through a few pages, noting the dates: August 3, August 6, and August 28. I flipped further back, wanting to know what he'd recorded about last spring, the most painful time, rationalizing that it would be all right for me to look because everything was so much better now.

I found pages dated right after the abortion and began reading. "I'm convinced we did the right thing. M. is gradually recovering. For a while I didn't think she'd go thru with it. Now I'm more in love with her than before." A few days later: "I saw Rick tonight. The same as ever. I wish I could share him in some meaningful way with M." And then: "Dare I say it? I want to love both of them. I do love them both."

The poet Donne's words came to me: "I can love both fair and brown." But what was Rob saying? My eyes flew over the words and I turned the page, where he'd written a poem. None of the pronouns was feminine—there was not a single "she" or "her"—but it was clearly a love poem, full of delight and sensuality, written for a man.

I lifted the notebook from the desk and sat down, rereading the frightening poem word for word. He's composed love poems for me, but this one is not for me. My throat tightened.

Remembering the young man Rob had met on his boys' nights out, I envisioned Rick at the door of our apartment, shaking my hand and grinning. "I've heard so much about you," he'd said. Now I recalled Rob's excitement, showing his friend around while I made tea in the kitchen.

So that was it. All of this was happening when we were in the midst of counseling with Father Bill, when they'd convinced me it was my fault our marriage was failing. All that time, they—our priest and my husband—had deceived me. I'd noticed the conspiratorial looks they'd exchanged from time to time. But I never suspected collusion. Now I was sure. Rob had been open with Father Bill. Together, they had sealed my fate.

I closed the notebook, slid it into the top drawer of Rob's desk, and picked up the phone. Through the half-open blinds I saw only darkness. I pictured Rob checking into his hotel and stepping out jauntily into the night. San Francisco. Perfect.

Outraged, I dialed Father Bill's number.

"Father Bill here," he said.

"Bill, it's Meredith. I know. About Rob."

"Ah, you know. Where is he now?"

"At the APA conference in San Francisco. What I want to know is: why did you hide this from me?" I leaned against the wall as tears streamed down my face. "He was seeing men when we were in counseling, when I had the abortion, and you knew it. Why did you deceive me?"

I heard him pulling on his cigarette. "I had good reason, Meredith. I believed it was an experiment, and he'd outgrow it."

"Oh, God!" I blurted. "Well, I don't know if he did."

"What do you want me to do, Meredith?"

"I don't know. We have to see you. When Rob gets back."

"As you wish, and Meredith, I'm sorry you had to find out."

"You know what I think, Bill? All the efforts I made to save our marriage were futile, because now I know the truth. You and Rob out-and-out betrayed me."

"But, I told you—" he said.

"You told me nothing about what was happening to me; you told me nothing about Rob, or how he felt, or who he was playing with. You told me to get an abortion. I killed my child because of you."

He said nothing. "We'll be there on the first, at two o'clock," I snapped, and hung up. I stood in the dark, listening to the silence. Then I went to the cupboard, took out a bottle of brandy, and poured myself a stiff drink.

The next morning, as soon as I was fully awake, I groaned out loud. One more day remained before Rob returned from San Francisco. I daydreamed, considering different ways our future might go. Though we'd been married less than four years, I couldn't even begin to picture myself without him. Our move had brought us closer together. I was sure of that. Or was I? I mulled it over. Rob didn't have a night out (or Rick in St. Louis), and we always went out together. Unless he was sneaking away during the afternoons, I did not believe he was still "experimenting," as Father Bill had put it. The idea of divorce sickened me, and I realized that an insidious hatred for both men was taking hold in my soul.

I got out of bed and opened the drapes. The morning sky was muted: a slate gray over the yellowing lawns that surrounded our apartment building. The trees stood barren, like stick men, inert, lifeless. In the kitchen I put water on for tea and glanced at the outside thermometer; the temperature was thirty-one degrees. While I gazed out the window, I prayed: God, I don't want to hate him. Today I feel more sad than hurt. Even if he's no longer sleeping with men, how soon will I begin to suspect him? How can I trust him again, even if I want to?

Needing to relieve my cabin fever, I dressed in layers. I spent twenty minutes choosing my clothes with all the care of a runway model—it was a relief to think of something else for a time. I moved slowly and deliberately. I did not need to hurry, and I certainly didn't want to sit and think.

Despite the life-shaking betrayals, I still sought water in the well that so far had proven dry. I drove to the chapel at St. Benedict's College, where they had a noon mass. I'd attended Mass every day of my life from the time I was nine years old until I was twenty-four. Fifteen years. I was sure to find peace in the familiar ritual.

With the students and faculty away on vacation, the chapel was nearly empty. Kneeling in the pews near the front were three women, their heads wrapped in woolen scarves, and an old man with curly white hair, bowed over his prayer book. A Christmas tree decorated with blue lights and ornaments stood in a corner with the crèche beneath it. Breathing in the fragrance of pine and incense and candle wax, I moved into the pew behind the old man. As the church bells chimed the Angelus, the priest, a baby-faced young man wearing black rimmed glasses, walked out to the altar and began. "The Lord is with you," he said.

I knelt, and stood, crossing myself, reciting the familiar prayers, and I received communion. After he said, "Go in peace." As much as I wanted that, it didn't seem possible anymore. Where was God? Was I losing my faith? I felt a hollowing in my chest, as if my heart had been removed. I left the chapel and drove to the library.

Back home, among my book and cigarettes, I had to distract myself. Big time. I was grateful to have a fictional world that allowed me to escape, at least a few moments every hour. I settled onto the living room sofa. Staving off the urge to drink on an empty stomach, I ate some crackers. I poured a small glass of brandy and put it on the coffee table, promising myself that I'd read ten pages between sips. The book refused to hold me. Images of Rob sitting in one of San Francisco's notorious bathhouses did. I pictured Rob being picked up by some bulked-up boyish-looking guy. Where did they go? Did they go to Rob's hotel room? What did they do? I fixated on these erotic scenes over and over again until I ran to the bathroom and retched. Then I threw myself on our bed and wept.

Right before I left I gargled with Listerine and tidied the house. As I drove to the airport, the night was cloudy and dark. I was grateful for the darkness. I would tell Rob about our appointment on the way home when he couldn't see the disgust in my eyes. Nor would I be tempted to look too deeply into his eyes, afraid of the anger that welled in me. Overwhelmed with hurt, jealousy, and anger, I stepped back into my role.

I pulled the car to the curb at the airport and waited. An elderly couple, walking arm in arm, made their way to the American Airlines door. I watched another couple, probably in their twenties, each lugging a large black suitcase, herding two toddlers—both blowing little toot horns from New Year's Eve parties—cross the street into the parking lot. Those little kids could be ours, I mused. How sweet the vision until

I glanced in the other direction. The light emanating from the airport entrance made everything inside look dull, deserted, a wasteland of silver chrome and beige tiles. At last I saw him jogging towards the car, and he opened the back door, calling out, "Hello!" as he tossed his bag into the backseat.

I reached over and opened the passenger door and he dove in, kissing my cheek. Our lips barely touched. I busied myself by turning the ignition key and making small talk as I pulled onto the street.

"Oh, it's good to see you!" Rob sounded joyful.

"How was the rest of the conference?"

"Great. I ran into John Fairchild and Charlie Morse and we had dinner, let's see, it was Tuesday night."

I nodded, barely paying attention as I envisioned Rob, smilingly leading a guy into his hotel, eager and more than willing. He closes the door to the room, perhaps hanging the "Do Not Disturb" sign, and then—well, I didn't know what to picture. As I drove I watched him, happily chatting. He may have looked young and innocent but now I knew better. He was ruining my life.

When we got home and walked into the kitchen, Rob dropped his bag and hugged me. "I'm so tired, so glad to be home. I think I'll sleep for days."

"Not too many days," I said, "because tomorrow we have an appointment with Bill at 2:00."

"We do? Why? What is it?" He'd left the water running and was reaching into the cupboard for a glass. I waited until he'd filled it.

"I, uh, need—we need to go." I turned and walked away.

Rob followed me into the bedroom. "I'm too tired to think, but if you want to go, we'll go." I heard the shower when I got into bed. The blue shaded lamp on his bedside table was on, and I turned on my side and closed my eyes. In a few minutes he got into bed beside me, turned off the light, and drew near, spooning his body against mine. For a second I considered that perhaps what I'd read in Rob's journal was all a fiction and that we were a normal married couple after all.

The next morning I dressed and went to the kitchen to make coffee. Around 8:00 I heard Rob pad into the bathroom, and I took a cup of coffee to him. The mirror was fogged up; he'd rubbed a spot clear and I saw his face, half covered with shaving cream, framed in a circle. "Here's coffee, I'll make some toast for the road," I said.

"Thanks, I'll be ready soon." He reached out and grabbed my wrist. "Why can't you tell me why we're going? It seems so—mysterious."

I felt the heat from the hot water and steam. I wanted to tell him, but didn't know how. I pulled away and shook my head. "No, no, I can't."

Soon we were on the highway speeding northwest, listening to "Bad, Bad Leroy Brown" and "Killing Me Softly." I was trying not to think. While Rob drove, eyes glued to the wheel and focused, I plunged straight back into my book. Rob didn't press me again, and we didn't talk much. Maybe he was catching on. If so, how did he feel? Cheating and lying. I could barely keep my mouth shut. I was surprised he couldn't sense my anger and disappointment. He was a fake, and I hated what he was doing to my life.

The traffic in downtown St. Louis was sparse, and we pulled in at exactly ten minutes till 2:00, with enough time to freshen up before we met Bill. In the lobby Rob turned to me and said, "We're here; what next?"

"You go first." I sat in an oversized leather armchair. The room was spacious but felt stuffy, permeated by the rancid odor from an ashtray spilling over with cigarette butts. With only a couple of lamps burning and heavy velvet curtains that blocked all the outside light, the space seemed funereal. I checked my watch. 2:01. When I'd telephoned him two nights before, Bill asked me what I wanted him to do. "Tell him that I know. And what I read. That's all."

2:09. He knows, now, I thought, realizing that the priest's next questions would be mine to answer.

Ten minutes later Rob sprang back into the lobby, his stride jaunty and his smile wide and joyful. I stood; he came close to me and put his hands on my shoulders. "So now you know. I've really wanted to tell you, Mer, I didn't like the deception. I'm glad you read my journal."

My eyes blurred. Rob drew me close and hugged me. I pulled away. "I guess it's your turn," he whispered.

I entered the dark smoky room and nodded to the priest, slouched in the chair behind his desk where he'd always sat during our months of counseling. Today he appeared grayer and older.

"Bill, thank you for seeing us so quickly." I was lying through my teeth. Why would I thank him? He had allied himself with Rob and they had deceived me. But at that time I was so conflicted I didn't know what to do. I just wanted to get it over with.

When he gestured for me to sit, I perched on the edge of the green armchair Rob usually took.

"As I told you, I'm sorry you had to find out that way," the priest said, lighting a cigarette. He drew on it and continued, "Now what do you want to do?"

I'd been unable to rehearse this answer; I had no idea what I would say. I surprised myself when I blurted, "I want him out!" But I wasn't thinking clearly because I hated the idea of divorce.

"All right. Can you tell him?"

I waited, thinking he might apologize for his part in lying to me, but he sat there, contentedly pulling on his cigarette. Meekly, I nodded. "I can't have a marriage with him 'experimenting,' as you call it."

"Then you know what you have to do," he said. "I really am sorry."

"I'm sorry? You're sorry? What do you mean you're sorry? You encouraged him to deceive me, and for all I know, also to experiment. What kept you, supposedly a man of God, from telling me the truth and letting me decide? You're a sham, Bill. A disgrace to your community."

I waited again, this time for some kind of priestly apology, but what was I thinking? Now that I was fully aware of the sham he'd worked, shaking the very roots of my core beliefs, I could not expect anything. Nor did I get it. At first Bill did not react, then he blinked a few times. I didn't know if it was his smoke or my fire.

I was tired of this oily used-God salesman. Disgusted and fed up. Why on earth had I insisted on seeing him again? Why did I cling to the childish notion that a priest could help us? Abruptly, I left the room.

Looking apprehensive, Rob met me downstairs. "I want to go now," I said. I hurried ahead of him, pushing through the lobby and outside feeling the cold slap me in face.

Rob drove all the way home. I didn't care if he was jet-lagged. Using my rolled-up coat as a pillow, I leaned against the passenger door and fell asleep ten minutes after we got on the freeway. Every time I woke, sordid images played in my head, scenes with Rob starring—and doing all sorts of lascivious actions to one man after another. I closed my eyes again and willed myself back to sleep. I did not want to see any more of that day.

As we neared our apartment, I straightened and stretched my arms. "You must be exhausted," I said.

"I am. But I'm worried, Meredith—about you and about us." He reached over and tried to stroke my hand. "Will you talk to me?"

"Let's get home and eat something. We'll feel better for a talk."

I heated up some of the vegetable soup I'd made and together we set the table, and ate soup and crackers. The soup tasted tinny and the crackers like cardboard. After a few nibbles, I pushed my bowl away. I wondered if it tasted okay to Rob, but didn't ask. We sat, our eyes fixed on the soup. While he finished his meal, I studied him. His eyes were red-rimmed with fatigue. He was still on California time and he'd driven nearly seven hours. I felt a pang of pity until my anger resurfaced. I steadied myself.

"Bill asked me what I wanted to do," I said, scooting my chair back. "I want you to leave, Rob. This is not my idea of a marriage." I burst into tears.

Rob got up and held me while I cried. "I'm sorry, honey," he said. "I'm so sorry."

Sobbing I said, "What did you expect me to say? You said you were glad I knew—about your lovers. Did you think I'd tell you to invite your lovers into our home?" I was beginning to see the hopelessness of the situation. I didn't like what I saw.

He went to the kitchen and poured me a shot of bourbon. "Maybe this will help," he said.

"Please, don't cry." He took my hand and led me into the bedroom. Silently we undressed and fell into bed, lying together spoon fashion. In spite of everything, I fell into a deep sleep.

In the night I heard what sounded like a groan of pain and sat up. The clock on my dresser read 2:16. Rob was tangled in the covers and moaning softly. I reached over to touch his head. He was burning.

I got water and aspirin and shook him awake. "Rob, you're feverish, take this." He drank, and sank back into sleep.

In the morning light he looked white, blanched, his eyes bleary, and he could hardly make it back and forth to the bathroom. I kept vigil, bringing him water, juice, and broth while he slept for the next two days and nights.

I used this time to sort out my own feelings. If he left, divorce was certain. I closed my eyes and saw myself, a banner reading *Divorced* draped across my chest like Hester Prynne's scarlet A, standing in front of my family, my friends, the nuns who'd taught me in school. Feelings of shame and revulsion roiled inside me. No one in my world was divorced. Besides, Catholics didn't believe in divorce.

If not divorce, then there was the matter of forgiveness. Could I truly forgive Rob? I struggled not to replay the tapes of Rob's telling me, "I have a new friend and I want you to meet him" and the memory of Rick and Rob laughing together. Why had that meeting occurred? Why had my husband brought his lover into our home? How many others were there? The bottom line was: could I trust him again? While Rob slept, I'd wrestle with what I'd learned about him, as the lines "Round and round, despair to drowning" from from Hopkins's poem spun in my head.

Finally, I decided that, if I felt sure he'd never lie to me again, I could forgive him. It was better than divorce. If I was sure he'd never lie to me again, I would learn to forgive.

The second morning as I was leaving his bedside, he reached for my arm. "Mer, honey, come here, please." He was using a term of endearment he hardly used anymore. I was touched, then revulsed. Did he think sweet talk could erase the pain? Did he think we could move blithely along, back to "normal"?

"I'm here, I'm right here." I knelt by the bed. His face was still pale. He's like a little boy, I realized. I knew I had to stop thinking like this. Revulsion, then love, desperation, ambivalence.

What on earth was driving me to love even now?

"Please, please, don't make me leave." His eyes filled with tears. "I don't want to be without you. I love you. Bill says I can change, and I promise you, I will. Please, let me stay."

Bill had also assured me that Rob could change—if he chose—with psychiatric help. I never imagined Rob would consider such a thing. Yet that's what he was saying. I knew he was ill and that when he recovered, I'd probably hear a different story.

But that didn't happen.

Over the next three days we talked for hours. He swore his promise was firm, and it was hard to hate a man willing to make such a promise. In a photograph taken at our Twelfth Night party—which we'd scheduled long before the events of the past few days—we look radiant. Rob's arm encircles my waist, and we appear completely in love.

The morning after, we stayed in bed past eight snuggling and dozing, but I wasn't yet ready to invite more than that. Because Rob had been sick and we'd been so busy preparing for the party, we still hadn't cleared the air.

"Let's eat something," I said, heading for the kitchen. "Big or small?" I asked, using our code for breakfast.

"Small, really small."

In the dining room, sunlight poured onto the gold carpet as Rob opened the drapes. Except for a couple of stray napkins, we'd mostly cleaned before we went to bed, so the house still had a spruced-up look. We took our coffee and toast to the table and sat so both of us could see a patch of blue sky.

"You did a great job with the party," Rob said. He was spreading homemade peach jam on his toast.

"Nearly everyone we invited showed up, I guess." I smiled, then frowned.

"Yeah, but you ended up doing most of the work. I'm sure glad I'm over that flu or whatever it was," he said, pouring milk into his coffee.

I let a moment pass, but it was time for us to address unfinished business. "Now that we've jumped that hurdle, we need to talk," I told him. "When you were sick, do you remember how you begged me to let you stay? Were you, or are you, serious?"

"I am serious, Meredith. I told you. Bill says with professional help I can overcome this—this aberration. Don't worry. We can be a real family with a house and children." He pressed his hands together as if he were pleading for his life.

"But it's such a big promise."

"I'll keep it," he said, squeezing my hand. "Then will you trust me? Give me one more chance?"

I squeezed his hand back. He appeared both serious and determined. I was beginning to believe that maybe we still had a marriage. "Yes, all right," I said. We stood and embraced. I closed my eyes and prayed to believe him.

While we were washing our dishes, Rob said, "Let's walk to the 7 Eleven and get a newspaper."

"Now?"

"Now! We need to start house hunting."

At the corner we grabbed the paper, hurried back to the apartment, and dropped our coats on the sofa. Rob laid out the real estate section on the table between us. Our search was on. He was trying hard to be the ideal husband.

Three nights later I woke during the night. The dim clock face told me it was 2:16. When I listened for Rob's breathing and heard nothing, I turned and saw his covers thrown back. I put on my robe and tiptoed into the living room. There, staring at a full moon, stood Rob. His intensity was palpable. He turned when he heard me enter.

"Is something wrong?"

He paused a few seconds before responding. "No, no, I couldn't sleep and came out here, and I guess I got caught up in the moon."

It was the pause that got me. And his stance before he knew I was there. He seemed to be peering out into the darkness as if he were searching for something, and I felt a tension when he spoke to me.

"Rob," I said. "Are you changing your mind about us?"

He came over and put his arms around me. "No, Mer. Let's go back to bed." After I lay down, I revisited the scene and realized that, although he'd put his arms around me, he hadn't drawn me close and hugged me as he always did. His arms felt limp on my back—his affection more like a placating gesture.

Beating back my negative reactions, I tossed the rest of the night. Was he changing his mind?

But somehow I stuffed my incipient loathing down, always aware of the terrible stigma of divorce. It was not what good Catholics did. No one in my family or his had ever been divorced.

The Century 21 agents who showed us Louisville properties were Nan and Howard Price, probably in their forties, both dressed in immaculate navy blue suits with gold-plated name cards pinned to their lapels. After they'd confirmed our credit rating, Nan, in her high, whispery Southern drawl, kept telling us, "Oh, y'all are such a cute couple. Imagine how beautiful your children will be! Howard, darling, we've got to find the perfect house." After the third time, Rob and I rolled our eyes at each other. Some sales pitch.

We traipsed through five houses on our first weekend tour, and agreed to meet again the following week. Nan called Wednesday: "We have three more places for you to look at. How 'bout we pick you and Rob up at 10:30?"

The last place we looked at was located in the Garden District. A two-story home surrounded by magnolia trees, it was crafted of stone and wood with a porch that extended across the entire front of the house. There was even a porch swing. Beveled glass windows graced the dining room, an ornately carved staircase curved from the second floor to the foyer, and the four spacious bedrooms upstairs each had a view of the verdant yard. The house had a woodsy feel to it. The day we found it, the trees were luminous with green foliage that made the street below almost invisible from the second-floor windows.

We fell in love with the place instantly. When the Prices ushered us into the living room, we gazed at what they called "great potential." Rob and I glanced at each other and simultaneously said, "It's charming."

We moved in May. Throughout June Rob pulled up the dark green shag carpets, painted all the rooms, and sanded the hardwood floors. It took me nearly a month to strip the staircase, caked with layers of ugly paints—brown, beige, and an olive green—down to its original state. Then we took turns prancing up and down the gleaming stairs as if we were Rhett and Scarlett.

We spent the summer remodeling. With the radio blaring, we sang along with Peter, Paul & Mary as we transformed our spacious living room. When we broke for lunch, we'd sit on the kitchen floor eating sandwiches and drinking Cokes. Rob seemed so happy. Sometimes he'd get out his guitar, strum a few chords, and make up lyrics to match his music: "This is our house, our very own house!" I'd sing with him and clap my hands.

In the South spring wraps its arms around you, leaving you heady with the scent of magnolias in full bloom. One evening I sat in our porch swing, reveling in the intoxication. Overhead the moon etched its thumbprint on an ink-black canvas dotted softly with sparkling stars. Suddenly I felt a familiar aching: the tug of a healthy thirty-year-old woman's desire. Rob hadn't touched me in weeks. He was upstairs in his study, honing his lecture on Immanuel Kant for the next day. At dinner he'd been excited about it, giving me sneak previews of his fresh insights. Now I sat alone on the porch, breathing in the night's fragrance, and remembering.

Almost four years ago, back when we were newlyweds, we'd pored over a "how-to" book called *The Catholic Marriage Manual,* written by a priest who began with a stern warning against the evils of birth control. Because it was the only book we had, we'd eagerly searched for instructions on sexual positions, but the information was scant.

After I heard about Germaine Greer's new book, *The Female Eunuch,* I had run to the college bookstore and bought it, and hurried back to my office, where Gwen was correcting papers.

"Gwen, you'll want to see this." I rolled my chair close to hers and caught a whiff of her new fragrant perfume.

"Oh, you got it! Another review was in the *Times* yesterday; it's supposed to be an even stronger polemic than Friedan's."

I was leafing through the book. "Listen to this: 'The ignorance and isolation of most women means that they are incapable of making conversation; most of their communication with their spouses is a continuation of the power struggle.'"

"That's what's it's all about, power. I sure hope some things will change," Gwen said.

I'd taken the book home and Rob and I studied it together. Sitting side by side on the sofa, I'd read parts of it aloud to him. Afterward, when we cuddled in bed, he whispered, "You can wake me up anytime you want me. Remember, I'm serious." He seemed earnest—he wanted me to experience the fulfillment we'd read about.

One morning I told him, "Last night when you were sleeping, I felt so randy. I decided to experiment a little."

"Did you—?" He looked shocked. I nodded, smiling. I didn't tell him, but it was the first time I had ever pleasured myself.

"Oh, why didn't you wake me?" His face fell. Strange for a man who seldom touched me.

But he'd made that plea months ago. Still, over time, I thought we were closer—emotionally at least. But what did I know? So often these days, I felt I was living with a stranger. Perhaps tonight, though, Rob would welcome my approach and wrap himself around me like the warm spring air. I pictured him as he once had been, hugging me tightly to him.

In a burst of courage, I raced upstairs to Rob's study. If we still had a marriage, he would welcome my advances.

I found my husband sitting at his desk, his books spread out and his writing tablet covered with notes. The pungent smell of his tobacco pipe filled the room. He turned. "What's up?"

"Rob," I said, "I hate to interrupt . . ." I was perched on a corner of the sofa.

"Remember when you told me, while we were still in St. Louis—you told me that if I ever wanted you, I should let you know?" My words came falteringly, but they came. Our marriage counselor had urged us to be open, to communicate with one another. I was communicating.

My husband blinked twice. "I know I said that then. That's what I felt then. That was months ago, Meredith."

"And now—it doesn't apply now?" My face flushed.

"If you're not satisfied, Meredith, take a lover."

My chest tightened as though someone dear to me had recently died. Feeling naked and ashamed, I ran downstairs. I crouched on the porch steps and stared into the sky. He was sending me mixed messages, and I had to restrain myself from going upstairs and slapping him.

I breathed in the magnolia fragrance still surrounding me, but half of the stars that had twinkled ten minutes ago seemed to have disappeared.

So much for thinking that marriage counseling and moving had saved us.

Without knowing I was even looking, I found Jason at a conference in Memphis. When I entered the auditorium he was merely a distant figure behind the podium, but I did notice that he was dapper and eloquent, and that was enough. After he finished his address, I stood at the rear of the hall waiting for everyone to file out. I was recalling the Joyce Carol Oates story, "Unmailed, Unwritten Letters," which laid out a similar scene: the narrator meets her lover after a captivating speech. In the story the woman has no name. Now I'd give her mine.

In the rear of the auditorium I stood, the conference program rolled in my hand, waiting. I was wearing black tights, a short red dress with a white collar and cuffs, my blonde hair swept back in a gold barrette. I had donned my costume and had taken stage left. As Jason Broderick—the man who would be my costar—moved steadily toward me, I saw a boyishly handsome man in a tweed sports coat with leather elbow patches.

Fully aware of what I was doing, I began fictionalizing my life—and distancing myself from what I was about to do. I was going to seduce this man.

"Hello." I extended my hand. "I really enjoyed your talk."

His face colored slightly. "Oh, thanks. And you are—" reading my name tag—"Meredith Baird?"

I nodded.

"I could use a drink," he said. "Will you join me?" As we moved into the hall he touched my arm, just at the elbow. He would never suspect that in going with him I was only following my husband's directives.

Jason and I drank well together; martinis and Manhattans bonded us that first night. I was so starved for lovemaking—it had been more than two months since Rob had touched me—I couldn't wait to get drunk enough to invite him to my room. Jason knew how to hold me, caress my breasts, take time to stimulate me so that when he entered me, I felt ecstatic. Jason knew how to make love—and we weren't so drunk we didn't remember it the next day when we crossed paths several times in the hallways and in the café. At the banquet the next evening, we sat properly, across from one another, squirming in our chairs and counting the minutes until it was over.

The next morning, unbeknownst to us, someone took our photograph. In February, months after the conference and when we were back in our separate lives, we opened our newsletters to find the picture: two slightly disarrayed thirty-something professors, huddled together over coffee and books. My hair looked unkempt, my jacket askew. There we were, for all to see. The morning after.

Jason and I managed to rendezvous several times over the next year. Because we both headed departments in our respective colleges, we attended meetings throughout the state. The dingy hotel rooms, the phony names, the flasks of gin, and marijuana, too—Jason made it a staple for us. Sometimes we would get so stoned we couldn't stop laughing. I'd count the weeks before we'd meet again, and grab his long sweet letters from the mailbox and devour them in my office. It may have been sordid, but I never gave it a thought. Jason loved me; he wanted me. Rob's words—take a lover—continued to ring in my head.

I also never considered Jason's wife, or worried that she knew or suspected. I never considered his little boy. I knew the story of his meeting his wife, Susan, back in college, and about his brothers, his childhood, but it was like hearing about characters in a novel. The gravity of our actions never once occurred to me.

Our meetings were so infrequent that Rob suspected nothing. He never asked me what I did afternoons, nor did I ask him. In my case, at least, I became an expert in lying by omission.

When Rob went off to Appalachia, solo—or so I thought—for a summer vacation of hiking and camping in the wilderness, Jason joined me. I brought him into our home, though not into our bed. Despite the nightmares after Rob had forced me to abort the child we had made there, and because I had convinced myself that I'd recovered from that trauma, I kept our bed sacrosanct. Instead, Jason and I stayed in the guest room on a foldout sofa.

Jason was my first real lover (I failed to count Greg, who was my soul mate), but he wasn't my last. While my husband did not find me physically attractive, I soon discovered that other men did. One of them, a gangly tanned tennis player I met at my neighbors' home, phoned me that day after we met. "Meredith, this is Lee Jackson, we met at Charles and Penny's yesterday."

"Yes, I remember," I said, grabbing a cigarette and cradling the phone with my shoulder to light it.

"I thought we might meet for a drink.'

"I'm married, Lee. Forget it."

"But wait—isn't there some way—you are one of the most beautiful women I've ever seen."

I was flattered, but I didn't like his pushy manner.

"I'm going now, Lee. I really am married."

"Let me know when you're not," he said, and hung up.

The timing couldn't have been more perfect. It was the early 1970s, with the advent of the pill, the women's movement, the proliferation of drugs and free love. With alcohol, amphetamines, Valium, marijuana—and the tacit consent of a husband I still strained not to hate, I moved forward. But for now, I still abhorred the idea of divorce, so I was playing *Happily Married* with Rob as my costar.

We finished the renovation a few days before classes started that fall. With the house all done up, Rob's parents brought his grandma to visit one weekend in October. The five of us sat around smiling at the house and at each other. I caught a remark Rob's mom Eve made to her husband as I walked by. "These colors! I've never seen anything like them," she said. Rob had painted the living room a trendy pale chartreuse and the matching trim olive green. After searching house décor magazines and paint samples, we'd selected the colors together. We knew it was rather mod, but we liked it. I didn't tell Rob about Eve's remark.

For Thanksgiving my parents drove in from Wichita. It was a balmy weekend, and after breakfast on Thursday, we went out to the porch. A few straggly leaves hung from the limbs of the big elm tree that umbrellaed the front yard. A barely perceptible breeze whispered around us. I sat in a chair I'd lugged out from the dining room and my parents sat in the porch swing. Rob was inside, talking to his sister long distance.

"This is really some house, sweetheart," Dad said. He pushed his feet against the floor and the swing began swaying. I grinned.

"I'm surprised you would choose such an old house," Mom said.

"Oh, but we like old—we like the idea of living in the same rooms where generations have lived, and imagining what they were like," I said. "You know Rob—or you'll know him better after this weekend—he's a poet, he lives in his imagination, so this house is perfect for him—for us."

"It does seem that you're settled now, both of you have good jobs. Isn't it about time you had a baby?"

"Mom," I said, "please—it's not a good time for this."

"But I thought you were waiting until—"

"I know what you thought, but please." I stood and walked over so I could meet her gaze. "Please, whatever you do, do not raise this issue in front of Rob."

Mom didn't answer, but I saw Dad reach out and touch her hand as though to quiet her.

While she and I and Rob worked together preparing dinner, the subject didn't come up again. When we went into the kitchen, I turned on the radio, loud enough to discourage conversation. I didn't trust my mother to keep quiet.

Rob and I, using another of Aunt Tilley's recipes, tore up cornbread and sautéed onion with bits of sausage for the dressing. Rob stuffed, trussed, and basted the turkey. While Mom was rolling out dough for the apple pie, I started peeling and slicing apples, tossing them into a large bowl of cold water. The room began to fill with various aromas: sausage, onion, apples, promises of a rich feast.

"Ah, now this turkey, my first, ought to be great," Rob said, sliding the turkey into the oven. "How many hours, Meredith?"

"It's by the pound, at least four. We can start checking at 3:30."

Rob went to the sink and washed his hands. "Okay, so we'll have dinner by 5:00?"

"Sounds good," Mom and I said simultaneously. All three of us laughed.

"I'm going to phone my parents now," said Rob, "before they go to Aunt Marlene's, so I'll leave you two here." Rob left the kitchen and we could hear his footsteps on the stairway.

"Meredith, I forgot to tell you, Trish is expecting again," Mom said. Trish was my cousin in Florida. She'd been married for at least six years.

"That's nice, Mom."

"Nice? It's a miracle. The doctors said she probably couldn't have any more children after little Mickey; you remember, she almost lost him?"

"Uh huh," I murmured. I didn't want to continue this conversation.

"Now, you know, they had Mickey as soon as Terrence got back from Vietnam, and their life stabilized." She took her time saying sta-bi-lized, for emphasis. She had laid the dough in the pie pan and was draining the peeled apples in a colander. Her movements were deft, practiced; she didn't need to think about what she was doing.

Ignoring her comment, I swept the apple peelings into the trash. "How about a glass of wine?" I reached into the refrigerator and pulled out a bottle left unfinished from the night before. Without meaning to, I slammed the refrigerator door and set the wine on the table with a thud, and then more gently took two wine glasses from the cupboard. I couldn't wait for the wine, and I knew my mom—she was longing for a drink too. I remembered how, when I was a little girl, she'd go into the kitchen, reach for the bottle of Four Roses Bourbon from the top shelf, pour a tumbler full of the brown liquid, and knock back half of it in one gulp.

Another time I'd walked in on her as she was screwing the lid back on the bottle, and she looked at me, and I was looking at the drink, and she said, "I'm getting something to calm my nerves, Meredith."

"Here you are." I set a full glass of Chardonnay on the cabinet next to her. She was cutting slits in the top crust.

"Thanks, Merry." Mom was the only one who could get away with that nickname. It had been a childhood term of endearment, so I let it pass.

"I'll go and say hello to the Bairds now, while Rob has them on the phone. Why don't you get Dad a beer and go relax?"

I hurried out of the kitchen and up to our bedroom, closed the door, and collapsed on the bed. Rob was sitting near the phone, laughing and talking. "Here she is now, she'll want to say hi," he said. He smiled and handed me the phone.

A few minutes later I joined my parents downstairs. I'd tried to watch how many glasses of wine Mom consumed, but after three I lost count. Shortly after 2:00 she and Dad went upstairs for a nap. In the meantime Rob and I set the table, and, settling ourselves on the living room sofa, we dove into our respective books. I sat sideways so I could stretch out my legs and lay my feet close to Rob's hip. I was deeply into Elizabeth Bowen's *The Death of the Heart,* while Rob was reading a recent biography of Emerson.

For an hour or so the only sounds were of us turning pages, lighting a cigarette, or sipping our wine, and the predictable groans of the old house settling. Then we heard the door upstairs open and someone padding into the hallway. At ten minutes to five, my parents came down the stairs. Rob and I put our books away, stabbed out our cigarettes, and joined them in the dining room.

We stood together for a moment admiring the table, set with the white bone china we'd received as a wedding gift and our best tablecloth and napkins. Rob had placed our newly polished silver candlesticks on the table and lit the candles. The fragrance of turkey and apple pie mingled and filled the house as we took our seats. It was nearly dusk and the candlelight gave the room an eerie glow, not at all romantic, probably because my mom's presence loomed so large.

We pulled our chairs in to the table and placed our napkins on our laps. As Rob reached for the electric knife to carve the turkey, I cut in. "Let's say grace." Rob wrinkled his nose. Even though we still attended Sunday mass, he was becoming more disenchanted with the vestiges of the religion we'd always practiced, and to which he'd dedicated four years of his life. The two of us never prayed before meals, but we'd decided we agreed to practice the old formulaic rituals for my parents, as we'd done with his family only a few weekends before. "Would you like to lead the blessing?" I asked Rob.

"No, please, you lead," he said, winking at me.

Folding my hands as Mom had taught me, I rattled off: "Bless us, oh Lord, and these thy gifts which we are about to receive from thy bounty through Christ our Lord. Amen."

I was reaching for my wine when Mom spoke. "We feel so grateful to be here celebrating with you two."

Uh oh, I thought. Her eyes looked slightly glazed. How many glasses?

Rob clicked on the carver and for a few minutes, its whirring stopped all talk. I told Dad to have some potatoes and gravy and asked Mom to pass the rolls.

Rob finished slicing and set down the knife. "Here it is, folks. I think we did it," he said, passing the platter of turkey. "Okay, now let's all eat before it gets cold."

As soon as our plates were filled, I scooped up a forkful of mashed potatoes. It was almost in my mouth when Mom cleared her throat.

"I wasn't quite finished," she said, "about being grateful on this first Thanksgiving in your beautiful new home." Barely pausing, she continued, "Isn't it about time for you two to start a family?"

I pushed the potatoes into my mouth and swallowed hard. No one said a word. Mom looked at Rob, who resolutely continued buttering a roll. Mom looked at me. I glared at her.

"So many religious leaving their orders." Mom frowned at Rob. "Whatever will the Church do?" She reached for her wine.

He and I shared a knowing glance. "They'll survive, Mom," I said. "Have some sweet potatoes, please, and pass them to me."

Back when Rob and I were courting, the topic of dancing never came up. And because our wedding was a simple one, without a grand reception, we'd never led a first dance as bride and groom. At least two full years passed before I ever even knew that my husband relished gyrating to popular tunes like "Love Train" or "You're So Vain."

Before our move to Louisville, Rob made a list of things that he found wanting in me. Besides the fact that my breasts were small and I didn't walk in a sexy way, he'd said that he wished I could dance. He had no idea how much I'd wished that too. In high school I'd taken ballroom dancing lessons with my friend Steven. For eight long weeks we'd shuffled around the high school gym, trying to master the fox-trot, the jitterbug, the waltz. We'd struggled to learn barely enough to get by in college. Fortunately for me, none of my college boyfriends were dancers either, so at events, we'd stand on the dance floor, moving our feet in small circles to "Moon River" or "Love Me Tender" and other slow tunes. If we'd had a few swigs of bourbon before we arrived, we'd swing around in our version of the jitterbug, giggling at our clumsiness.

Once Rob and I were settled in Louisville, he brought up dancing again. "I really miss dancing, Meredith. Do you like to dance?"

I cringed. "I don't really know how." My voice sounded like that of a ten-year-old, tentative and high-pitched.

We were in the kitchen and he turned away to open a cupboard. I sat down at the table. "I figured," he said. I could hear the disappointment in his voice.

"I could try. Is there somewhere special you'd like to go?" Damn him, I thought. He's testing me. It's like the breast thing, only now he expects me to turn into frigging Ginger Rogers.

He brought his glass of water to the table and sat beside me. "Maybe we could practice."

"Where?" I reached over, fiddling with the salt and pepper shakers.

"Here! There's plenty of room if we push back the table and chairs in the dining room, and we've got those records Jeannie gave us." He was grinning.

"Great idea," I lied. I was terrified of dancing with Rob. This was a man who accomplished everything he set out to do with ease and enjoyment. Even writing a research paper, a daunting task for almost everyone I knew, was a delightful experience for him. Often, when I went to bed early, I'd kiss him goodnight while he sat at his desk typing away without a whisper of anxiety.

After dinner the next night I heard Rob shoving the furniture around in the dining room. Then "You're So Vain" blasted from our little record player.

I was drying the last dish when he came back into the kitchen. "Okay, Meredith, we've got our own dance floor. Let's go." He pulled me into the dining room and started dancing."You're so Vain" was still playing and I couldn't stop myself from thinking how appropriate the song was for my accomplished husband.

My body stiffened. I stared at him, all arms and legs gyrating around with the music. "Loosen up, Meredith, listen to the music," he said, pivoting around me.

I tried to concentrate and sway this way and that, as Rob was doing. I was relieved when he circled around and danced facing the opposite wall, so he couldn't see me. Inevitably, the minute the song ended, he turned around.

"You really don't like to dance, do you?" He walked over to the record player.

"I can practice, and I'm sure—"

"But Meredith," he said, "it's all about finding the rhythm. You've got to listen for the beat." He shuffled through the albums, and put on Simon and Garfunkel. "Are you going to Scarborough Fair," they sang. Sprawling on the sofa, Rob said, "I think I'll sit this one out."

I curled up at the other end of the sofa and we listened together, joining in on the parts we knew so well.

At least I knew I could sing.

More often than not Rob and I talked about our classes over dinner. The first time he mentioned her I barely took notice. "It's great having older students," he said. "They have such a different perspective from the twenty-year-olds."

A week later he remarked, "This woman's brilliant in philosophy."

"This woman?" I sat up straighter.

"You know, the woman I told you about." His eyes lit up. "I've been curious about her and today she came to my office."

"What's her story?"

"Oh, typical re-entry, married young, divorced, no profession, came back to get a degree." He cut into his meatloaf. "She said she really likes my class and has never had a better professor." He chuckled.

I concentrated on my salad, thinking: He's so transparent. Does he actually believe he's fooling me?

One Friday afternoon I left work early to purchase a bottle of champagne. Rob and I had another reason to celebrate. That morning I'd received a letter from the president of the Literacy Association of America inviting me to speak at the opening session of the national convention in October. My work the previous two years designing programs for students new to the college experience was highly regarded, the president said, and they would be pleased to have me share it with my colleagues. Before I left the office I'd shown the letter to Maryann and Janet, my friends who taught history. Reading it, Maryann leapt out of her chair. "Hooorah, Meredith, at last!" Janet grabbed the paper and headed out the door. "I'm xeroxing this and taking a copy to President Allen's office," she said. The two of them insisted on treating me to lunch and toasting to my success.

Still, I was eager to share the news with Rob. Driving by the Humanities Center, I decided to stop by and tell him in person. Maybe he'd be ready to leave and we could go for a drink. As I walked down the corridor, I could hear him chortling. Nearing his office I heard someone speaking too softly for me to distinguish the words, but the voice was clearly female. There was more raucous laughter. I hesitated a moment before I rounded the corner and stuck my head in Rob's open door.

"Oh, Meredith, what a surprise," Rob said. I caught a strained phoniness about his voice. And he called me by my full name, which seldom happened. The room reeked of a mix of sickly gardenia and overwhelming tobacco. From the doorway I saw a woman sitting in the straight-back chair next to Rob's desk. She had short, dark wavy hair and silver hoop earrings, and she wore a snug black sweater that accentuated her large bust. Her face was heavily madeup. We stared at each other.

"Meredith, meet Gloria. I've told you about her." Told whom about whom, I questioned.

I plastered a smile on my face. "Hi Gloria. Glad to meet you."

"Same here, Meredith," she said. Her voice was deep and gravelly.

I felt my face blazing. "Well, I thought I'd wanted to stop by and say hi—I'm on my way now. Nice meeting you, Gloria." I nodded at her again, trying not to gawk. Her face looked hard, as if she'd suffered a lot or smoked too much. I guessed she might be in her late thirties, perhaps eight or nine years our senior.

"See you in an hour," Rob said, sitting back in his chair and giving me a little wave.

I flew down the stairs, my heart racing. She's exactly what he wants, I thought. Perhaps a 38D, and dressed the way he'd like me to be: in tight sexy jeans, tight sweater, leather boots, and gypsy hoop earrings. She reminded me of Cher, with a few more pounds. Mentally I replayed his first mention of her, telling me: "She really likes my class."

Has Gloria replaced Rick? I was confused. Rick? Gloria? Where do I fit in? Does Rob think Gloria can change him? How can I possibly still think our marriage can be saved?

I'd completely forgotten about the letter.

Back when I'd had hepatitis I'd encouraged Rob's "nights out"—which I deeply regretted now. The second year In Louisville, he started coming home for dinner and announcing he had plans for the evening. "I'm going out later with Pat and Nigel," he'd say. Since they were his colleagues in the philosophy department, I was never surprised if his plans didn't include me. Then one night Rob rushed into the kitchen slightly out of breath. I was busy making a salad.

"There's a new bar," said Rob, enthusiastically. "It's got a clever name—'Pit of the Seventh Olive'—and it's down on Olive Street. Pat and Nigel and some others went there for drinks. They're going again tonight."

"Oh? Some others?" I said casually, blotting wet lettuce with a kitchen towel.

Rob leaned against the counter. "Meredith, you and I, we—well, we never go to clubs together. Anyway, you probably wouldn't enjoy it," he challenged.

Something about his tone made me so curious that for once, I opted to join him. Besides, going might give me another chance to see Gloria.

When we walked into the pub that evening, Suzy, Pat, and Nigel waved us over to their table. A young man with a long red ponytail took our order. "Two double martinis," Rob scanned the room. "Oh, look who's here." Acting surprised, he called out to a woman several tables away, "Hey, Glo, come on over!" Glo—when had she become "Glo"? He waved her over.

Rob stood to pull a chair out for her. Again she was wearing a tight dark sweater, snug-fitting jeans, and the same large hoop earrings I'd noticed that day in Rob's office. Her red lipstick looked black in the soft light, accentuating her full mouth. "I think you know everyone here, right?" said Rob. "Suzy, Pat, Nigel, Meredith?" We all nodded and I managed a "Hi" to Gloria.

The waiter brought our martinis and set them on the table. "Anything else?" he said.

"What are you drinking?" Rob asked Gloria.

"A Manhattan, please."

I took a sip of my martini and fished my cigarettes from my purse. Rob didn't touch his glass. The jukebox started playing Paul Simon's "Kodachrome" and Rob came to life. "Any of you ladies want to dance?"

Without making eye contact with me, or even waiting for a reply, Rob took Gloria's arm, headed for the dance floor, and disappeared into a fog of cigarette smoke.

"I think I'll go sit at the bar awhile," I said, leaving the others. A hot flash flared in my cheeks. My husband had blatantly ignored me, right in front of his friends. Perhaps they knew more than I did. I wanted to disappear.

On my barstool, far from the dance floor, I sat staring into my martini. When the glass was empty I ordered another. Olivia Newton-John was crooning, "Have you ever been mellow?" I wasn't even close to mellow. I kept lighting up Marlboros as a means of self-defense; the smoke created a haze that seemed to separate me from everything. Letting my mind wander, I drank one martini after another. When Rob came to tell me it was time to go home, I could barely walk.

A few days after my humiliation at the Pit, I grabbed my colleague Frank Jones as he passed me in the hall. Frank was a well-groomed guy with dark curly hair, and the youngest member of our department. His specialty was Victorian literature, but he was always bragging about how well he danced. "Frank," I whispered in his ear, "Will you teach me to dance?"

"Oh, I'd love to!" he said. "Dancing's my favorite thing next to poetry and making love." He spoke the last three words in my ear and we chuckled conspiratorially.

That night I packed up my little red-and-white portable record player and a few 45s. After we finished teaching our Wednesday classes, Frank and I cosseted ourselves in an empty classroom. "Rock, around, the clock tonight," sang Bill Haley as I studied Frank's feet closely, noticing how they kept time with the music. Strong and lithe, he moved me around him as we sang and clapped and danced. Dancing with Frank came easy; his enthusiasm spilled over. Maybe I could do this.

"You're doing great!" he said. "Now keep it up! Practice makes perfect." After about an hour we were perspiring and short of breath, and I honestly believed he'd taught me to dance. Really well.

Sunday night I waited until Rob had gone upstairs to prepare a lecture. Then I tiptoed into our dark living room, turned on a corner lamp, and put on "Rockin' Robin" very softly, so it wouldn't bother him. I began to dance, wiggling my hips as Frank had instructed. Repeatedly, I moved my feet across the hardwood floors Rob had so carefully sanded and refinished. Trying my best, I envisioned Frank and abandoned myself to the music. Practice makes perfect, practice makes perfect, practice makes perfect.

Halfway through the third replay, I heard Rob's door open, then his footsteps pounding down the stairs. Ignoring the impulse to stop the record and still my body, I continued dancing. When my husband reached the bottom step he stopped and gaped at me, a dead look in his eyes. "What are you doing?"

"You said you wished I could dance, so I'm practicing." I tried to smile but before I could say another word, Rob brushed past me and into the kitchen, closing the door behind him. I stopped the record, listening. I heard the refrigerator door slam and water splashing into the sink. I clicked the player off and ran upstairs.

An hour later, he came into the bedroom. I said, "Rob, we need to talk."

"We need time apart," Rob said. "That's what we need."

I got into my side of the bed and pulled the covers over my eyes. When he didn't spoon his body close to mine, I felt my chest contract. I waited until his breathing steadied, then crept out of bed and over to my closet. In a shoebox I'd hidden a quart of vodka. I unscrewed the top, brought it to my mouth, and took three huge gulps. It burned as it went down my throat, but I had to have it. My days of trying to cut down were over.

One bone-chilling January evening, I was driving Rob home from the library where he'd been meeting with students. The streets were full of ice and I was taking my time. I glanced at Rob, staring out his window. We hadn't turned on the radio and our silence was broken only by cars rushing by and the occasional groan of a braking big rig. I started thinking about Jason, wishing that one of these days Rob would take me in his arms and ravish me the way my lover did. In spite of the recent Gloria sightings, in spite of what he'd said that night when he found me dancing, I still had hope. I was willing to do anything to avoid divorce.

I jolted back to reality when Rob cracked the window on his side and turned to face me. A cold rush of air burst into the car.

"How do you think we're—our marriage—is going?" he asked.

He caught me by surprise. I wondered what his question implied. "Okay," I said. "I think it's okay."

He cleared his throat. "What if you think you don't want to work on your marriage anymore? That there's no point?"

I kept my eyes on the road. "You're saying 'you' for yourself?"

"I am," he said. His voice sounded resolute.

I sat with his statement a minute or two. "If that's what you think, it's time for you to go." I could scarcely believe my words. But what else could I say? My heart fluttered with dejection, but I kept my eyes on the road. I refused to let Rob know I felt utterly crushed.

He said nothing.

When we got home, we headed upstairs. Rob clomped up two steps at a time, hurried into his study, and shut the door. I changed into my nightgown and robe and took my psalm book from the bedside table. The psalms always consoled me.

Back downstairs, sitting on the sofa with my legs wrapped in the afghan Rob's mother had knitted for us, I opened the book. *Look on me and answer me, Lord, my God,* I read, but it was impossible not to keep replaying our conversation in the car. Even after I'd let his pronouncement sink in, I hadn't cried. I hadn't cried then, and I did not feel like crying now, though I felt the cold paralysis of despair—doomed to divorce, failure. Finally I shut my eyes and prayed using my own words. It was what I had been taught and the only thing I knew to do. Gradually, I felt myself relax.

I was dozing—but in only a few minutes, the chilly memory of Rob's words pierced my lethargy, and I rose, went into the kitchen, and did what I knew I could do: took a large swig from the Smirnoff's bottle. I slowly ascended the stairs. Rob was already in bed, his head buried under a pillow. At the door I paused to listen to his breathing; he was sleeping soundly as I slipped into my side of the bed. Settling in, I wrapped my arms around myself and recited my new mantra: God is with me, I am not afraid. But where was God anyway? And who was I fooling? I was afraid. After two restless hours, I finally slept.

Despite Rob's announcement in the car, I woke the next day determined to give it one last shot. I refused to see that I could not doff my rose-colored glasses.

Our third year in Louisville Rob had taken a job at another university which offered him opportunities to teach more courses in his field. The following semester I'd been invited to teach a course on women's literature there. The study of literature written by women—reflecting the emerging women's movement—was brand new to the academic scene, and I was flattered by the offer.

After class one day Lauren Broderick, a full-bodied, sandy-haired senior from Kansas City, approached me. She glowed with anticipation.

"Dr. Baird," she said, "I'm so excited that you're here. I had your husband last year for Modern Philosophy, and I think it's so neat that you're both professors."

I smiled and nodded. "I'm happy to be here, Lauren."

She shifted the books in her arms. "Well, I'm on the newspaper staff and I'd really like to interview you as a campus couple."

I thought she was joking. "Campus couple?" I said. "You seriously want to interview us?"

"You're the only married couple teaching here, and I've already talked to the editors. They gave me a green light. So what do you say, Dr. Baird?"

"I'm flattered, but we need to check with my husband. You're the reporter, why don't you ask him?"

Lauren grinned. "Gladly." She gave me a little bow. "I'll speak to him this afternoon. Oh, you'll see, it'll be great!"

Her enthusiasm spilled over me and for a moment I believed it could be great: a story about us might solidify our marriage and lend it meaning, even as we struggled for solid ground.

Nodding again, Lauren rushed off to her next class.

Hours later, pouring Rob a glass of wine, I said, "Did Lauren Broderick approach you?" We were in the kitchen after work.

He laughed and sipped his wine. "Yeah, about an interview. I don't know, Mer."

"I guess she's taken by the fact that we're married professors teaching on the same campus. You know, she's right, Rob, we are an anomaly there."

"Okay, let's go ahead with it," Rob said, surprising me. I hadn't thought he'd like the idea. "You'll see Lauren first, so why don't you tell her?" he said. His agreement fed the smallest hope I foolishly continued to keep alive.

The Valentine's Day issue of the *Campus Monitor* featured a two-column story headlined "Dynamic Duo on Campus," along with a photograph of us at the Christmas faculty dinner: Rob wearing his navy blue suit, his arm around my waist, and me in a black and white satin gown cinched with a black cummerbund. No clues about our troubled selves are apparent as we smile jubilantly for the camera, as if we'd won an Academy Award for best couple in a family drama.

The story was published the day after I finally realized our marriage was over. I'd tried everything I could think of and nothing had worked. Now I brought the newspaper home, folded it, and secreted it in the bottom drawer where I kept the lingerie I'd bought to please Rob. Neither of us ever said a word about it.

That night as I lay in bed, all sorts of imagined fears raced through my mind: I saw our family members, friends, and colleagues, each one aghast at our news, each one blurting, "But you're such a great couple. Why?" I visualized the next edition of the *Campus Monitor* emblazoned with a new headline: "Dynamic Duo Self-Destructs."

By the end of February I was still fretting but had a rough plan. If we kept things a secret until the end of the semester, our news would trickle out during the summer months, and maybe when school reconvened in the fall, reactions would be tempered by time. Since our families lived miles away, they wouldn't know until we told them by letter or phone.

Mostly to placate me, Rob agreed to a separation agreement. One night in early March, after dinner, I brought paper and pen to our kitchen table, and we produced a document to make our separation official—at least to me. In it we agreed to a six-month trial, said when we'd contact our families, and listed a few close friends who could be told immediately.

Notably missing from this document was the issue of dating, which was already happening. Never in our solemn deliberations did we write or even speak the word *divorce*. Our strict Catholic upbringing prohibited our even thinking about it. Or was it simply denial that things might reach that point?

A few days later I was grading essays when Rob came in from work. He was whistling "Yankee Doodle"! How does he find it in himself to be so obviously happy, I asked myself. Maybe he'd had another paper accepted for publication. "Oh, Mer," he said, setting his briefcase down and taking off his jacket. "I found a great place today. It's close—around the corner of Central and Grand, a one bedroom—and I'm ordering furniture."

I remembered all the things we'd picked out together so carefully, less than three years before. "But—don't you want anything from here?" I swept my eyes around the room.

"No, only my desk." He picked up his briefcase and started up the stairs. "Since we're not sure this is permanent, I want to leave everything here. In case, you know..."

My fingers flew to my throat. "But you're ordering new furniture. I mean, how is that logical? Where would we—" I found myself standing, flailing my hands in the air like some madwoman.

"Oh, we'll think of something. Later," said Rob, continuing up the stairs. "Oh, by the way, I've written Mom and Dad. You might want to write your folks."

The following Friday the scent of mown grass floated in through the open window. Rob had already left for the college and I stood in our bedroom, gazing out at the street recalling Williams's poem "Spring and All." To myself I whispered, "Lifeless in appearance, sluggish dazed spring approaches," and realized my spring is dazed and even muddied, and I'm about to become a separated woman. Separated! A vision of all my body parts hanging separately in space vanished when the telephone jangled, startling me.

"Meredith, is that you?"

I recognized my mother-in-law's voice. "Yes, Eve, how are you?"

"Well, Meredith, I'm—we're both stunned. We got Rob's letter. And I—we can't believe it. Rob says you kids are separating." Her voice became soft. "Honey, please tell me it's not true."

"Oh, Eve—yes, it's true. Rob started looking for an apartment on Friday."

"But Meredith, why? We can't understand what he's told us. He says—let me read from the letter—'We've grown apart and we're headed in different directions.' Meredith, what does he mean?"

"I can't speak for Rob, Eve." I sat on the bed, made up with the dark blue chenille spread Rob and I had ordered from the Penney's catalogue. Eve sighed. The phone felt heavy in my hand.

"We're terribly upset, Meredith. And I told Len—this is Rob's idea. I'm right about that, aren't I? This separation is Rob's idea, isn't it?"

I knew I had to tell her something, but definitely not the truth: Your son loves men, and maybe women too, but he no longer wants me. He's said hideous things to me, and told me to take a lover. I took a deep breath. "Yes, it's his idea. But I can't say more than that. You know I can't speak for Rob, Eve. Please try to understand. Rob needs to talk to you himself."

Eve sniffled. "We are so sorry. Remember—no matter what, you're our daughter and we love you."

Holding back my tears, "Thanks Eve," I said. Replacing the phone, I saw the clock: 9:07. I had to rush.

Even after all that had happened, we still ate dinner together. That evening I beat Rob home and headed straight into the kitchen. I was heating the beef stew he'd cooked over the weekend. I cut three pieces from a fresh loaf of bread and set the table. I was filling water glasses when I heard the door open.

"Hi Meredith," Rob greeted me. He pecked my cheek.

I said, "I'm glad you're here early." I set the glasses on the table.

Rob leaned against the wall, his briefcase in one hand. "Why? What happened?"

"Your mom called. This morning. Right after you left."

"Oh, now it comes. She waited for me to leave this morning so she could talk to you, didn't she?"

"Maybe. Yes, probably. Sit down." I waved him into a chair and put steaming bowls on the table.

"Meredith, I'm sorry you got stuck with her. What did she say?"

Nervously fingering my napkin, I said, "She wanted to know what you meant in your letter, about us growing apart." I took a bite of meat.

"Oh, God," Rob groaned, "I knew they wouldn't get it." He pounded his fist on the table.

He wants it all to come off so easily, I thought. He thinks it's not hurting me. Here we are, sharing a meal at the table his parents gave us, like any married couple. "Oh, you'll need other stuff for your apartment," I said, "like cleaning materials and dishes and pots and pans." Despite all that had passed, I yearned to be part of his life. "I can shop for you if you want."

"That would be great, but I don't want to put you out."

You are putting me out, I thought, but refrained from speaking.

Rob devoured the last of his stew and began mopping the bowl with his bread. I looked at my bowl and found I had no appetite.

Rummaging for a pen and notepad in the catchall drawer, I said,

"You're not leaving for a while, so why don't you tell me what you need?"

Rob glanced up at the calendar on the wall. "Not really. Meredith, I'm leaving Monday. I've already called Alan. He's coming over to help me."

"Monday?" I heard my voice break as the tears came. I pushed away my plate, laid my head on the table, and sobbed. We sat together, only inches apart. I kept waiting for him to touch me, to say something to make me feel better, anything.

I waited.

Stepping inside the house, I gazed around. The lamp I turned on cast shadows into all the corners of the living room, but everything appeared the same as always. I took a deep breath, hurried up the stairs to our bedroom, and flung open the closet door. All the clothes and shoes on his side—gone. The stack of books on his bedside table—gone. I continued into the study. Only blank swaths of wall showed on the bookshelves where Rob's library had been. His desk looked naked, too, stripped of all pens and notebooks. Also gone were two framed photographs: one of me pregnant and buxom, and one of his parents standing side by side in front of Rob's childhood home.

Next I checked the medicine cabinet in the bathroom: empty shelves. I sniffed the towel he used after shaving, hoping for some trace of him. Nothing. I turned on lights in the spare bedroom and poked my head inside. Nothing changed there. Back downstairs I reached into the liquor cabinet and pulled out a full bottle of Christian Brothers Brandy. I filled a glass tumbler, headed back to our—my—bedroom, and wrote in my journal: "God, he's gone."

From the rocking chair I watched as twilight chased gray shadows from the corners. I needed to find some modicum of comfort. I felt terribly sad, terribly disappointed, but not desperate. I recalled Miriam, a character in Marge Piercy's novel *Small Changes*. Miriam had acquiesced to her husband's demands, and even given up her doctorate-level career for the security of marriage. Although he disapproved of almost everything about me, Rob had never tried to discourage my professional ambitions. He understood my passion for learning and teaching. Noticing the elm tree in the front yard, its limbs strong and muscled with age, gave me the first moment of clarity since I'd come home to the empty house: I had every right to be proud of myself. Despite our marital woes, I'd kept my management-level job and earned distinction for my research.

Following in my mom's footsteps, I knew to find comfort in a couple swigs of brandy I kept under the bed. The brandy burned all the way down my throat, and I coughed. Who was I kidding? I may have done well in my profession, but coming home to a darkened, empty house was something I didn't know how to handle. I raised the bottle a second time, this time stopping to savor the earthy, woodsy bouquet. I was starting to feel better. Ever since our problems had started almost four years ago, I'd taken solace in alcohol. Its comfort level never changed. It's there for me, now, I remembered, and I ran downstairs and brought up an unopened bottle of Christian Brothers brandy, secreting it in the cedar closet right next to my bed, under a pile of blankets. I wondered aloud: Why are you hiding this, Meredith?

From the college one Friday afternoon I called my colleague Maryann. "Let's go see the new Woody Allen tonight." Then I pedaled my bicycle five and a half miles home. As I rode, the humidity started playing serious catch-up with the heat and hugging me tightly. Sweat streamed down my face, and twice I had to stop and wipe my blurred, stinging eyes. At home I took the stairs two at a time, pulling off my shirt soaked clean through. I turned on the tiled shower Rob and I had updated to COLD, shrugged out of my bra, slacks, and panties, and stood under the downpour.

Wrapped in a towel that Rob had favored, I ran downstairs to the kitchen and opened the refrigerator. The air blew cool against my freshly scrubbed face and shoulders. I pulled out a head of lettuce, a six-ounce package of farmer's cheese, a bottle of diet Coca Cola. I dug through the contents of the iced-over freezer until I found a pack of Newport menthol cigarettes. I tore three leaves from the lettuce, unwrapped the plastic from the cheese, and using my finger smeared it, sparingly, on the lettuce. I pulled the cap from the Coke, and leapt back from its raspy sizzle. Aloud I began counting the calories: cheese 100, lettuce 2, Coke 0. I threw everything I didn't need back into the refrigerator, and slammed the door, walked out of the kitchen and back up the stairs. On the way I nibbled on my lettuce sandwich and swallowed huge gulps of my drink. That was supper. It was also the first meal I'd eaten all day. I was seldom hungry anymore and it didn't hurt that I was losing weight. Maybe, when I had dinner with Rob on Sunday, he would notice. I was never fat before, but now thin was in.

Maybe he preferred thin.

After Rob moved out, I made sure I was home alone as little as possible. As head of my department, I gave myself a punishing schedule, teaching three classes a day and having four office hours. I started at 8:00 a.m. and finished at 8:00 p.m. When sleep eluded me, I had many choices: marijuana (I kept a baggie and a small pipe next to my bed), whiskey, wine, or drugs like Seconal, Valium, or Librium, which, thanks to my physician friends and generous colleagues, I had in abundant supply. Most mornings I woke to find I could barely remember the night before, but I staggered out of bed, pulled on shorts and a tee shirt, and ran five miles before I went to work. I was determined to prove that I could do it.

One bright spring morning I half woke to a faint buzzing. I covered my head with my pillow but the noise persisted. When I realized it was the telephone and stretched my arm to grab it, I felt as though I was reaching across a wide chasm. My body refused my commands, and I strained for the receiver. The phone jangled, one, two, three grating rings. I was counting them, one by one, and blinking, trying to rid my eyes of a blur. Eight, nine, ten rings, and finally I grabbed the receiver and held it close to my ear. It felt so heavy I nearly dropped it. "H-h h—," I stuttered. "Hello" floated in my mind but stuck like lead in my throat. I knew that something awful was happening to me. I clutched the receiver and tried again to speak. Nothing.

"Meredith, Meredith, are you there?" It was Walter, my boss. He was shouting.

I tried a third time. "I'mherecanyouhearme?" My words shot out staccato-like, one following another, in a high-pitched tone. I sounded like Daisy Duck.

Walter's response, "What did you take?" gave me sudden clarity. I laid the phone on the pillow and picked up the medicine packet on my bed table.

I fell back on my pillow, gripping the receiver. "Tranquilizers," I said, yawning into the phone. "WaltI'msotired."

"Listen to me." His voice sounded serious, authoritative. "Tell me you're listening."

"Y—y—e-s," I muttered.

He ordered me to get out of bed, drink the strongest coffee possible, telephone my doctor, and call him back. "By the way," he added, "you're forty minutes late for the interview with Joann Jameson, but do what I said. I'll take care of everything here."

When I told my doctor I'd taken three or four of the pills, he chided, "The normal dosage is one. What were you thinking?"

I couldn't tell him the truth. I wasn't thinking. I was only trying to stop feeling the sense of loss that swept over me every time I was alone, in my bedroom, imagining my baby, and the terrible thing I'd done in vain to keep Rob from leaving.

After six months, Rob and I talked divorce. The simplest way in Kentucky was for me to file a plea for "Abandonment and Non-support." Ever the dutiful wife—even doing what I most dreaded, I trotted downtown to a cheap lawyer (to save my husband money) whom friends had called adequate. I sat in his office, the beige paint peeling off two walls, the other two lined with shelves overflowing with books, an old rolltop desk piled with papers and huge law tomes, and gazed out a window so streaked it made the sunny day seem gray. It's come to this, I mused, remembering our wedding night and the poem Rob wrote on creamy vellum: "You are the one I will not learn to lose." Now he's losing me, his choice, but I'm taking care of the dirty details—because this is the easier way. He's at fault, under the law, the abandoner, and I the one wronged, deserted. But I'm the one here, sitting in a gray vinyl chair meant to be part of a kitchen set, signing the papers, handing the lawyer a check for $175 which Rob has signed.

Eight months later I drove to the courthouse, my friends Janet and Maryann at my side. I'd dressed in a cheery green polyester suit I'd bought for the occasion. Green was the color of spring and rebirth, and I wore it to assure myself that better times awaited me. Daydreaming in front of the white-haired judge, I was startled when he banged his gavel and drawled: "Granted."

The three of us walked down to the Main Street Bar and I gulped three martinis. I knew my friends were appalled, but I rationalized my behavior: both women were happily married; they had no way of understanding my overwhelming sadness. Despite my best efforts, I was a divorced woman, a pariah in my family and among all my old school chums. I felt disgraced and humiliated. After the second martini I'd been able to laugh, and with the third I became almost hysterical. I could see Janet was eager to get me out of there. She'd stared wide-eyed when I'd ordered my third drink.

Back at home I called Rob. "It's done," I slurred.

"Thanks for letting me know," he said. "Remember, we'll always be friends."

"Sure," I said. I hung up the phone. Friends? It seemed a stretch but I was willing to keep up appearances because I was so ashamed of the stigma of divorce.

The next weekend we met for dinner. Rob said we should celebrate our "amicable" divorce at my favorite restaurant, Vincenzo's, a carefully restored Victorian in midtown. That night I primped, taking special pains with my makeup—especially my eyes—and hair. I smiled over and over again into the mirror, making sure I could hide my feelings of hatred, and rehearsed what I'd say when I greeted my now ex-husband. I was glad for the shadowy dining room. As I had every time we met since he'd left, I relied on my acting skills to present a persona that appeared composed, even content, counter to the deeply wounded, angry woman I really was.

Once we were divorced, Rob continued teaching, dating Gloria and (I suspect) others. I took refuge in my work. I taught five courses. I wrote grants to help black students new to higher education. I held workshops for local teachers. Twelve- to fourteen-hour workdays became the norm. I welcomed speaking engagements across the country—in Seattle, Cleveland, and Pittsburgh—anything to keep me in constant motion. My efforts earned the college prestige, and, a year after our divorce, the president announced my promotion to dean of humanities.

All of these events may have been exciting in other circumstances, but for me they were only distractions helping me hide my grief and shame.

Though Rob and I kept in touch with occasional phone calls and dinners, I found that I rarely missed his company. Nearly two years passed before he mentioned meeting a handsome guy named Nolen.

Part Three

One gloomy February afternoon I was working late in my office when the phone rang. It was Professor Harold Billings, calling from California. We'd met the previous summer when Notre Dame sponsored a national conference and he gave the keynote address, describing the work he'd done to diversify the University of California. After his talk I'd walked up to the podium to meet him.

I shook his hand. "I've taught disadvantaged black students for ten years," I told him. After listening to his talk I knew that he understood that such work was arduous, sometimes discouraging, and often tiring. Professor Billings and I made an instant connection and chatted throughout a forty-minute wait in the lunch line. Since then I hadn't heard from him. Now here he was, telephoning, six months later. I was shocked and flattered that he even remembered me.

The professor came straight to the point. "I'm hoping you'll be interested," he said, "in coming out here to work for me."

Interested? My heart skipped a beat. I desperately wanted out of Louisville, away from Rob and the house that held such painful memories. Craving a fresh start and ready for big changes, I told Dr. Billings that I was more than interested.

"We have to get you out here," he said. "We'll want you to come for a few days after classes are out. You can stay on campus and get a feel for things, and of course meet some of my staff."

In my head I was already on the plane, and I began counting the weeks until my trip to California.

At San Francisco Airport, I was welcomed by a dark-eyed beauty who told me her name was Rosario Rodríguez. She was so young and petite I doubted for a moment that she could handle the imposing van she escorted me to. I need not have worried, and I relaxed as we cruised south until we reached Highway One.

I was dazzled by the beauty of the coast: the jagged cliffs overlooking the Pacific, frothy waves curling onto sandy beaches, and the lush green foliage lining the road. Through the van's open windows the cool sea air felt bracing.

After an hour and a half, we drove in the rear entrance of the UC Santa Cruz campus, through sweeping fields of summer-dried grass, and parked near a sign that read "Clifton College." Six three-story brick buildings were nestled among massive redwoods. A swath of bright green lawn, dotted with flowerbeds full of golden California poppies and blue hydrangeas, was the centerpiece of it all. Due west lay the Pacific Ocean. Its vast blueness took my breath away.

A man wearing a baseball cap and khaki pants stood waiting for us. "That's Gil, the proctor," Rosario told me. "He'll show you to your rooms." I thanked her and climbed out of the van.

Gil pumped my hand. "I'll take it from here. Thanks, Rosie." Gil picked up my suitcase. We both waved as Rosario pulled away.

"You'll be staying in one of our student apartments," said Gil. He led me down a long sidewalk, up two flights of stairs, and into a spacious suite of rooms.

I took in my surroundings: a living room furnished with orange upholstered chairs and sofa, and a fully equipped kitchen with floors polished to a bright shine. The place smelled like wax and Pine Sol.

"The bedrooms are down that hall," said Gil, gesturing to three closed doors. "Choose any one you like; there's nobody else here, now that it's summer."

Gil beckoned me to the picture window. "Step over here a minute. Professor Hal's invited you to his place for dinner." He pointed to a smallish house with architecture matching the other buildings. "It's right over there. But take your time and get settled in."

That night I dined with Hal and his wife, Georgia. Hal was a large man, broad-chested, his black curly hair flecked with gray. When Georgia offered me a glass of red wine, I was relieved but wary. God, I prayed, don't let me drink too much.

My first official interview was the following morning. Hal met me outside the main building, handed me a typed schedule, and walked me to an office with its door closed. "Today you'll be having lunch with my assistant, Jim Piper. He'll drive you through the campus to give you an idea of its enormity—two thousand acres of redwoods overlooking the Monterey Bay. You can't beat that, can you?" he said, knocking at Jim's door.

A sandy-haired man in pressed Levis and an Oxford button down shirt waved us into his office. "Hello there. You must be Meredith." Jim gave me a firm handshake. "Hal's told me about you."

Jim seemed about my age but when I looked closely at his face, his blue eyes were all I noticed. Trying to hide my attraction, I smiled and shook his hand.

After a few minutes of small talk, Hal headed for the door. "Okay, Jim, let's meet again this afternoon at 3:00. You two enjoy the university tour and lunch."

As we drove though the sprawling campus, Jim kept up a running monologue. He told me he'd worked with Hal for six years and gave me an overview of his academic life: private schools in Los Angeles, bachelor and master's degrees from UC San Diego. And then, as if it were essential to completing his profile, he said: "I'm divorced. I imagine you are too?"

Divorce? Holding my breath, I waited for Jim's next question, and breathed a sigh of relief when he quickly changed the subject.

For lunch Jim chose the Crow's Nest, a popular restaurant near the Santa Cruz yacht harbor. Its patio seating afforded spectacular views of Monterey Bay. The sparkling sunlit waves were so blue, they appeared almost unreal. Sailboats floated by, seagulls and pelicans flew overhead, and I could smell the ocean. The whole scene played movie perfect.

"Do you see anything here you'd like?" Jim asked, jolting me back to reality.

As I stared at my menu, the line I fixed on read: "Free glass of house wine with lunch."

By the time we'd finished our generous servings of shrimp Louie, both Jim and I had enjoyed our free glass of Chardonnay, and several glasses more. I glanced at my watch, saw that it was 2:45, and leapt out of my chair. "My God!" I said, grabbing my purse and pulling on Jim's arm. "Let's go, please! We'll be late."

Jim remained calm. "Oh, don't worry about Hal. He's cool. You're on California time now, anyway." He sauntered over to pay the bill and gestured for me to wait while he entered the men's room. I chewed on my thumbnail.

While Jim drove us back to the university, I was anything but calm. Several times I squeezed my eyes closed, desperate to shake the blurriness I felt overtaking my brain. Through a wine haze I realized two things: that I was heading for a very important interview, and that I was very, very drunk.

During the meeting I sat ramrod straight, occasionally pinching myself to stay attentive, and enunciating my words carefully. Jim sat in the room with Hal and me but I avoided looking at him. At the close of the interview, Hal told me to meet him in the parking lot the following day at 6:00. "We can jog along West Cliff Drive," he said. "I think you'll find it stunning."

"All right," I said, but couldn't wait to get away. I hurried back to my room, fell into bed, and slept straight through the night.

The next morning I awoke to a twilit sky. Shortly after daybreak, Hal arrived, and drove us to the seaside cliffs only a couple of miles south. We parked at the edge of a three-mile pathway skirting the ocean. Waves crashed on the shore below us, and above, gulls wheeled and cawed. This was a most unorthodox setting for an interview but I figured a brief running stint would put me in good stead. Thick summer fog blanketed us as we pushed off.

Hal wore dark blue shorts, a white tee shirt, and a nylon windbreaker with the Stanford University insignia. I remembered that he'd studied for his doctorate there. Loping along with Hal, distracted by the scenery and my hangover, I struggled to concentrate on Hal's words. We ran six miles—three down and three back—while he outlined specifics on the position he had for me.

Is this man for real? I questioned, grateful that he jogged slowly enough so that I had no trouble keeping up. *But what about yesterday? How could he hire me after I showed up for the formal interview intoxicated? Did I manage to bluff him?*

We drove back to Hal's office and gulped several glasses of water. Hal's face streamed with perspiration. My red tee-shirt was plastered to my chest and, worried that my nipples were showing, I discreetly tried to stretch it so it wouldn't be too clingy.

But Hal's attention was elsewhere. He kicked off his Nike shoes and slid his feet into slippers he took from a file drawer. Wiping his brow with a handkerchief, he said, "How I love a good run." He sighed, smiling. "Glad you could join me."

Nodding at him, I gulped more water.

"Now, there's one more thing," Hal said, leafing through the papers scattered across his desk.

Beads of sweat gave my face a grimy feel and I wanted to run from the room and go wash up. Instead I shut my eyes, listening to the sound of Hal shuffling papers on his desk and his heavy measured breathing. *There's no way he'll hire me after yesterday. Smashed in an interview.*

Hal swung his chair around to face mine. He had a paper in his hand. "The salary schedule," he said. "Let's talk salary."

I barely held myself back from shouting.

A couple of days later I flew back home to prepare for my move. The next six weeks were a blur of activities: turning in my letter of resignation and meeting with the dean, putting the house on the market, saying goodbye to a few friends. Every morning I rose before the sun, gulped a cup of strong coffee I'd brewed the night before, and headed out on an eight-mile run. Then I'd come home where Janet and Maryann showed up, every morning for a week, helping me sort out, throw away or pack everything I could transport in my little yellow Datsun.

In the middle of the week the three of us were sitting right next to the air conditioner in the dining room, wolfing down sandwiches and cokes. "Whew," said Janet. She leaped out of her chair and positioned her face directly in the path of the cold air. "This is heaven! The radio said it would be ninety-five today, and at least 100 percent humidity."

"Speaking of heaven, tell us about your promised land, Meredith," said Maryann.

"Yeah, and while you're at it, what about that Piper guy you met?" Janet chuckled. "We know our girl won't waste any time."

I blushed. These two women had supported me since our move to

Louisville. They knew almost everything about Rob and me. "All right, ladies." I chortled. "There's no humidity in Santa Cruz, and his name is Jim. And yes, he's quite good looking."

While I was scrubbing the cupboards one morning, I got a call from Jim. I was excited to hear his voice.

"I'll see you in August," he said. "Hal is sending me away."

"What? You're leaving?"

"He's been talking to my ex-wife, and he told me I had to get sober or I'd lose my job. So I'm off to a rehab hospital in Oakland."

Rehabilitation hospitals for alcoholics? Poor Jim, I thought. He's been found out. Now I, too, would have to get serious about controlling my drinking. I was so grateful for my new job, I was willing to do anything. Working in California meant at last I'd get away from Rob and Gloria and Nolen and all the shame I felt with my divorce. Maybe I wouldn't need the comfort of alcohol in California.

I decided a solemn promise was in order: No drinking in California. Ever.

The next week, my trunk crammed with boxes, suitcases, and four bottles of Chardonnay, I set out for the Promised Land. Each night when I stopped on the drive across country, I drank one bottle. On the third night, after I'd crossed the California border, I had to amend my promise: Once I begin my new job, I will never drink again. When I reached Santa Cruz, I mustered the courage to toss the last bottle into a dumpster.

Another week passed before I saw Jim, on the day after he'd been sprung from the Oakland rehab. He was every bit as handsome and charming as I remembered, and when he invited me to dinner, I was ecstatic. Even though I was excited about my new university position, I'd driven three thousand miles across the country and found myself more alone than ever.

"I can smell the roses again," Jim said on our first date. I thought his remark was corny but kept my mouth shut. Sitting at a window overlooking the bay, we ordered fresh salmon and sipped water with lemon slices. He told me that in the rehab clinic he'd been introduced to a group called Alcoholics Anonymous. They had meetings all over, and he'd been to one the night before. "I'm committed," he said, "to attending a meeting several times a week."

I was squirming inside, hoping to avoid mention of my own need for such a group.

He didn't continue in this vein, and he drove me home. Pulling up in front of the college, he drew me close, and we kissed. "I'm so glad you're here, Meredith. We'll have some good times together."

Running up the stairs to my apartment, I realized it had been at least three days since I'd thought of Rob and Louisville. Now remembering Jim's eager kisses, I was feeling better than good.

I saw Jim a lot those first weeks. We attended the same college meetings and met for dinners or movies downtown in the art theatre. At the beginning of October, he drove us down to Big Sur, a stunningly beautiful area an hour south of Monterey. At dusk we dined at the Nepenthe restaurant, a structure that Orson Welles had built for Rita Hayworth. It was nestled right into the mountain with jaw-dropping views of the Pacific, and he told me of the famous writers—Hunter Thompson, Robinson Jeffers, Henry Miller—who'd been Big Sur residents. I could see why. It was the most spectacular place I'd ever seen.

That night, back at Jim's house, we settled in his living room. I eased into a brown leather armchair while he got us cokes from the kitchen. He sat on the shabby gray sofa. I was beginning to feel very at home with this man, and so what happened next took me by surprise. Jim lit a cigarette and took a long pull on it, puffing the smoke out in slow swirls. He looked at me. "How much do you remember about our lunch before your interview with Hal, back in July?"

I blushed. What did he expect me to say? "Hmm," I hedged, knowing I couldn't lie. He'd been there too. "Um, how much we drank?"

Jim nodded and paused. "Yeah." He let another moment pass. "Have you heard of the twenty questions?"

I shook my head. "Some kind of inquisition document?" I joked, wishing this whole conversation were a joke. It was getting too serious for me, and I writhed inside.

"Not at all." After putting out his cigarette, he pulled a small pamphlet from his shirt pocket and slowly unfolded it. Right away I noticed the Alcoholics Anonymous logo at the top of the page. *Oh great,* I thought.

"Now what you do"—his voice became enthusiastic, like he was trying to convert me—"is read this list. Keep track of how many questions you say 'yes' to, and then you'll know."

"Know what?" I was starting to resent the intensity of the blue eyes I'd found so attractive only a month before.

"Whether or not you're alcoholic. Obviously, I failed the test, or passed it, depending on how you look at it. Don't you want to know?"

I'm trapped, I concluded. *Well, I could give it a try. But if you don't have a problem, Meredith,* I heard a voice say, *why did you make that solemn promise?*

I took the paper from Jim. "At least don't make me do this here. I'll read it later," I said.

An hour later we were sitting together in my living room on campus. "Are you going to read it now?" Jim asked. I felt that he was harassing me and decided I had to read it so he'd stop nagging. Taking the pamphlet from my purse, I moved to a chair on the other side of the room. Jim sat on the sofa, watching me.

To these questions I answered yes:

Have you ever felt remorse after drinking?

Do you crave a drink at a definite time daily?

Do you drink to escape from worries or troubles?

Do you drink alone?

Have you ever had a complete loss of memory as a result of drinking?

When I finished I met his gaze. "Only five yeses."

Jim smiled. I couldn't really tell if it was a smile or a smirk. "Did you read the boldface line at the bottom of the page?"

It read: "If you have answered yes to three or more of these questions, you are definitely an alcoholic."

"Okay, okay." I put my hands in the air. "I surrender. Give me your meeting schedule and leave me alone." I wasn't about to thank him for the dinner or for the enlightenment.

The next evening I tiptoed into a first-grade classroom at Sea View Elementary School. Seven people were already there. I perched on a small chair in the corner and searched each face, looking for a hint of normalcy. There was a huge bear of a man dressed like a cowboy, who talked with a southern accent. Across from him sat a diminutive lady who was knitting. As the meeting began, a handsome couple entered, he a tall dark-haired Steve McQueen, and she a short busty blonde with blue eyes and curly hair. Surprisingly, no one here even remotely resembled a drunk.

When the group's leader asked for newcomers to raise their hands, I didn't respond. I wasn't ready, yet, to have a bunch of proselytizing folks shoving brochures at me. Since I sat as close to the door as possible, the moment people stood to close the meeting, I raced out to my car. I'd take a drive to clear my head.

As I turned south onto the freeway, I drove through pockets of fog and began to question myself. Maybe it had been only at Jim's insistence that I'd found myself in a meeting. Maybe I wasn't an alcoholic. Still, I had to admit that after Rob moved out, I'd begun an alcohol-fueled life, one that took me so far from the young girl in Kansas that I hardly remembered her. My mind was crowded with hazy memories of a life that repeatedly took me into bars and beds with men I hoped never to see again.

Even had I understood what I was doing, I could not have stopped. One night in Louisville a close friend I'd known since grad school had taken me to dinner. While we were sipping our after-dinner coffees, Lorraine came right to the point. "I'm terminating our friendship," she said. She waited until I set my cup on the saucer. "I cannot continue to watch what you are doing to yourself." A ball of resentment lodged in my throat. How dare she? She has no idea what I've suffered with the abortion and Rob's betrayal. Good riddance, I thought. So much for friendship.

I never considered getting help. After all, I didn't have a problem. My denial fierce, my drinking continued, and it was a miracle that I'd found a position in California. I glanced at the freeway sign and saw that I was fifteen miles from home. Replaying scenes from those ugly times, I turned off the freeway at La Selva Beach and headed north toward home. I kept seeing the knowing glance Jim had given me after I had busted myself.

Yes, I had to admit I was an alcoholic. The next afternoon I drove to Holy Redeemer Church. There, the group convened in a stark basement room furnished with a couple of long tables and a dozen or so folding chairs. When I walked in, I noticed a gray-haired woman in a blue denim dress sitting alone. She was crying and holding a handkerchief to her nose. Three older men sat at the other end of the table, talking and guffawing.

What is this? I thought. I looked around. One person crying while the others joke around? I could understand the crying because I wasn't happy to be there either. But laughter? I assumed that this recovery stuff was supposed to be serious business. Life or death.

My puzzlement must have been obvious because an elderly woman with heavily rouged cheeks approached me, her gray eyes kind. "Are you new?" she asked. Before I could answer she said, "I'm Maggie." Her face crinkled in a smile as she put her arm around me. Patting my back, she added, "Welcome home."

Home? I was about to dash off again, but then I remembered: If you can answer yes to three or more of these questions . . .

During this meeting we read and discussed a chapter from what they called the Big Book, a hefty tome with a bright blue cover, which explained how to live without alcohol. It had been written years ago—in the 1940s—when AA was still in its formative stages. Small wonder I had never heard of it. Books about sober living were never on my reading list. I sat beside Maggie and listened. This time when the group's leader asked, "Are there any newcomers here?" I raised my hand.

"I'm Meredith; I think I'm an alcoholic." I wasn't quite ready yet, but what was I doing sitting on a folding chair in the moldy basement of Holy Redeemer Church?

"Hi Meredith," all the others said in unison.

Well, it wasn't quite the Mickey Mouse Club, but close. Even so, I was determined to take whatever counsel these people offered as quickly as possible so I could get back to drinking, like my sister did, like a normal person.

Not long after Rob and I had divorced, I was on a flight from Dallas back to Louisville when a flight attendant brought a tray holding a mini-bottle of Seagram's Gin and a small bottle of tonic.

"Oh, but I didn't order anything," I said.

"I know," she said. "The pilot sent this. I think he saw you boarding the plane in Dallas."

After we landed I waited in my seat until the pilot emerged from the flight deck.

"I'm Sean Manchester," he said. "Is Louisville your home?" He was imposing in his dark blue Delta uniform.

I nodded and thanked him for the drink.

"I'm hoping you'll have dinner with me sometime when I stop over. May I call you?"

"Okay, sure." I sat back down, pulled a notebook from my purse, and scribbled my phone number. Handing it to him, I observed his strong square face and reddish brown sideburns. I hoped he'd call me.

A couple of weeks later I met Sean at a nightclub not far from the Louisville Airport. Again I thought him handsome and distinguished looking. The place he'd chosen was thick with cigarette smoke, but the music sounded soft and sultry, and the food was delicious. We ate beef Wellington and drank martinis, and danced to songs from the fifties and sixties. I tried to keep count of my drinks but soon lost track. When Sean glanced at his watch and said, "Gosh, I've got to grab some sleep," I was actually relieved.

Sean walked me to my car and kissed me chastely before I drove off. The clock on the dashboard read 2:40 a.m.

I traveled a few miles down the freeway before turning onto city streets with familiar names. I had to keep blinking to stay alert, and when I began seeing stop signs instead of streetlights, I braked. Peering into the darkness, trying to read unfamiliar traffic signs, I realized that I was a stranger to these roads. I must have made a wrong turn.

I peered into the rearview mirror and saw a small blonde woman, alone in her yellow Datsun hatchback. I was lost—in the worst part of town, where I'd never go, even in the daylight.

The next day, as I lay drowsing in the early morning sunlight, city garbage trucks creaked and rumbled, jolting me alert. I could only half remember the night before. Where was I?

I was dressed in my nightgown in my own bed. I got up and crept downstairs, where I was enormously relieved to see the front door locked and chained. I hurried through the house, out the back door, and to the garage. My car was parked there, apparently undamaged, the garage door closed.

Somehow, driving drunk, so smashed that the next day I remembered nothing after that moment in the intersection, I'd returned safely. I never told anyone about that evening and shoved the memory as far down as I could.

Four years later, at an AA statewide meeting in the Civic Auditorium, a well-spoken man who identified himself only as Jerry K told his story to three hundred sober alcoholics. Toward the end he confessed, "One night I started drinking in San Francisco and woke up in Salt Lake City, in an unfamiliar bed. The sheets were rumpled and reeked of cheap perfume. I found my keys and an airline ticket on the bedside table. I was alone, without the slightest idea how I'd gotten to the Sleep Tight Motel."

The people around me found this hilarious and burst out laughing, but I was mortified. Jerry K was forcing me to recall a certain night in Louisville.

"Whenever I drank," Jerry continued, "I always blacked out. When I woke up and didn't know where I was or how I'd gotten there, I'd vow never to drink again. Until the next time."

These people had a name for it: blackout. My face reddened with guilt.

After the meeting, I ducked out quickly. I couldn't wait to get home and reflect on all I'd heard. What I'd taken as a one-time miracle was actually commonplace among drunks. At home I fixed myself a cup of peppermint tea and climbed into bed. As I sat recalling Jerry K's words, I felt strangely calm. The people laughing in those rooms, they talk of serenity. And, even when they've done terrible things, they seem to be onto something.

Realizing that I'd been taken care of that night, delivered to my bed, and even locked inside my house, I had my first glimmer of hope.

When I first heard "serenity" mentioned at the meetings, I had a vision of myself leading a serious, boring life. How would I ever have fun without alcohol? This serenity stuff sounded dreadfully dull. After only six months of sobriety, I told my first Alcoholics Anonymous boyfriend, Carl, who had been abstinent for fifteen years, "I think serenity is boring."

Carl gave me a weak smile, gazing at the floor as if searching for some appropriate response, but it never came.

Even so, a month later I felt brave enough to speak up at a meeting. That particular day's topic was a suggestion that we ask God to remove our character defects.

"I drank too much because my husband deceived me," I said. I wasn't about to tell them what I'd done to my baby. That would hurt too much.

After the meeting, Maggie, the petite Irish woman I'd met early on, took me aside and whispered, "Honey, you've got to let go of those resentments. They're killers—killers of the spirit. It's like swallowing poison and expecting someone else to die."

When did I admit to feeling resentment?

Then Maggie took my little blue notebook and printed on the front page in bold capital letters: LET GO AND LET GOD.

These people spoke so often of serenity, I finally decided to look up the word in the dictionary. It said that serenity was tranquility, calm, the absence of stress and anxiety. Spiritual-minded folk claimed that it was a by-product of honesty, tolerance, and unselfishness. I didn't understand any of this, but I could hear excitement in the voice of a fellow member who announced, "One day I was flooded with serenity, and I realized this was the spiritual awakening I've been waiting for, all these years."

I wanted my slice of serenity too, but I had no idea how to get it.

My biggest resentment was the same one I'd held fast to for over three years. How could I stop resenting Rob for what he'd done? He'd tried to remake me, lied to me, tricked me into an abortion, lied to me some more, and finally left me. I despised him. The priest deserved some blame too, but I directed most of my rage at Rob.

When my mentor challenged me to write about my resentments, I reluctantly agreed. When I first spotted Adrianne sitting in front of me at a meeting, I had been put off. Perfectly coifed and sporting a stylish black pantsuit and pumps, she could have been Lauren Bacall's twin. I had chosen her as my mentor, mostly because she laughed at the same remarks I did. But she wasn't laughing when she told me not only to list my resentments but also to admit my part in each of them.

My part? Horrified, I fiddled around, making excuses and avoiding the task. When I called one morning to tell her I had stayed home with the flu, she gave me no sympathy. Instead, she said, "Well, now you have time to make your list. Get to it!"

Outed, I had no more excuses. This time the list was different. Sure, Rob had lied to me, but I'd lied to him about Greg. He'd tricked me into an abortion, sanctioned by the priest. That was a tough one. I tried to be open-minded; maybe Rob felt he had no choice. Maybe he didn't know who he was at that time, maybe he was groping in the dark. Coming to terms with homosexuality in a culture that denounced it had to be overwhelming. But why had he been so cruel?

I sighed, feeling overwhelmed. I was more confused than ever.

Making peace with Rob and the priest did not happen overnight.

I kept remembering what former Black Panther Eldridge Cleaver had written: "The price of hating someone is to love oneself less." I did not want to continue this way and I wanted to stay sober. My only alternative was to let go.

In my second year of sobriety, when a couple of women asked me to mentor them, I was skeptical. I had barely finished studying the steps of the program myself. I believed I wasn't ready. But Adrianne thought otherwise. "You're here to give back what you've been given. You're ready, Meredith."

The following week when the young ponytailed Melanie asked me to be her sponsor, I agreed, even though I was groaning inside. She was only the first. Over the years many women asked me to guide them, and I learned that Adrianne was right: those women taught me much more than I ever taught them.

But my journey was far from finished.

"I've taught black students for ten years." That was how I'd started my first conversation with Hal Billings. I don't recall what else I'd said, but whatever it was, it got me to California and opened the doors to my new life.

In my on-campus interview that followed, Hal had said: "Your job will entail interviews with students enrolled in our special programs. You'll be asking them about their past lives—and their university lives—and writing a lengthy report on what you learn."

When I arrived, I knew my task, but had only a vague idea of how to go about it. I'd never done this type of research. I rushed to unpack my twenty-two boxes of books, and got directions to the university library.

On my way there, I jogged along, stopping often to stare up at the cathedral of trees that surrounded me. When I spotted the library building, I gasped. Set in the middle of a redwood forest—the tree trunks soaring as high as skyscrapers—the building was magnificent. Constructed of stone and redwood to harmonize with the environment, it reached four stories, each one with floor-to-ceiling windows. Inside, I spent nearly three hours burrowing through the labyrinth of stacks to find studies similar to the one I was to conduct. I was relieved. I could do this.

When Hal offered me the opportunity to live on campus as a proctor, I jumped at his offer. I knew I had to create a visible presence so students would get to know—and trust—me. Besides the interview project, I taught a course on ethnic literature, where I met students from all different cultures; some were the first in their families to attend university. There I found volunteers to participate in our study. After four weeks, I brought my list to Hal.

He scanned the names, nodding as he took them in. "What you find out," he said, "may radically change the face of higher education."

"I hope so," I said. The past ten years had taught me that higher education had a lot to learn when it came to teaching nontraditional students—those whose families had little or no college, high school, or even grammar school experience. And many of them certainly didn't have the financial resources to send their kids to college. I was meeting a new kind of college student.

One fall afternoon after I was well into my research, I sat grading essays in the college cafe. With the lunch rush over, the place was deserted except for a couple of girls poring over thick textbooks on the far side of the room. The aroma of roasted coffee beans hung in the air. I was sipping my iced tea, riffling through the stack of essays, when I heard a voice."Meredith." I looked up to see a broad-shouldered Latino with huge brown eyes and thick shaggy dark hair. "Meredith, I'm glad I found you." He sounded out of breath. "We need help. With Juan."

The young man was Enríque González. He and his high school pals, Julio Muñoz and Juan Rodríguez, were all in our study. The three hailed from Hayward, a town near Fremont where their fathers worked in the General Motors plant. They were the first in their families to go to college, and here on campus, popular and admired.

I waved him into a chair. "Sit here, Enríque. Tell me."

"It's his old life, Meredith." He lowered his voice and scooted in closer to me. "In high school Juan was in a gang. We thought he'd quit his old ways, but last night he told me, when he goes home on weekends, they hassle him. 'Come back with us,' they tell him. He's thinking about it. Will you talk with him?"

I nodded. "Of course. Can you ask him to come to my office?"

"I think so." Enríque wiped his brow with the back of his hand.

"Will he be upset that you've told me?"

"I don't know." His eyes looked sad. "But he'll come—if I have to carry him."

I spoke with Juan, Juan met with Hal. We listened. We talked. And listened. The following weekend, when Juan returned to Hayward, I had a hard time getting my mind off him. Would the lure of the gang be too much for him? Did he realize the opportunity he had at the university? Would he return to us?

He did.

Juan was not alone with his challenges. Painful as it often was, in the privacy of my office, I heard a litany of student woes. Students worried about fitting in, about their intellectual abilities, about their finances (many of them sold their blood to send money to impoverished parents), about their girlfriends and boyfriends, and most of all, about the overwhelming doubt: can I do this? They lacked role models—parents or uncles or aunts who were university graduates—and they needed support, which was exactly what this college was providing: tutoring, counseling, advising. And my job was to discover if the services were indeed helping them succeed.

Hal's assistant Jim Piper came to my office a few days after I'd made the first report on my evaluation project to the faculty senate. He and I were no longer a couple, but I saw him frequently at AA meetings. "Hey, Meredith." He poked his head inside the door.

"Come in. Sit down," I said. I noticed how relaxed he seemed, so different from when I'd met him and we both were fighting alcohol addiction. He didn't even ask to light a cigarette.

"I want to congratulate you," he said.

"For what?"

"My God, Meredith. You've done it. You're clean and sober *and* you're doing a fantastic job with these interviews. I heard your senate report. And I talked with Hal."

I blushed. "Thanks."

After he left, I daydreamed, imagining all my students, gowned in bachelor's robes, receiving their degrees, their families and friends cheering them. Jim was right. This job was a gift of my newly found sobriety.

But there were more.

Years after Enríque's visit on behalf of Juan, I sat at my desk sorting mail: four textbook ads, the latest *New Yorker*, and a thick envelope, hand addressed. The almost minuscule handwriting looked familiar, but there was no return address. Tearing it open, I found an invitation on fancy parchment: "Please join our family to celebrate our son Juan Nariño-Rodríguez, MD.

Tears flooded my eyes. Two months later I drove to Hayward, to a mega-hotel a block from the freeway. I wandered the halls of the enormous building until I found the Grand Ballroom, opened the door, and stepped into a cavernous hall, full of tables and chairs, festooned with balloons and flowers. I barely got inside when Juan bear-hugged me. He wore a white guayabera with a little red pin that said *Sí se puede*—Yes, you can. Juan was still the handsome guy he'd been in college, but I saw he carried himself a little straighter now.

"Come with me, Meredith, please." He took my arm. "My parents are waiting to meet you."

"*Muchas gracias para ayudar nuestro hijo Juanito.*" Many thanks for helping our son Juan. His mother, her face lined with wrinkles, clutched my hand. Juan's father, slight and bent from years on the assembly line, bowed. His eyes shone. "*Gracias, profesora, por todo.*"

Then Enríque appeared, and Julio.

I thought that celebration was my finest hour, but I was wrong. Fifteen years later, a number of students from my special group returned for a reunion. Teachers, doctors, dentists, nurses, business professionals, professors, scientists—they came to share their stories, as they'd done with me in our research study.

I have a picture of us that afternoon. *Mis tres hijos,* my three sons, all doctors now, are sitting with me, under a colorful banner with the message *Sí se puede. Yes, you can.* We're looking straight into the camera over platefuls of rice, beans, and tortillas on a table in front of us. They are smiling. But not me. I'm grinning.

That was my finest hour.

One foggy Santa Cruz afternoon in 1988, the screeching brakes of the mail truck distracted me, and I went to get the mail. The sky was darkening to dusk and a chorus of seals yelped from the ocean a few blocks away. I fished the white envelope from the mailbox, instantly recognizing the tiny controlled script of my longtime friend Ann Marie, who'd mentored me in graduate school. We'd kept in touch since the '70s, and I'd visited her in St. Louis only a few months before. But we used the telephone, and never wrote letters. I was curious about what she had to say.

Ripping open the envelope, I pulled two papers out. On one, a light-blue sheet of stationery, she'd written: "I wanted to make sure you saw this." The other was an article cut from the *St. Louis Post Dispatch*:

"Priest Indicted in Sex Charges." The priest was Father Bill. The article said that fifteen men—all whom he'd taught at St. John's High School—were suing him and the Church, and that the Jesuit order had already paid out more than $550,000 in restitution.

Really.

Had Bill molested Rob at some point? Had a twisted relationship with Rob motivated him to tell me abortion was not a sin? A tsunami of rage rolled over me. It all came back: splitting hairs with St. Augustine, lies he encouraged and participated in. Along with the boys he'd damaged, I too had been gravely injured.

I pictured him now in his eighties, his bulbous nose swollen and red, his spine curved over a shapeless body, ensconced in some posh retirement home for priests, hidden from public view.

Decrepit or not, he had hurt me. Badly. I wanted to report his crimes against me. I telephoned Ann Marie. "I don't blame you," she said. "But think about it. He's old and feeble by now, unable to harm anyone else. What good would it do?"

"But—" I started.

She cut me off. "What about you? Bringing it back will open all the wounds. It's you I'm concerned about."

I told her I'd sleep on it. In the morning I knew what I had to do. No more. No more. I called Ann Marie. "I need to see Rob, one last time. As for Bill, I'm letting it go."

When I'd first connected with Alcoholics Anonymous, I thought my longtime Catholic practices gave me an edge. Surely all those years on my knees had to count for something.

I'd been wrong. I soon realized that even with hundreds of Masses and rosaries under my belt, I was no better prepared for this journey than anyone else in those rooms. Out of habit, I continued to attend

Sunday Mass and recite familiar prayers. After a few years, I began to realize my thinking was changing. At each meeting, my fellow members shared their experience and hope, and sharpened my vision of spirituality. The program emphasized letting go of the past, and forgiveness—of oneself and others—in ways that had never occurred to me. Gradually I came to see this new pathway enhanced the religion of my youth, and that the new path forged perfectly with the old. I didn't have to give up my old beliefs; time would teach me to see how they interfaced.

For nearly five years, I had ignored—at least where Rob was concerned—the program's step to make amends to those we had harmed by our actions. My anger and resentment toward my ex-husband had continued to fester in me.

In the beginning, I'd wanted to take action to prove I was earnest about the twelve steps of the program. A year after I started attending meetings, I'd flown back to see my parents, to my sister in Chicago and to my brother in San Diego. In each meeting, I'd clutched my blue recovery book as I admitted my wrongs and years of selfish behavior. This felt a lot like confession, but far more intimate and certainly more humiliating. My siblings and my father had shrugged and said, "Sure, don't worry about it," and hurried away as if they were embarrassed. Making amends was not part of our family routine.

Mom, wearing her customary bright red lipstick and red polished nails, had laughed and said, "Oh, honey, you've never done anything hurtful to any of us." She missed it. No wonder, as she was the one who'd taught us the fine art of denial. In our family no matter how outrageously we behaved, the next day we acted as if nothing had happened. It had seemed to work, and apparently still did for her.

But now, five years in, my conscience and my sponsor kept dogging me. I knew I had to make amends to Rob for my infidelity with Greg.

I had lied and deceived him. I could simply have written him a letter, but my sponsor insisted that all serious amends be made in person. At meetings, I flinched when I heard people say: "I feel so relieved now that I have made all my amends, even those I feared most." Imagining what seeing Rob would require of me, I lay awake nights, painting scenarios in my head. When I came to the scene of a face-to-face reunion, my stomach knotted and I'd curl tight into a fetal position. How would he look? Would he smile? Kiss me? What about the moment I confronted him. Did I dare? Would he walk away, enraged?

Every morning I resolved to make a plan. The thought nagged at me at odd times, as I brushed my teeth or poured a cup of coffee. In a few days, the idea had morphed into an obsession. I had to go.

A year or so previously, Rob had written that he and Nolen had bought a home in Brooklyn where they were teaching. I wasn't keen on flying from San Francisco to New York City only to see Rob. It was an arduous trip that required a plane change, so I jumped at the opportunity to attend a conference at Columbia University in New York City. The night before we met, I slept fitfully. In edgy nightmares, the faces of Rob and Greg whirled like phantoms casting icy stares. Those images disappeared, and I felt my body thrown into a black hole and falling . . . until I awoke, fearful and anxious, my pillow soaked with sweat.

Though Rob had told me to take lovers while we were married, I thought my admission that I'd been in love with Greg too might anger him. Then there was the matter of Father Bill sexually assaulting his young students. Was it my right to question him about sexual involvement with the priest? Could I confront Rob with his dishonesty? I had spent so many years pretending that I was "past" it all. I'd even defended Rob repeatedly: "He was caught in a terrible dilemma . . . he didn't know how to get out of an untenable situation . . . in the '60s and

'70s gays were ostracized and demeaned, especially in the Midwest." Now in the '80s and living on the East Coast, it might be easier.

I was afraid. Of confrontations. And of anger, especially my own.

I'd arranged to meet Rob on a Thursday afternoon at a bookstore a couple of blocks from Columbia. He strode up, a briefcase in one hand. I wondered if he had brought something to show me. He looked no different after nine years. He set the case down and hugged me. We kissed the way old friends do, briefly touching lips. "You look great," he said. Still Prince Charming, I saw.

He picked up his briefcase and we strolled a few blocks to an Italian restaurant on Amsterdam. As we entered the foyer, the subdued lighting lent everything a romantic glow—including Rob. I recalled the dinners we'd shared as newlyweds in St. Louis. I'd been so proud to be squired by such a catch. Then I stopped. Stay in the moment, I said to myself.

Seated in a corner, a white tablecloth and candlelight between us, we ordered and caught up on family news. After a few minutes, I was slightly more comfortable.

When the waiter cleared our plates and brought coffee, Rob reached into his briefcase and brought out a photo album. "I wanted you to see how we've remodeled our place," he said. He put the book on the table and opened it. He showed me pictures of a two-story Tudor covered with snow, and before-and-after shots of rooms they'd redone.

"It's lovely," I said of the light-green living room decorated with Asian art. "It's almost the same color you and I chose for our living room."

"I guess it is," he said. He seemed surprised. Maybe he didn't remember. He turned the page. "The next ones are of our kids."

Children? I felt blood drain from my face.

Rob pointed to a photo: large hands cradling a pair of tiny gray-

and-white kittens. I felt the blood come back; I breathed again. He was talking about cats. Cats!

"Your kids—they're darling," I said. "I didn't know you liked cats."

"I didn't know either but Nolen insisted, and he was right. I love them."

My mind raced: What if I had insisted? What if . . . I glanced at my watch. It was getting late.

"Rob," I said, "I need to say something."

He nodded, and closed his photo book. He looked straight at me, giving me his undivided attention. I took a deep breath. He covered my hand with his. The demonstration of affection shocked me. I wondered how long it would last.

"I have two matters." I took another breath. "I need to make amends," I said. He started to interrupt but I put up my hand. "Rob, all those years I was with you, I was—uh—also in love with Greg."

I'd said it. My ex-husband now knew about my affair with our friend.

His eyes widened. Then he laughed. "Really? Well, you know what?"

I shook my head and braced myself.

"All those years, I always assumed Greg was gay."

Oh good grief. I sighed. "Please let me finish. I want you to know that I was wrong." I picked up my napkin and wiped my lips, ready for him to ask me for details. Surely he'd want to know: What did you do? When did it start? What happened after our divorce?

But he asked nothing. He also didn't say, "It's okay, I always suspected," or, "It's all right, I forgive you." He just reiterated his first incredulous response: "I really believed Greg was gay." And laughed again.

"But I want to be truthful." I paused. "All the years since our divorce I was only pretending to be friends with you." He removed his hand. "I wanted so much to believe we were still friends that I was willing to write letters, and send Christmas and birthday cards. But on my part it was all an act." He edged slightly away from me.

"You wanted to be friends, and I wanted to hide the shame of our divorce, so I went along with it," I confessed. "The truth is I was devastated. I despised you. I knew you plotted to make me leave even before the abortion. You conspired with Father—if I can call him that—Bill to persuade me to abort our child! You gave me no choice and you deprived me of a child."

"But I thought—" he began, and I interrupted again.

"I need to finish." I straightened and knotted my napkin. "I've worked hard to forgive you, but I can't forget the cruel ways you treated me, putting me down for not walking sexy, for not wearing the right clothes, and for not having large breasts, for God's sake. Can you imagine how I felt when I opened that weird contraption you ordered to enlarge my breasts? I was ill, Rob, thin as Twiggy and emotionally a wreck."

I sipped my water. "I couldn't tell you then, that the drugs I was taking inhibited my ability to concentrate. I couldn't even read a decent book. And you made fun of me when your mother brought me what you called 'housewife lit.'"

Rob was staring at the table. I leaned forward, and spoke quietly, intensely. "You never stopped trying to make me into someone else—someone with huge breasts, who could make you forget the fact that you wanted men."

I was vaguely aware of a disconnect. I had wanted this meeting to make amends. What was I doing? But anger goaded me on.

Someone across the room broke out in peals of laughter. "I've thought a long time about who we were then," I said, "and how hard it must have been to be gay. Still, you had no right to be so mean and ugly to me. You told me, 'I do not want your children.'"

I held back tears. "You think any woman could ever forget that?

I know you could have found a better way . . . you could have told me who you were and that you needed to leave our marriage. You knew how to be gentle and kind—I've seen that in you. Yet you showed me no compassion. You were hard, ugly, and mean."

Silence lay heavy between us. We stared at our empty cups, and glanced at the couple next to us, whispering with bent heads, giggling and sharing intimacies. He looked at his watch and frowned. "Well, that's a lot to take in. I don't know what to say. I had no idea you felt that way. I thought you agreed with Bill, that it was not the time for us to have a child. I thought his counsel relieved you. I remember how closely you focused on St. Augustine. And—I thought we were still friends."

"Bill? What kind of a priest was he? Rob, I was grasping at straws. . . . How could I do such a terrible thing without something to hold on to?"

"But you told me you could do it, and when I offered to come to New York—" he said.

"Oh, come on. Don't put that on me. I couldn't let you know how I felt because I was only following orders. Yours—and his. But I can't bite my tongue anymore."

"I can see that." He glanced at his watch again, clearly wanting to leave. Tight-lipped, he shoved back from the table.

I was suddenly indignant at his noncommittal response. "Wait. Don't you think you owe me an apology—for any of it?" I didn't realize I'd totally lost track of what I'd come to do—make amends for my shortcomings, not to harass him for his.

The waiter approached with the check. "Will there be anything else?" he asked. We both realized: there would never be anything else. Rob took out his wallet and laid several bills on the check.

"Well, Meredith." He raised his eyes to mine. "What do you want me to say? You weren't so perfect yourself."

"But I gave everything I had. I tried to follow *your* rules, to make *you* happy."

He glanced at his watch a third time. It angered me further. "You don't get it, do you?" I grabbed my nearly empty water glass. I threw it at his chest. He ducked aside, and it fell on the thick rug several tables away and lay there.

Dumbfounded, he stared, along with the startled couples around us. Everyone stopped talking and waited for what might come next.

I stood, grabbed my purse, and snapped, "Sorry if I got your shirt wet." I fled. I didn't look back.

For the first time, I'd stood up for myself, and standing outside I felt liberated. By the time I'd hailed a cab, I felt I'd finally let go—of Rob, of losing a child, and of my desire for vengeance. That evening I believed I'd finished with him, that I was ready to bury my past. I slept deep, free of the ugly imaginings of the night before.

When I awoke in my hotel room the next morning, I felt empty, hollowed out, as though I'd lost something valuable, or some vital part of me had been removed. I moved restlessly around the room, starting to pack my things. Still in my robe, I ordered a pot of coffee from room service and sat in front of the mirror to brush my hair.

I looked at the woman there—she looked tired. She'd survived a couple of trips around the block, and this morning it was beginning to show around the edges. I didn't feel liberated; I didn't feel free. I brushed absently, and mused.

Then I knew.

I'd crossed the country to make amends; instead, I'd thrown Rob's shortcomings and failings in his face. I'd lost myself in a storm of rage, and then believed I'd freed myself of my anger and shame.

Burying anger was not what I'd learned to do in AA. I knew I had to forgive. Lashing out at Rob had felt good, but it wasn't right. It wasn't going to free me. Making amends required me to acknowledge my own shortcomings, not someone else's.

I needed to try to make things right. I needed to forgive him, as completely as I could. If I couldn't forgive him, I could never forgive myself. His shortcomings didn't diminish me or frighten me. My own did.

My hair was still disheveled. A splayed lock poked out over my ear. I set the brush down on the glass-topped desk and reached for the phone.

CPSIA information can be obtained
at www.ICGtesting.com
Printed in the USA
LVOW12s1943220516
489467LV00012B/710/P

9 781604 948967